MW01243933

Pretender '56

Also by Jane Kelly

Meg Daniels Mysteries
From Plexus Publishing
    Killing Time in Ocean City
    Cape Mayhem
    Wrong Beach Island
    Missing You in Atlantic City
    Greetings from Ventnor City

A Meg Daniels Bonus Mystery
    A Fear of Seaside Heights

Writing in Time Mysteries
    Swoon '64

Widow Lady Mysteries
    Widow Lady

Pretender '56

By Jane Kelly

Benday Publishing, LLC

Phoenixville, PA

Disclaimer

This is a work of fiction. Names, characters, places and incidents either are the product of the author's imagination or are used fictitiously. Any resemblance to actual persons, living or dead, is entirely coincidental.

Copyright ©2015, 2021 Jane Kelly
ISBN: 978-0-9963340-5-1

Dedication

To the Class of 1962

St. Athanasius Grammar School

Acknowledgments

Thanks to those who shared recollections of life in Philadelphia in 1956 especially Anne Tanner who verified that my recollections were not crazy.

Rick and Beth Kelly read the first draft of the story even before Aunt Julia took the case. Thanks to those who reviewed later versions: Marilynn Benz, Debbie Wernert and Carole Turk.

Chapter 1

At first glance, I found her beautiful. Then, I realized she simply looked rich. Really, really rich. Well-worn jeans, a simple white shirt and modest silver jewelry could not hide the confidence that enduring family wealth bestows at birth which, in her case, I calculated to be about twenty-five years earlier. The Italian handbag didn't even attempt to hide that this was a person of means.

The graduate student had approached my niece, Tracy, a woman who has trouble saying no. So, she didn't. She said, "My Aunt Julia used to work in a private investigation firm and sometimes helps me with cases. Maybe she could talk to you. She has time on her hands." Which Tracy, in the midst of a career change, did not. So, on a bright fall morning, I was the one sitting in a back room of the White Dog Cafe near the University of Pennsylvania campus watching a young woman stride towards me with her hand extended, but no smile on her face.

"Julia Tracy?"

How had Tracy described me? She couldn't have told Antonia Sadoski to look for a twenty-something, long, lanky blond with large blue eyes and skin like silk—which was how she described the student to me. No, she must have said something like *My aunt is sixty-ish, five-foot-four, average weight, dark blond hair. (Wink, wink.)* She wouldn't have mentioned my eye color. No one ever does. For the record, according to my driver's license, my eyes are hazel. "It's autumn, so nine times out of ten she'll be wearing blue jeans, a white blouse or t-shirt and a blazer, probably navy blue with a matching scarf." The description proved accurate that day. The woman headed right for me.

"Antonia?" I asked.

"Yes. I'm Antonia Sadoski." She seemed to take pride in the information.

"Nice to meet you." I extended my hand and her firm grip convinced me the girl had no issue with confidence.

With incredible grace, she slid onto the seat across from me, crossed her long legs so one ankle wrapped neatly around the other and, without further social pleasantries, launched into an explanation of why she had approached my niece. "I contacted Tracy Shaw because my mother had heard of her. I followed up and read about her work. Well, her avocation. I thought she would be interested in information I found about two murders, one double murder actually. She said she had another project right now, but you might be able to help."

I told Tracy I would like to try. I told Antonia I would like to hear more.

Across the table, the graduate student grew more relaxed. She leaned back in her chair. "What did your niece tell you?"

I didn't repeat everything Tracy had told me, "Antonia Sadoski is a Ph.D. student who stumbled on a case through her research. She has no personal involvement in the crime. Yes, this story might be a good opportunity if I found out something new about those murders, but without a party with a vested interest, nothing would prod me to keep digging. This case might be interesting, but I have to focus on teaching if I want to be invited back to Wallmann for another semester. Before I tell her no, I thought I would check with you in case you would like to do a little rooting around. Maybe you could act as my screener and determine if this story is one I should follow up on in the future."

I told Antonia Sadoski, "Tracy mentioned a double homicide in a lover's lane on Cresheim Valley Road in Chestnut Hill. That's all she said, that said you found information suggesting the cops got it wrong."

2

Antonia nodded and opened her mouth to speak, but then turned her attention to the waitress. When she welcomed the server with a broad smile, she revealed an impressive array of teeth, straight and white, worthy of a movie star. Yet, her demeanor suggested no trace of drama as she ordered her water by brand. She remained cool, calm and collected, a stereotype of the remote golden-haired goddess.

When she turned back to me, her smile faded and her bright blue eyes grew darker. A harbinger of bad news? No, she had just turned away from the light. "The police declared it a lover's lane murder, but the couple wasn't really a couple."

The few people I'd met in similar situations always sounded anxious, but I didn't expect a display of nerves from this young woman and didn't see one. And not simply because of her persona. Unlike others whom Tracy helped, Antonia didn't have to relate the story of her brother, daughter or parent. She told a story about two strangers.

"All the victims had in common was a prominent Chestnut Hill family. The father sold the cops a story that a carjacker got the two of them."

"Did these rumors hold him responsible for the deaths?"

"Absolutely not. No one said that. Just that the big shot interfered with the investigation."

"Do you have the big shot's name?" I asked the logical question.

"All you have to do is check the newspaper and you'll see. A man named Henry Parry."

"Do you believe he committed the crime?"

"Oh no." For the first time, I observed emotion in her presentation: defensiveness. "That is not what I am saying. I would never make an accusation like that against anyone." She paused. "Although I do suspect that is what some of my sources think. My take? A stodgy old-school kind of Philadelphian wanted the entire episode buried, didn't want scandal to touch his household. So, he came up with a theory

3

and put a little pressure on the police to accept it. He wanted the case to go away. And in doing so, he robbed the two victims of justice."

"What's your connection to the case?"

"My thesis topic involves crimes against women in the mid-twentieth century. When a few people I interviewed told me this story with the same twist, I realized I might be onto something. I've never been involved in anything like this before. A murder." She shivered. "You don't expect to uncover an unsolved capital crime when doing sociological research."

I understood her surprise. None of us think we are going to be involved in a murder, even a six-decade-old murder of strangers.

"I'd read about Tracy and her course. Actually, my mother did. When the same rumor—how the cops blew the investigation—came up repeatedly, I thought Ms. Shaw might be interested. I did a quick check of the newspaper to verify the rumor. The story, as I view it, illustrates the social environment here in Philadelphia in the 1950s. And, from what I've read about the course she teaches, that is what she is looking for." She made her position clear. She was doing Tracy a big favor. She handed me a plastic sleeve containing a printout of a newspaper article. I checked the top of the page: *Philadelphia Bulletin*, April 22, 1956.

"Did you do any more research on the killings?"

"No. I only read the one article to confirm that the events really happened. The story is tangential to my research. I didn't have the time to follow up." I sensed her relax and spotted the trace of a smile on her lips. "This is my second year working on my thesis and it isn't getting any easier. I tend to be a perfectionist. I am researching so many related topics, I can't think about doing more, but I felt someone should. Besides, I wouldn't know what to do with any additional information I found, except what I did: bring it to Ms. Shaw and, now, you." She made it sound as if she were

4

giving me a gift.

Whatever expression showed on my face, she read as doubt. "The murder happened."

I detected a touch of desperation in her tone.

I glanced over the article expecting to see two young faces, but there were no photos on the sheet. Only seven paragraphs with basic information. "The only reason you brought it to us is that you happened upon it in your research? You have no other interest?"

She appeared startled by my question. "I simply put two and two together. The murder and Tracy Shaw."

"I wouldn't happen to be helping with your dissertation research, would I?" I'm not usually that suspicious. Well, yes, I am usually that suspicious.

"I can understand why you might think I have an ulterior motive. My research is on crime statistics, on crimes against women, but I got what I needed about this particular case." She sounded a bit petulant. "As I said, I thought someone should follow up on the rumors."

"Okay, can I keep this?" I held the plastic sleeve aloft.

"And you'll share it with Tracy?"

"Of course." I couldn't blame her for sounding apprehensive, or disappointed. And, she sounded both. She didn't know me. She didn't know my investigative career had involved working closely with a New York PI. I didn't pull out my background in an effort to impress her. After all, I'd only worked with him for a brief time in the 1980s. Besides, I had other value to add. I'd actually been alive at the time of the incident. Maybe under the age of reason, but alive. I doubted that information would alleviate the young woman's concerns. She wanted Tracy, the one with her name in the paper, the one with the book on the shelf, the one who occasionally showed up on cable TV in a documentary about the unsolved mystery in her life. Antonia wanted Tracy Shaw to check out her case and I didn't blame her. Unfortunately, I was the best she was going to get. At least for starters.

"That is everything I have." She nodded at the folder. "It happened so long ago. If you don't do something soon, it will be too late. Any witnesses will be dead."

I harbored a suspicion most already were.

"What about the people who told you the rumors."

"They asked that I not share their names. They spoke to me in confidence. Besides, none of them had any first-hand knowledge. I told you. I heard *rumors*." She not only sounded anxious; she sounded imperious. "If anything is going to be done, someone has to do it immediately."

Maybe Antonia Sadoski wanted to be a hero. Maybe she just wanted to do good. I didn't try to find out. The case sounded interesting. And, as Tracy pointed out, I had time on my hands which she didn't. I told Antonia Sadoski I would look into the *rumors*.

Chapter 2

Why did I have time on my hands?

I retired from my career at forty. While some opt to retire with sufficient funds to see them through their golden years, I opted to retire with enough money to see me through the summer. Then, I went back to work at intermittent consulting jobs that always left me with time for fun. Not a lot of cash, but loads of time. I got good at finding cheap entertainment. The newspaper morgue at Philadelphia's main library offered free time-travel via old newspapers— one of the main reasons I enjoyed helping my niece with her investigations of past crimes. And now I had my own case. Or might, if I found something indicating Antonia Sadoski's suspicions were well-grounded. Or at least grounded.

The double murder of Cassie Kelly and Jonathan Brien happened in 1956. The *Bulletin* article Antonia provided cited the basics of the crime and asked good citizens to come forward if they knew anything about the car theft that resulted in the deaths of two people. The story did not include photographs, and Antonia provided nothing else with the printout. No file of clippings. No list of contacts. When family members were involved, they usually arrived loaded with old pictures, yellowing pieces of newspaper, and lists of potential witnesses or suspects. Antonia Sadoski gave me no head start. I looked to the local press to do that.

In April 1956, Philadelphia had three newspapers. I began my search with the morning *Inquirer* for the date Antonia provided. The story wasn't hard to find—if you were looking. Really looking. And since I was, I found a short article reporting two bodies had been found. Scant coverage for the discovery of a victim in Chestnut Hill, a rare occurrence in 1956. I thought the discovery must have happened shortly before the reporter's deadline.

I expected a bigger story by the *Evening Bulletin* and found the article Antonia had provided under a large headline *Lovers Found Murdered.* Smaller text underneath explained there had been a *New Car Ride to Death.* This news, however, wasn't plastered across the front page. The big story in that day's paper was the royal wedding in Monaco where local girl, Grace Kelly, married Prince Rainier of Monaco. I had to page through section two to find the story about the murders of Jonathan Brien, born John O'Brien, law student from West Philadelphia, and Catherine "Cassie" Kelly, maid from Germantown.

The two met at the home of a Henry Parry in Chestnut Hill. I didn't know Henry Parry but I did know Philadelphia, at least 1950s Philadelphia, and could figure out what being Henry Parry of Parry, Shippen, Weathersby and Baron meant in 1956. Whatever he said back then would have gone. And, he said the Brien kid visited the Parry house and offered the maid a ride home. He assumed the two stopped for a little hanky-panky along Cresheim Valley Road, a lovers' lane even I had visited, admittedly over a decade later. I'd never heard a peep about a murder at the locale.

The article went on to provide specifics about the scene, details that, although they supported the cops' theory of the crime, did not rule out other scenarios. Based on the account, I concluded that, in under twenty-four hours, the police had made up their collective mind and were searching for what modern-day authorities would call a carjacker. The article devoted a lot more space to the achievements of Henry Parry and earlier generations of his esteemed family than it did to the accomplishments of the two victims who were defined according to their relationship to the *bigwig,* as Antonia Sadoski called him. Catherine "Cassie" Kelly was the lovely maid at the Parry house. Jonathan Brien became the handsome visitor who offered the family's maid a ride.

I moved onto a brief piece in the *Daily News* that provided no more insight into the victims or the crime.

I checked the following days' news. I didn't find another word about the two victims until the day of Cassie's and Jonathan's funerals. A picture of each victim and the mourners at their gravesites accompanied an article stating simply where and when the two had been buried with their family and friends in attendance. A brief summary of the investigation indicated no progress had been made.

At least this story included photos. I studied the victims. The press described Cassie as lovely and she was. In what must have been her high school graduation portrait, she sat with her back to the camera and, with dreamy eyes, gazed over her shoulder into her future. Jonathan's picture, most likely his college graduation photo, showed a serious young man, or a young man doing his best to look serious. He too stared into the future, but one that dreams had nothing to do with. He leaned forward as if demonstrating he knew where he was going. Of course, I made all this up. I had to. The reporters gave me nothing concrete to work with.

I printed the articles I found and used the library's Internet access for a few searches, including my usual checks of the weather and moon phase on the night of April 21, 1956 before setting out for Germantown to share my information with Tracy.

Chapter 3

I took a small detour on my way to Tracy's house which, by my definition, means I went completely out of my way. Trolleys like the ones that carried Cassie Kelly along Germantown Avenue to her job no longer rolled up and down the street, but cars still had to straddle tracks that had outlived their usefulness. My car slipped back and forth across the metal strips until I reached the corner of Cresheim Valley Road where I expected to find a spot to pull off and park. I made a left but saw no picnic area. I continued my drive. I recalled a space for picnicking right off the road. Maybe I had it wrong. Maybe? Clearly, I had it wrong. The space I envisioned was not there.

The visits I remembered were from a time, so distant, when I shared a few kisses in that park. Actually, more than a few kisses with a boy for whom I thought I had strong feelings. At the time, I assumed they were feelings. I now know they were urges and I had no feelings for him. But still, I recalled our time in the park. Didn't I?

I remembered driving by the spot recently. Well, recently if you count the nineties as recent. Or maybe the eighties. What did it matter? Clearly, the locale—if I drove to the right one and not a product of my imagination—had been altered, redesigned, repurposed. There would be no chance to sit in the place where Jonathan Brien and Cassie Kelly shared their last kiss—alleged kiss—the one during which they had supposedly been attacked and murdered. I would not be able to employ Tracy's technique of standing where the victim stood, or, in this case, sitting where these victims sat, to gain insight into the event. Not a huge disappointment. Even though she used it religiously, my niece swore the tactic never worked. Not once. So, despite circling a few times expecting the familiar spot to reappear miraculously, I didn't feel too concerned. I moved on.

The drive to Tracy's gave me time to theorize about what had gone on between Cassie and Jonathan. I had been a little kid during the fifties and I bought into the naiveté attributed to the era. Viewing movies from those years as an adult, however, raised my suspicions that things weren't as innocent as I believed. After all, crowds flocked to see *An Affair to Remember,* not *A Dinner and Dance to Remember.* Moviemakers made sure I didn't actually see anything. Had Cassie Kelly been just as naïve? Or had she been up for a romantic interlude with a man she barely knew?

When I arrived at the stone Victorian Tracy was housesitting, her housemate answered the door. "She's not home yet, but I am." Alex gave me a loose hug and a light kiss I could hear but not feel. "The sun's almost down and the autumn air is getting a little chilly. If I am not mistaken we are drawing perilously close to happy hour. Please join me and get happy. Tracy should return in three martinis at the most."

He shuffled across the living room, dragging his feet like a two-year-old wearing his father's boat shoes. When he wasn't dressed for his job in finance, Alex generally looked as if he had just hopped off a sailboat, although I'd never actually known him to sail. That day, despite the autumn chill in the air, he looked the part in khaki shorts almost covered by a shirt as oversized as the shoes that appeared to have been stretching for decades.

I'm not a martini drinker, so he set me up with a red wine and a tray of assorted cheeses, crackers and grapes in the long living room lined with overstuffed bookshelves and artifacts of world travel—none of it belonging to Tracy, the house sitter, or Alex, her houseguest.

"I'm helping Tracy with a project." I grabbed a cracker and pulled my legs up under me and settled in for the wait.

"Who brought this case to her?" Alex exaggerated his exasperation. "Someone with money I hope."

"Appeared to me she has plenty. However, I don't think we're going to see any of it. She is a student. Even if she is filthy rich, she might have nothing in her own name while she waits to inherit a fortune."

"Or she could be poor as a church mouse but good at faking the rich girl look." Alex raised a glass to toast Antonia Sadoski.

"Also possible."

"Probable. People with money don't have problems for Tracy to solve." He sighed theatrically. "If only they did."

I touched my glass to his. "Maybe they do but they don't need Tracy's help. They hire professional investigators. The people Tracy helps need her."

"Go ahead." Alex offered a slice of cheese on a water cracker. "Eat my Camembert and make me feel guilty for being so mercenary. Although technically, it's Tracy's Camembert."

"There's not enough public information about this crime to make a good case study without an extensive investigation. I don't think Tracy will change her mind about investing time in it. The student only happened upon it when doing research for her thesis. You know Tracy needs to be pulled in by a friend or family member of the victim or the unjustly accused."

"Are you asking if I understand that she is a sucker?" He didn't wait for my answer. "I do."

"But the lure of a broken heart hasn't come up in this case. I doubt it ever will but I did basic research to lay the groundwork in case Tracy wants to jump in." I dropped the copies I'd made at the library on the ottoman that served as a coffee table. "There isn't much there but the story is kind of interesting if you want to read."

He curled his lip to tell me he did not. "I'll look at the pictures. You can fill me in."

I did. "From what I saw in the newspaper, not much to tell, the investigation concluded the perp attacked the couple in the car, dumped the bodies on the ground and took a little joyride. All the papers quoted Henry Parry's theory that someone wanted the car, a 1956 Thunderbird convertible."

"A really sweet ride." Alex didn't own a car but when he rented he never went for the compact Ford sedan. He upgraded, as far as a rental company could go, to a fancy vehicle loaded with luxuries. Somehow or other, any time he delivered Tracy to my apartment he managed to do it in a luxury car, once a pale blue Bentley convertible. "What color Thunderbird?" He asked.

"Peacock blue."

"That car would be a big hit with the ladies." Alex nodded. "Or, in my case, with the boys."

"Even with the top up?" I doubted the entire carjacking scenario. "I checked the weather. The temperature hit the mid-fifties during the day but this happened after dark—on a cloudy night with no moon. Not the perfect time for a joyride which might explain why the police found the car with the roof closed."

"I might have indulged in a joyride with the top up especially if I didn't want to be spotted." He paused. "But I wouldn't have. I would have put the roof down and cranked up the heat." He made a great show of wrapping his brain around this dilemma. "Okay, I agree that even in inclement weather keeping the top up is a pretty conservative approach to joyriding. But then again, I don't have much hair to worry about. Maybe that guy did, or maybe he liked ladies with fancy, fifties hairdos. A girl with a French twist might want to keep it out of the wind." Alex patted his soft brown waves to mime a woman protecting a tall hairdo. "Did the newspaper confirm a single perp?" He asked proudly. "See, I pay attention to everything Tracy says. I am learning the questions to ask."

"The article speculated that more than one person could

have been involved. As far as I can see, the cops wrapped up this case rather quickly. The newspaper said the car had been wiped down but, later on in the same story, it mentioned the cops were following up on fingerprint evidence. So, maybe the perp, or perps, missed a couple of prints. I assume the police never found any matches."

"Weapon?" Alex pointed to himself proudly to reinforce the idea that he knew what questions to ask.

"Heavy object. Unknown at the time of the articles. Not found at the scene. Jonathan Brien had been badly beaten. It only took two blows to kill Cassie Kelly. I've been thinking about that. If the guy went down in a fight, the perp might have felt he had to kill the girl, the only witness."

"Or, the perp might have killed Cassie first."

"If so, where was Brien? Why wasn't he defending her?" I sipped my wine. "The cops found blood in the trunk. If it belonged to Brien, maybe he went for a weapon, a tire iron, a jack, something to defend himself. Of course, there is another, more horrifying, option. It occurred to me the killer might have put him in the trunk and taken his time with Cassie."

"Any sign of sexual assault?"

"I don't know how straightforward the cops were with the press, or the press was with the public in those days, but none is mentioned."

"Was there room to stash the guy back in the trunk?"

"From what I found online in an old ad, the space could easily hold two bodies, even three if needed, which offers another possibility. We can't assume they were murdered in the park. If they weren't killed where they were found, the perp might have locked both victims in the trunk to transport them."

Alex studied the newspaper photo. "Pretty girl. One thing I learned from all this gruesome business Tracy gets me involved with?" He paused for dramatic effect. "Always have a current photo."

"This one is probably her high school graduation picture. Dreaming about her future."

"Really?" Alex sipped his wine and studied the newspaper picture. "I think she's older than eighteen. Did she go to college?"

"Not that I read. She died at twenty while working as a maid."

"The drape low around her shoulders is kind of seductive. I don't know what she's dreaming about but I don't think it's something the good sisters at St. Mary's of the Modest Neckline High School would have liked in their 1954 yearbook." Alex studied the picture.

"Funny, I didn't see that school in her bio."

"You weren't reading between the lines of the young Kelly girl's bio." He studied the photo. "Sad. Such a pretty girl." He glanced at a wedding photo of the new princess of Monaco at the bottom of the page. "Almost as pretty as Grace Kelly."

"Pretty close." I studied Cassie's photo. I noted the same cool elegance that I saw in Grace Kelly. And, in Antonia Sadoski.

"What about the guy? He looks okay too. Kind of serious."

Jonathan didn't appear happy in his photo. I had no clue if that was true or not. "The article doesn't give much away about either of them. He was a law student at Penn who had changed his name. At some point, John O'Brien became Jonathan Brien. There's a comment about his father and brother cooperating with the police and a long shot of them at the funeral. So I know he had family. All they say about Cassie's family is that they buried her. There are a couple of photos of the gravesites in the article *Murder Victims Laid to Rest*."

"I wonder if the perp came to the funeral. I bet he did." Alex squinted at the pictures. "Not that these photos would give him away."

15

"It is odd. The newspapers covered the stories but not heavily. I know the story had to compete for space with Grace Kelly's wedding, but I wonder if they held back on sensationalizing it because of pressure from the Parrys. The family would not want their names in the paper except in the Society pages."

"You think the family had that kind of power?" Alex's tone suggested he thought they might.

"Power might mean social connections. Not necessarily sinister."

Alex sighed. "That girl who came to Tracy should have gone to the police. They work on unsolved cases."

"Technically, this case is probably still open, but I don't imagine it has gotten much attention in decades. I'm not sure how happy a police department suffering under budget constraints would be to spend resources on a sixty-year-old murder based on rumors a graduate student heard."

"Sixty years. That's a long time. You might not be able to find anyone from back then who is still alive."

I stared at Alex long and hard. "I was around back then and I am still alive."

I watched as he did some quick math in his head. "Not for long."

"Why? Did you put something in this wine to kill me?"

Alex remained puzzled for only a moment. "I mean back then you weren't alive that long. You weren't old enough to be a good witness."

"I remember Grace Kelly's wedding. A friend of my parents went and sent us a postcard that I kept for years. It had portraits of the Prince and the Princess with scenes of Monaco in the background. All black and white but I loved it."

"You remember that card because you had it for years. You saw it again when you were ten, twelve, maybe even sixteen. Otherwise, you might not have remembered it."

"But I recall the day it arrived. I think if I'd seen someone

get murdered that same day—as long as I was not a baby—
I would remember."

Alex, unconvinced, shrugged. "Maybe. Maybe not."

"Maybe not what?" Tracy was home.

Chapter 4

Tracy staggered through the door, dropped her bags on the floor and flopped on the couch. Even her dark-brown ponytail that usually bounced cheerfully behind her looked tired. I swore it had lost its usual texture and shine.

"Bad day, dear?" Alex asked. "I'll get you a glass of wine."

"That would help." Tracy turned to me. "I want to continue with this career change." Her tone added: *I really do, but it's killing me*.

When she wanted to make a change, Tracy knew she could look to me for encouragement. Unlike her parents, I didn't worry when she worked her way through her twenties at a number of seemingly random occupations. I, probably projecting my personal feelings, worried when she turned thirty and felt that she had to settle into a business career that she appeared to hate. I was happy to see her trying to escape the business world. "Basically, I love teaching, especially the adults I have in my Saturday class. But this term?" She forced a shudder. "There is one know-it-all."

I suspected there would always be one know-it-all.

"He wears me out. Next term I am finding a way to check ages so I pick a case solved ten years before the birth of the oldest student."

In the class Tracy taught, called *Writing in Time*, she presented the students with an actual crime. Then she guided their research while they wrote a fictionalized scenario using the basics of the murder and the details of the era.

"The usual problem . . . . Did I say problem? I mean challenge. The usual challenge is kids having absolutely no idea of the years we're dealing with, but, in this class, I have the opposite situation. One guy claims to know it all. He's a veritable Forrest Gump. To hear him tell it, nothing happened in 1960 that he did not witness. No one, including me, believes a word he says."

She took a glass from Alex's hand but didn't stop talking to take a sip. "And, he tells every story in real-time. 'So, I remember that morning as if it were yesterday. I got up at about 8 AM. A little before eight actually. I like to get up with the sun but, at that time of year, the sun comes up too early for me. So, the old clock on the wall said close to eight o'clock when I threw back my covers, you know not covers like we have covers now, back then we didn't use comforters, we used . . . ."

"Please stop," Alex begged as he handed her a cracker. "Eat this."

"We get the picture," I assured her.

"I've spoken to other instructors about techniques to shut him up, but he is immune to the normal approaches."

"You could say, *why don't you shut up, you ignorant old goat, you're boring everyone to death,*" Alex offered. "I assume he is."

"He's boring me."

"How old is he?" Alex asked.

"Old," Tracy stated emphatically and then blushed.

"My age?" I asked.

"Probably." Her tone apologized.

"Hey, Aunt Julia. That might be a hot date for you." Alex offered.

"Next topic." I pointed to the folders on the ottoman and filled Tracy in on my meeting with Antonia Sadoski.

Tracy picked up the newspaper clippings. "I would have thought that in an era less inured to crime, the murder of a beautiful young couple would have caught the public's imagination."

"Maybe it would have if the press had not been so preoccupied with the happy news of Grace Kelly's marriage," I explained.

"But *we* think the Parrys shut the press up," Alex added.

"Or at least caused reporters to behave with a certain decorum." I slipped a cracker into my mouth.

"The Parrys might have just wanted to avoid notoriety. Henry Parry was an attorney. He would have known that classifying the crime as a random act focuses the investigation on the victims' activities. The cops would be looking for a timeline, not motives within the Parry household. He probably prized his privacy." Tracy suggested.

Alex offered another theory. "And, if the cops view the victims as a single entity, a couple that is the victim of a random crime, they might not feel as compelled to delve into the details of each victim's life."

"Even if they weren't viewed as a single entity, no one would ever know if one party was the target and the other an innocent bystander." I threw out another point to consider. "That complicates things."

Tracy leaned back and stretched her legs along the couch. "Parry, the attorney, knew all of this and could have used that knowledge to direct the police away from a crime in his household. But then again, he might just have been a snob who didn't want to see his family name in the newspaper connected with something so unseemly."

"Which is where we started." Alex sounded frustrated.

"Do you think this case would be good for your class?" I asked Tracy.

"I think it has the potential to be great," Alex answered.

Tracy and I stared at him.

Unfazed, he explained why. "I like the idea of the class distinctions that were so blatant back then. The murder itself may turn out to be cut-and-dry but I bet some of the underlying issues would make great fodder for studying the fifties. A striving young law student. A maid. A millionaire."

I agreed but waited for Tracy to offer her opinion.

"Or," she paused for dramatic effect, "the murders could simply have been what the authorities claimed, a random act, with none of those elements playing a role in the crime. Calling the murder of two young people with no significant connection to one another, a carjacking eliminates the need to uncover a motive in the killing of either. That might be a win for the Parry family, but it's a real bonus for the murderer." She nodded at the heap of bags she had lugged home from her teaching job. "I do not have the time right now to take this further."

"Too bad." Alex sounded truly dejected.

Tracy eyed him with amazement. "You never want me to take these projects." She paused. "I need to be motivated. This one has no strong personal driver."

Alex proclaimed that to be the good news. "That might be a positive. I've seen you get ripped apart by sad stories from decades ago. With this case, you can't get too involved with a damaged party, because there isn't one. All that happens is you end up with a great story for your class."

"Well," I spoke tentatively, "maybe I could stick with it, take a little look-see."

Tracy turned to Alex. "Now see what you've done. You've dragged my aunt into this. I don't want her out there talking to strangers on my behalf."

"I can help her. I help you all the time." Alex turned to me. "I perform bodyguard duties. Not all the time. We have rules you see."

Tracy smiled. "Yes, *we* do."

"The most important one is *never approach anyone who might be the real killer without me,*" Alex explained.

"That is not actually the rule, but Alex does go along on interviews that I suspect might present a problem."

"Or *I suspect*," Alex said. "I am a little more suspicious than Tracy is."

"I don't want to push . . . ." I made a weak protest.

Tracy waved her wine glass at me. "Go ahead. I can tell you're interested."

"They were such attractive young people who could be alive today." I felt an attachment to the two victims developing.

"Although no longer young and possibly not that attractive."

Tracy and I shut down Alex's ruminations with matching scowls.

He changed his approach. "I'll be happy to help although don't get too fond of them yet. They might have become total jerks. The kind of people who monopolize the discussion in Tracy's class."

"Or maybe they'd be warm, wonderful friends who routinely offer perceptive insights and listen attentively to others." Tracy raised her glass in a toast.

"I'm going with that." I clicked my glass against hers. "Until proven otherwise."

Chapter 5

Tracy claimed to be too busy to call at John Brien's grave with me. She never wanted to go on cemetery visits—a point of contention between the two of us. I always tried to cajole her into making a trip but she protested every time. "What would we possibly learn there? Sometimes, most times, the victim has never been there. What do you think will happen? We'll drop by decades later and find the perp kneeling at the grave lamenting aloud, 'I am so sorry I killed you?'"

I wasn't that foolish. Although the fantasy did occasionally play in my mind, I was seeking inspiration and motivation, not to mention some facts about the family. This trip to Holy Cross Cemetery served a specific purpose: find Jonathan Brien, buried as John O'Brien, maybe with relatives in a family plot. I would have preferred to visit Cassie first, but finding information on Jonathan proved easier.

The weather made it a perfect day to visit a cemetery—a true metaphor for death. Fallen leaves. Gray skies. A chill in the air. An appropriate atmosphere for wandering through the rows of headstones—which was fortunate because finding the gravesite location online proved easier than finding the physical location on the ground. I walked through the headstones seeking the grave of Jonathan Brien.

"Oh man, if this is the right spot, Jonathan would hate it." I stopped at a Celtic cross taller than any of the surrounding monuments. The headstone of the O'Brien family. Mother Margaret. Father John. Son John. The years etched into the stone matched. I had found the grave of John O'Brien.

If Jonathan Brien could get a message to me from beyond

the grave, I felt pretty sure I knew what he would say. *I spent all my money and made a huge effort to become Jonathan Brien and my father puts John O'Brien on my tombstone and tops it off with a huge Celtic cross just in case anyone missed the fact that I was an Irish Catholic.*

A wind swept across the cemetery and I pulled my coat tight around me. I swore I could feel Jonathan's anger. He wanted so much and worked so hard to become a new person. And then someone stole that image from him and left him under a cross that signified everything he wanted to escape.

My sympathy remained qualified because he should have appreciated being laid to rest with people who loved him, the same people he felt ashamed of. To fight my feeling of annoyance, I cautioned myself that what I felt was nothing more than my emotions reacting to the little my brain had learned about him. I realized that my subconscious was speaking through music when I heard humming *The Great Pretender*.

I told myself to keep quiet. I had a long way to go to know Jonathan Brien. But the trip proved to be a worthwhile first step that led me to an obvious second step. I felt confident that I had identified the right O'Brien family.

Chapter 6

No matter how many times I helped Tracy, I felt excited but apprehensive about several of the tasks involved, e.g., confronting strangers, accusing strangers—who was I kidding—simply approaching strangers made my palms sweat.

I had butterflies in my stomach as I drove across the bridge to the barrier island that was Ocean City, New Jersey. A typical reaction. The sight of the ocean with the sun glimmering on its rumpled surface did nothing to calm me. Neither did the presence of my friend, Liz, although she tried.

"Why are you nervous? You say he is not a suspect. You don't even know we are headed for the right guy."

"I'm pretty sure. Not one hundred percent but confident." At least about my target's identity.

Without giving myself a chance to chicken out, I drove straight to the address on Central Avenue. Summer visitors had departed, just when I needed them. No pedestrians in the crosswalks to stop me. No cars looking for parking spaces near the beach to block me. We sped right along. Well, cruised. I stayed under the speed limit and still the ride passed alarmingly quickly. I was dismayed that we reached 27th Street in record time.

I hopped out of the car, at least a sixty-year-old's version of hopping, and stood on the street making a great show of looking for the right address. Spotting the oversized numbers on the front door of the duplex directly in front of me killed my excuse for lingering by the car. I took a deep breath. "Let's do this."

Liz trailed me up the few steps to the first-floor

apartment that I hoped was Timothy O'Brien's. In case of an unfriendly reception, fleeing from a downstairs location would prove easier.

I knocked and waited thirty seconds. "Guess he isn't home."

"Knock again." Liz reached past me and banged on the door.

"Darn." When no one answered her knock, I painted a look of disappointment on my face. Truth was, no matter how far I traveled, I often felt relieved when the person wasn't at home. "I wonder where he is."

"In the apartment upstairs?" Liz made a good point.

"Maybe." I eyed the first-floor mailbox.

Liz noticed. "Isn't it a federal crime to mess with the mail?"

"I'm not going to mess with it." I lifted the flap and peeked inside. "Largely because there isn't any mail."

I checked out the mailbox at the bottom of the steps to the second floor and spotted a yellow envelope sticking out of the top. I sauntered over to the foot of the steps that climbed along the side of the house, peeked in and twisted my head to read the name on the label. *Current resident*.

"You are acting like a criminal." Liz walked over with long confident strides and hit the envelope with a sleek red nail to reveal the next piece of mail. "Look at that. A strong gust of wind must have knocked that forward."

I craned my neck to peek in. "Sylvia Woodson."

"Might be his girlfriend." Liz knocked another envelope forward.

"Harry Albright," I read.

"So, I think we are at the right door down here. Looks like no one is home. Maybe you should have called."

I couldn't resent that Liz suggested the obvious. "Tracy prefers catching people when the element of surprise makes it harder for them to say no." Although it also makes it easier for them to slam a door in my face. I didn't share that with

Liz who did not enjoy confrontation, let alone rejection. "I don't want to get sidelined by a phone brush-off. I want to see the person's face even it turns out their face is hostile."

"Let's see if his car is here." Liz led me down the side of the duplex.

"I wonder if that is his Subaru." I pointed to a sun-bleached station wagon that had once been red. "I see wash on the line." I stepped onto a cement driveway. The half that did not house the Subaru served as a clothes dryer.

"An athlete." Liz looked at the sweat clothes. "Jogger." She pointed to two pairs of sneakers airing on the small back porch.

"Do you think he's out for a run?"

"If he is, he must be naked. There's a lot of laundry here."

I checked out the hanging clothes. "There are two black outfits and one pair of black sneakers. There are two turquoise suits and one pair of matching sneakers. There is one green suit."

Liz followed my train of thought. "So we should be searching for a man in a green suit and sneakers."

"That would be my guess."

"Do you have a feeling about where he would be running?"

We spoke in unison. "The Boardwalk."

That was when we heard the voice. We both spun around but didn't find the source.

"Up here."

We tilted our heads back and raised our hands to shade our eyes. A man about the same age as Liz and I leaned over the railing of the second-floor porch of the house next door. "If you want O'Brien, you'll probably find him up on the Boardwalk jogging. Left about half an hour ago. If it's his wife you want, you're out of luck. She is visiting her mother."

"Thanks." I smiled although part of me resented his

butting into what I considered impressive detective work.

Beside me, Liz muttered. "We knew that."

"Who should I say stopped by?"

"Oh." That was a good question. I could hardly say a friend of his brother's. I stretched the single syllable into a sound that said don't worry about it. "We'll stop back."

"Yes." Liz grew flirtatious. With her carefully coiffed hair and tastefully made-up face, she could carry off a coy response. She wagged a well-manicured nail at him. "Don't you say a word to ruin our surprise."

We offered insincere thanks to O'Brien's neighbor and drove the few blocks to the end of the Ocean City boardwalk at Twenty-Third Street. I couldn't help noticing that we rode by Grace Kelly's childhood summer home. The Spanish-style structure no longer reminded me of the movie-star-turned-princess. It reminded me of the aspiring star, Cassie Kelly, whose death shared space in the newspaper with the royal wedding.

Chapter 7

In the autumn without a crowd, the boards provided a perfect place for a jog but as we stared down the long wooden walkway that stretched for two and a half miles, we saw no runner as far as we could see which, in Liz's case, was farther than I could. She is one of those people described as *seeing ships before they come over the horizon*.

"How far do you think he runs?" Liz asked.

"Couple of miles?" I had no idea.

"How long would that take?"

"It would take me several days. I'd stop at the Port'o Call and get a room for the night." I leaned against the railing.

"If I ran, I'd run on the beach down by the water," Liz said as she settled onto the bench that faced the length of the Boardwalk.

"You hate the sand."

"Only the soft stuff. I'd ask Tony to carry me to the hard stuff." Liz had a very accommodating husband. "But for now, I'll just sit here on this bench." Through her oversized designer sunglasses, she watched the wooden walkway that laid a path to her feet.

I gazed over the beach in case Timothy O'Brien, like Liz, liked to run along the water's edge. Even though the day was gorgeous, the beach and the Boardwalk were all but empty. I looked south and spotted tiny figures in the distance. Two human. One canine. I turned north and saw no one. Too bad. The ocean breeze swept across the wide expanse of sand and rustled the tall dune grass to lay a soft soundtrack on top of the rumbling of the rolling surf. A tiny bit chilly for those of us who were standing still, but close to a perfect day for a runner. I felt happy to be there. My apprehension level

29

dropped.

"There's a store I like on Asbury," Liz pulled out a nail file and began an accounting of the inventory the last time she had strolled along the avenue visiting shops. She described the stock of a half-dozen stores before she called out, "Green jogger approaching." She sounded excited, not because we might have found our man but because, if we had, we might get to move on to shopping.

The man moving towards us, with a gait closer to a walk than a run, might have been in his seventies, the right age for the man we wanted to see. When he came closer I saw that, as an older person, he did not resemble Jonathan Brien, and I doubted he had in his youth. The shape of his face was rounder, the cut of his features was softer and I could see traces of red in his white hair. Jonathan's brother could as easily have had brown or black hair but red was the stereotypical color for an O'Brien. I had a feeling we were about to meet our man. I steeled myself. I'd have to approach him. Talking to Tim O'Brien was why I came.

The jogger didn't notice us, although we were the only people not only on the Boardwalk but as far as the eye could see. He stared forward, oblivious to Liz's and my presence.

"Timothy O'Brien?" I stepped away from the railing but stopped short of blocking his path.

The man started before his face contorted into a frown. Plotting his getaway? That's how I read his expression, but he answered. "That's me." He ran in place for a few seconds before leaning over and pulling his shirt up to wipe the sweat from his brow. Staying bent over he dropped his hands to his knees. After ten seconds in that pose gathering air to speak, he straightened. "Who wants to know?" He didn't seem fearful, just a bit curious and more than a little annoyed.

"My name is Julia Tracy. I wanted to talk to you about your brother, Jonathan."

"Did you know Johnny?"

I detected no smile on the man's face but found it in his tone. I hated to disappoint him. "No. No. I didn't. I was only a kid when . . . when . . . ."

"When he died." He went back to ministering to his sweaty brow. "So was I. If you didn't know him, what's your interest?"

"I was asked to check into the circumstances of his death."

His eyes narrowed and his lips constricted into a tight grin. "What's the rush? He's only been dead for sixty years." He waited for his sarcasm to sink in. "Why you? You a cop?" He sounded doubtful and looked even more skeptical when he glanced at Liz ignoring us in favor of her nails.

"No, it's complicated. My niece, Tracy Shaw, has done investigative work on old cases. I help her out sometimes."

"She a cop?"

"No. No. She's a teacher. People come to her for help on old cases."

"Why?"

Good question. One that Tracy herself asked. "A few years ago she wrote a book about her attempt to find a missing friend. Ever since then, people come to her for help in finding the truth." Which she had done several times. "Now she teaches a class called *Writing in Time* at Wallmann College."

"Criminology?"

"No. English. Writing." I sensed a total lack of comprehension on O'Brien's part. "She guides students through the process of writing fiction based on a real crime. She shows them how to research and represent the era. On occasion, she has uncovered significant information about the case."

"Who wants to find the truth about Johnny's death?" He sounded suspicious.

"A student who heard about the double-homicide."

"What did they hear?"

"Rumors, really. She—my source was a young woman— wouldn't be specific but she said people told her that the killings did not happen the way the cops said." I decided I'd better not say anything about the bigwig, Henry Parry, for fear of turning the concerned brother into a vigilante. "My niece asked me to contact people about the event." I hated to use the word, murder, to the family although Tim O'Brien knew full well what that *event* was. "So I thought I would talk to you."

"About time somebody did."

"According to the newspaper, the cops did talk to you back in 1956. An article I read said you were very cooperative."

"Did the newspapers note that I told the cops there was no way on earth that Johnny went to a lover's lane with a kitchen maid?"

"Your family too good for the domestic help?"

"Not my family. Johnny."

"How so?"

"My brother wanted the right girl, the right clothes, the right car. A big house on the Main Line or in Chestnut Hill." Tim's intonation made it fairly clear that he did not share his brother's goals.

"It appeared that your brother was doing okay for himself. Villanova. Penn Law School. Nice car. Fancy friends."

"You're right. He was doing okay. Especially for a poor kid from West Philly. He could have made money for himself and had a nice life, but that wasn't enough. He wanted to be part of Philadelphia Society. Can you hear the capital S? Society where you mingle with the right people— not their maids."

My knowledge of 1950s Philadelphia said that would be a stretch for an Irish kid from West Philly.

"When most kids read the sports page, Johnny devoured the Society columns."

That time I heard the capital S.

"Never got his picture in the paper but he did wangle a couple of invitations."

"He and his friends?"

"He moved on from his old friends."

"New friends?"

He stared across the ocean for a second before he answered with a touch of sadness. "I never met any of them."

"Did he have any time for girlfriends?"

"No time. No money. Not for regular girls, not for girls from the neighborhood. He didn't even go to his prom. He showed no interest in anything or anyone that did not move him towards his goals."

"He must have needed money to fit in." My statement was really a question and O'Brien answered it.

"I swear he still had his First Communion money when he died. As long as I can remember, he saved every penny he got. When he was old enough to work, he took every job he could get. Smart kid but he studied like a madman for scholarships. Villanova came through so he went. My father felt so proud but Johnny didn't like the idea of a Catholic college. When it came time for law school, he made sure he got to Penn. He wanted Ivy League. Even with his tuition paid, he didn't relax. From senior year of high school on, his favorite job was to stack groceries at night. Know why he worked the late shift?"

I shook my head even though Tim did not expect an answer.

He shook his head with a look of disgust on his face. "So no one would see him." He gazed out over the waves. "Johnny had to have the right thing. Not just a tennis racket, the right tennis racket. Not just golf clubs, the right golf clubs. The irony? The cops think he was killed with one of his fancy golf clubs. The putter was missing." He used his shirt to wipe his brow again but found no sweat. I suspected he was hiding his emotions. When he revealed his face again, he appeared composed. "Johnny was on a mission. He bought the kind of clothes that those people, the rich ones, wore and then he washed them over and over again so people would conclude he owned them for years."

"Sounds as if he worked hard on his image."

"24/7."

I guess I had to ask but I knew the answer. "Is that why he dropped the O from O'Brien?"

"Broke my father's heart." O'Brien sounded both bewildered and sad. "Poor guy found out when he went to Johnny's college graduation."

Timothy settled on the bench beside Liz as if his heart had also been broken, just then, there on the Boardwalk. "Johnny had dreams."

Liz stopped fiddling with her nails and turned to listen.

*****Timothy O'Brien*****
O'Brien Home
Philadelphia, Pennsylvania
April 1956

Johnny's tuxedo didn't fit in. Not in their living room, not next to the beat-up couch and the armchair with frayed upholstery. Maybe if his mother had lived. Maybe then the living room would be pretty like the neighbors' with soft pillows with embroidery and white curtains with ruffles. Sometimes his friend's house even smelled of flowers. The O'Brien house smelled of cigarette smoke. He heard people on television talk about a woman's touch. That was what their house needed, what their house lacked, a woman's touch. His memories did not include life with his mother, so he couldn't remember if there had ever been a woman's touch at the O'Brien house. If there had been, any signs had long since disappeared. He might only be a kid but he knew. Johnny's tuxedo would have looked better in the house next door.

"Listen to me, Timmy. You're lucky. There's a lot you can learn from me. I had to discover everything for myself."

Timothy didn't understand why Johnny bothered showing him how to dress for dinner. He didn't need a monkey suit to eat TV dinners on a tray watching Douglas Edwards deliver the news, but he paid attention. Johnny was really smart. Everyone said so.

"You're sixteen now, Timmy. You need to learn these things." Johnny studied his tuxedo in the mirror. "Never rent a suit. It's important to have your own tuxedo if you want to go anywhere in life."

"Where would I go?"

Johnny smiled. Not a mean smile. Timothy thought his brother found his questions funny but not dumb. "There is a lot more to the world than the block we live on. No more than ten miles from here there are beautiful people wearing beautiful clothes in beautiful houses. I want to go there, Timothy. In . . ." Johnny put an arm around his shoulders, guided him towards the door and waved his arm with a dramatic flourish. ". . . my beautiful new ride."

Timothy ran towards the turquoise blue car parked along the curb. He recognized that it was a 1956 Thunderbird and that a Thunderbird was a nice car. Everyone knew it was a nice car. He liked that on the warm night the neighbors sitting on the porches of their row houses saw Johnny's new wheels. The ones that weren't would hear that Johnny O'Brien got himself a new convertible.

"Wow. That's yours? When can I take it for a spin?"

"Not while you're driving on a learner's permit. I shelved a lot of groceries to pay for this car, Timmy. And, I look great in it." He slipped into the driver's seat.

"It's really cool, Johnny."

"I want to look more than cool. I want to look classy." Johnny turned to face him as if he had something important to say. "I met her, Timmy."

Timothy, confused, climbed into the passenger seat. "Who?"

"The girl who is my ticket out of here."

"Is she pretty?" Timothy figured that was what love was all about. Sooner or later he would meet a pretty girl, one who liked him back.

"She lives on this huge estate in Chestnut Hill with a pool and a pool house and tennis courts and a guest cottage as big as our whole house. They even have a pond that freezes in the winter so they can ice skate in their own back yard."

Timothy guessed she must be pretty. "Do you like her?"

Johnny ran a hand along the dashboard. Timothy didn't know how his brother felt about the girl but he knew Johnny loved that car. "I'm going to marry her, Timmy. I'm going to marry a socialite."

*****

"I thought being a socialite was like being Irish or Italian, only better." He snickered at his youthful naiveté. "And I guess, in a way, I was right." And then I heard the only indication of bitterness toward his brother's desire to leave his roots behind. He patted what I suspected had been brighter red hair and flashed an insincere smile. "At least he didn't have to worry about his Irish red hair."

"Did your brother tell you who the girl was?"

He nodded. "The daughter of a big-deal WASP lawyer who married a Catholic. Johnny figured that a guy like that couldn't be too stodgy. Johnny wanted to join this guy's law firm, meet his daughter and marry her. Although not in that order. He had already met her."

"Did he give you a name?"

"Sure. Parry—the family the other victim that night, Cassie Kelly, worked for."

Chapter 8

"You know you are a puzzle to me," Liz said over her scallops.

I asked for clarification.

"I studied you today while you were talking to Timothy O'Brien."

I let my eyebrows express my concern so my mouth could work on my crab cakes.

"Clearly, you love the idea of helping Tracy, but just as clearly you are uncomfortable talking to family members, not to mention witnesses, suspects, whatever. Let's call them persons of interest."

Apparently, I was not so clever about hiding my discomfort as I'd thought.

"If we couldn't find Timothy O'Brien you would have gone home, somewhat relieved, and told yourself this case was too old and wasn't going to work. But by the time you finished talking to him, you were hooked. You saw a brother's pain and you reacted to it. I watched. His pain became your pain. You can't walk away."

"I didn't plan on walking away."

"Good, because you can't. You gave him hope. Not that he gave you much to go on."

"In a way, he did. He was adamant that no one in his brother's life would want to hurt him. He couldn't relate a single incident or provide a single name. That says a lot although I won't have any facts to report to Tracy."

"When are you seeing her?"

"Tuesday night. I'm a guest at her class tomorrow. A witness to the era."

"You might have more by then."

But I didn't. I had no bombshell revelation to share as I drove to the Wallmann campus for my first visit to Tracy's class as a guest participant. Not a guest speaker. I would simply join the circle of students as an expert on the year they were studying—expert being defined as someone alive at the time. In return, Tracy would treat me to an early dinner in the cafeteria that I tried to find based on markers such as the Class of 1905 Memorial Garden and the Hilary Barkley Meacham Class of 1927 bench.

Walking across the Wallmann campus made it easy to get into the 1960 mood, the year her current class was investigating. It would have been easy to get into the 1860 mood, but I only had to go back to the last century for purposes of my class visit.

Aside from the height of the trees, the center lawn of the campus had not changed since 1960, when the school's population of young Catholic women who, except for a few brainiacs aiming for medical school, were not viewing college as a stepping stone to a great career. But if the landscape remained unaltered, the school had changed since then, and so had the attendees. The students strewn across the lawn on the unseasonably warm day did not fall into any one category of gender, race, religion or age. Their clothing categorized them no more clearly—although most of the outfits had one thing in common. They would have shocked the class of 1960.

The cafeteria, old-fashioned yet charmless, would not have shocked the 1960 graduates. I suspected the main station had not changed since their day, but they would have been surprised by the addition of a wide variety of ethnic specialties at other counters scattered around the room. I added my favorite 1960 standards onto my tray and planted myself in the middle of the room until I looked towards the taco stand and spotted Tracy's ponytail.

"That's all you want?" She eyed my selection with bemusement. "Remember, I am treating."

"Just the Brussels sprouts are enough to make me happy." I didn't quite understand why but the vegetable satisfied a developing obsession.

We found a seat at a table with a view of the lawn.

"I realize I've only done one interview so far, and Alex is right. I do think this alleged carjacking would make a great case for your class. The cast of characters might lead to interesting discussions of the 1950s. As far as the crime goes, although I am not sure what answers I'd find, the story does raise some relevant questions."

"Why did you start with Jonathan's family?"

I had a simple reason. "I haven't discovered any of Cassie's relatives. I made a lucky guess with Tim O'Brien. Well, a lucky guess after hours and hours of research." I didn't mention the trip to the cemetery. "His brother proved more than willing to talk. He's pleased to know someone remembers Jonathan. He calls him Johnny. In O'Brien's eyes, the original investigation left a lot to be desired."

"Could he point the finger at any suspects?"

I shook my head and pursed my lips to convey my disappointment.

"Did he say why he thought the cops jumped to conclusions?" Tracy held a taco in her right hand and leafed through my file with her left.

I worked my way through the Brussels sprouts that, like all items from the entrée station, were badly overcooked, precisely the way I liked them. I had to chew before I could answer. "He felt the cops didn't want the neighborhood upset by a brutal crime. A familiar story. They wanted everyone's approval. The city's population. The politicians. Their bosses."

"And the bigwig?" Tracy asked as she scanned printouts of everything I could find on the Internet about the people, places or things involved in the deaths of Cassie Kelly and Jonathan Brien—which wasn't a lot.

"He figured Parry felt embarrassed by his association

with a crime. He wanted the story to go away, so he gave the cops a theory that they liked and ran with."

With an abrupt motion, Tracy leaned across the table. Her bright brown eyes stared into mine with an intensity I found surprising. "Please, listen to me as if I am telling you the most important thing in the world. Stay focused on me and pretend that I never enjoyed Mark Twain that much, myself, until I read a *Connecticut Yankee in King Arthur's Court*." She nodded at me as if it were my turn. Her eyes begged me to speak.

"Laughed myself silly." I suspected that her intense interest in our conversation had to do with a dark figure hovering at the corner of our table.

"Yes, and I think that is what a lot of people like about Twain. Humor and social commentary. Now, you may not agree but some scholars feel that Twain is responsible . . . ."

"Ahem." The sound was guttural. And loud. And followed by, "Excuse me. I don't want to interrupt you ladies."

But he did. A moderate size man about my age with pretty blue eyes and stark white hair.

"I've read a lot of Twain. I didn't mean to eavesdrop, but I couldn't help overhearing."

He couldn't help overhearing after he stationed himself at the end of our table.

"I thought this might be your mother and I'd like to meet her."

Now, the funny thing is that despite knowing that I am old enough to be Tracy's mother, I felt offended that this guy realized that.

"No. No, This is not my mother." Tracy smiled far less than politely at the man. He didn't notice. He kept talking.

"I see a family resemblance."

"Thank you," I said. I didn't like being dismissive but I could tell this guy bugged Tracy. I could help get rid of him.

"Are you her big sister?" He locked eyes with me but

40

nodded at Tracy.

I imagined that my niece felt the same way about being mistaken for my sister as I did at being mistaken for her mother. This guy attained the status of equal opportunity offender.

Tracy's innate politeness overcame her desire to diss this guy, whoever he was, which turned out to be the dreaded student. "Ed Hayley, this is my aunt Julia Tracy."

"Julia Tracy? And you're Tracy Shaw?"

"Tracy is my mother's maiden name," Tracy explained.

"I am the sister of Tracy's mother," I explained a little more.

"Wait, Tracy is your maiden name. I can't believe a sweet thing like you isn't married."

"I know. Shocking, isn't it?" I showed my teeth in what I hoped would be taken for a smile.

"No harm in being single. I'm single." The man leered.

Go figure, I said—but only to myself.

"Is there something I can do for you?" Tracy asked.

"Just wanted to say hello." He strained to see what we were looking at. "Nineteen-fifty-six Thunderbird convertible. You a collector? Oh, no. I bet this has something to do with next term's project, doesn't it? Well, I have the solution. A lot of people would kill for that car. It's worth a bundle."

Now, I thought. Not in 1956 when the current year's Thunderbird was expensive but not exorbitantly priced.

"Maybe I should repeat the class next term. Having ridden in one of those sweet chariots, I'll be way ahead of the others." He smiled at Tracy to give her time to comment on how wonderful having him back in her class would be. When she didn't, he said good-bye. "I'm on my way to the library. Got to stay in 1960, so I'll be ready for class."

I smiled.

"Maybe I'll see you again sometime." He made a peculiar gesture, half wave, half salute.

I didn't bother telling him that I would be in class that night. "I imagine you will."

After another awkward pause, he moved on.

"It isn't so much what he says that is offensive as the way he says it," I observed.

"If you spent more time with him, you'd realize it is also what he says."

"It's a shame because he is rather attractive." I watched him walk away. "And dresses well."

"Probably has a lot of first dates," Tracy observed.

"Well, at least he solved our case for us. Everyone got it right in 1956. Simple carjacking. Ed Hayley says so."

"Now I am convinced." Tracy paused for effect. "Of the opposite. There is no way this was a simple carjacking. I can't accept that Mr. Hayley would be right about anything. Do you want to dig any deeper? Do you have the time?"

Time was not my issue. "Nothing in my consulting pipeline."

"We don't owe Antonia Sadoski anything. However, I do think I could use this case at some point—if I manage to hold on to this gig. But, don't feel you have to take this on for my benefit."

Tim O'Brien's face flashed in front of me. "I don't know what I can accomplish for him, but I think Jonathan's brother would appreciate any attention to the case. I don't know if you ever have guests, aside from me, but I bet he would be happy to come to class." I stopped to take a breath. "I'm getting way ahead of myself, aren't I?"

Tracy nodded. "I try to keep the students away from anyone directly involved in the crime. I don't want them to play vigilante. I make sure they know this is a writing, not a criminal justice, course. They are getting graded on their fiction, not their investigative skills. Theoretically, they can lose points if they are too aggressive. So far none of the students have come close to overstepping. Grades are always a good control mechanism. Now, we have to get our heads into 1960."

I pulled out a notebook. "I'm ready for some time travel."

I loved my visit to Tracy's class. I marveled at the way she guided the conversation, gently reminding students that in 1960 one had to find a phone booth to make a call and that an elderly character in 1960, born in the nineteenth century, might not speak exactly the same way her grandchildren did. She kept the tone light and respectful, and, more importantly, kept Ed Hayley in line.

I kept myself in line. As tempting as regaling the students with tales of my childhood felt, I had been invited as a guest participant, not a guest speaker. I stuck to the intangibles. Anyone could find facts on the Internet. What I could add was how it felt to live in that year.

"Nineteen-sixty was an extremely constrained time. There were rules. Not written ones but the expectations for each of the characters you are creating would be deeply rooted in their city, neighborhood, social class, and religion. I suppose there were always free spirits, but not as many were visible." My thoughts turned briefly to Cassie, who lived under these same constraints, but I brought them back to the case at hand. "Even among the teenagers. A lot of them conformed—or at least faked conformity. And, think of the grandfather character Tracy mentioned. Born in the 19th century, all the rules that seem silly to us now represent the reality he and his contemporaries grew up with. Trust me. You did not wear white after Labor Day, even if the temperature reached 110 degrees in the shade. If you did, you were judged."

We laughed at stories of things that were done and, more significantly, *were not done.* "*People don't do that* was a big phrase back then. If you are dealing with average middle-class characters, they were living under those restrictions. Rules. You may have believed in them or you may have questioned them, but you adhered to them. To break them, or to have your children break them, would be painful and have consequences."

Did I hear myself offering sympathetic words about bigwig Henry Parry and his need to avoid notoriety? I was describing the era of his maturity. Sure, he was a stuffed shirt, but he believed in all that stuffing.

I didn't have much time to ponder my thoughts about Parry. Ed Hayley was speaking.

"It will happen to you, kids. Just wait and see." He offered a follow-up to my statement, and I feared it was going to be a long one.

"But for now," Tracy interrupted, "let's not worry about the future. Let's try to feel the past."

Chapter 9

I didn't know the Parrys, but that didn't keep me from judging them harshly. I stereotyped the Parrys of the 1950s as WASPs uninterested in meeting those outside their own crowd. My opinion was largely based on old movies, although my mother had held the same opinion and she had witnessed some of the archetypical behavior. She'd told me the story about dinner at the home of a friend of the Muffy-Buffy ilk. "I had been puzzled by her father's comments. 'I used to play with the Irish kids.' 'We had Irish kids who lived in town.' At least he didn't mention their maid was Irish, although she *had* recently arrived from Dublin." My mother, whose family hadn't been near Ireland in many generations, became painfully aware of the woman's brogue. She thought she was *one of the gang*, but she worried that her hosts saw her as someone different, an outsider, an oddity. She worried if they expected her to clear.

I had, however, gathered facts to support my conclusions about the snobbishness of the Parrys. I'd checked Parry, Shippen, Weathersby and Baron's website and found that Parry, et.al. did employ one Italian, one Irishman and one African-American. No partners, but associates, each of whom appeared to be under forty, so I figured the change had not come early in the firm's history. And, I speculated, not easily. But they *had* changed. I am sure most of the Parrys and their associates kept up with the times. At least, I hoped most of them kept up with the times. I'd heard one of his class, social class, tell a joke not too long before. The positive reaction by the group indicated that at least a good number of the proper WASPs present had not accepted the equality of Jews, Catholics, and African-Americans. Fifty years ago I imagine everyone in the room would have laughed, including Henry Parry. Was I misjudging the man? I saw only one way to find out. I'd have to find a way to talk to him.

I read up on the now elderly lawyer. He appeared to keep his personal life out of the press, but his professional accomplishments were well documented. I hated to admit it but he was, in my grandmother's language, a tad on the extraordinary side. A blurb in an old *Philadelphia* magazine honored him on his ninetieth birthday for still keeping an eye on the law firm that bore his name, visiting his office at least three days a week and eating lunch at the Philadelphian Club on workdays, just as he had for the last sixty years.

I hoped that after several more years a man with such a sense of tradition still kept the same schedule and would be willing to talk to any self-proclaimed historian—my proposed cover—writing about the glory days of Philadelphia. Even me.

The question remained how could I get the request to him. I'd never get into the fortress that was his law firm. I bet they protected the old guy with the same zeal the government guarded Fort Knox. I had no doubt the reception at his house would be chillier. That left the Philadelphian Club. And I couldn't run into him there. When I say *I couldn't*, I mean I was not able to get inside to stage an encounter in the private club, the very private club, the kind that never considered renting space for a social or business event. Compared to the Philadelphian Club, Fort Knox looked like an easy mark.

"How do I get into the Philadelphian Club?" I asked myself but since I was sitting in Tracy's living room waiting for her to return from class, Alex heard the question and answered.

"Philadelphia or Philadelphian?" He stressed the n at the end of my second choice.

"Philadelphian." I dragged the *n* out for clarity.

"Aside from gender reassignment surgery?"

"I had hoped for a simpler solution." I paused. "You're kidding about the gender issue, right? That isn't legal anymore, is it?"

"Legality hardly matters. Why join a club where all the members have sworn not to speak to you?"

"Have you been there?"

"Not really a big gay hangout."

I got his point.

"Too bad Parry doesn't eat at the Union League. You could take a tour and then drop out and go corner him at lunch. Of course, you could get a job as a waitress at the Philadelphian Club. Although you'd have to dye your hair gray and acquire some sort of accent." Alex matched my sigh. "At least that's what I hear."

"How do you hear?"

"What?"

"You said 'that's what I hear.' How do you hear about the Philadelphian Club?"

"I . . . someone must have mentioned it once." He gave an unconvincing performance.

"You know someone who belongs, don't you?"

"What makes you think that I would know someone who belongs to a place like that?"

I stared him down.

"Maybe a couple of my friends belong." Alex cracked easily.

"Like who?"

"Trey. Trey Trowbridge. You met him at the pool party Tracy and I gave last year. You remember the pool party?"

Who wouldn't? You don't get invited to many pool parties where the hosts are still inflating the swimming pool when you arrive.

"You must remember Trey Trowbridge. He had on surfer gear and carried a surfboard. Very loud. His outfit. Not

47

him."

I remembered. Trey Trowbridge was a perfect gentleman.

"Don't even think of asking him to take you to the Philadelphian Club." What Alex really meant? Don't expect me to ask Trey to take you to the Philadelphian Club.

Until a few moments before, I never knew Trey's last name. Now, I needed him to be my best friend. "I can't believe someone who is so much fun would bother belonging to such a stuffy place. Especially someone of your generation."

"His father probably pays his dues."

"Does he use his membership?"

"I think he goes once a year or so to keep it in force. Just in case he ever decides to get serious about business." Alex tried to disappear behind the latest *Architectural Digest.*

"Hmm," I said.

"I'm not interceding for you." He stared hard at the magazine.

I wasn't concerned. I could plead my own case. "I'll ask him. Why don't you invite Trey over?"

"Because . . ." After a long pause, Alex stumbled through his next sentence, "He would ask me why I didn't take you."

"You belong to the Philadelphian Club?"

"Kind of." His eyes never met mine. "My father pays the dues and hopes I show up once a year."

"And do you?"

"I make sure I do. Once." He turned the page with a leisurely motion.

I saw an opening and went for it. "Have you been there yet this year?"

I've found that when you are the same age as a person's mother, especially a young man's mother, they are reluctant to disappoint you. Alex dropped the magazine and invited me to lunch at the Philadelphian Club.

Chapter 10

I didn't believe climbing the three steps to the small, unimpressive door of the Philadelphian Club accounted for the perspiration on Alex's brow. He ran a finger around his shirt collar, straightened his tie and pushed a button in a rhythmic code.

"Secret code?" I asked. He didn't answer. The door that popped open did.

In the 1950s, the Philadelphian Club was the quintessential men's club of the decade. In the 2010s, the Philadelphian Club remained the quintessential men's club of the 1950s. I surmised that little had changed in sixty years, and Alex confirmed that not much had changed in the century and a half since its founding by a clique of Philadelphia lawyers who felt the other clubs in town were beginning to accept undesirable elements such as merchants and politicians. Since then, the male descendants of this self-selected group had huddled in leather wing chairs set on Persian carpets to drink single malt Scotch and smoke Cuban cigars under the watchful eyes of former members immortalized in a collection of oil paintings that all but obscured the highly polished wood paneling. Frowning from their spots on the wall, none of the founders looked particularly happy to see me, or actually anyone.

Alex led me past the library to the dining room where the darkness was broken by the white linens on the tables. Since we were dining during the twenty-first century, I wasn't the only woman in the room. I couldn't tell if the other one noticed me. The maître d' seated Alex and me a few tables away from her party and not far from the kitchen.

"Am I the reason we got this table?" I whispered when

the waiter gave us time to review the single-sheet menu.

"You don't help, but I'm the real reason. I'm not exactly a regular." Alex leaned across the table. When he spoke, his voice barely rose above a whisper. "I hope that you aren't horrified at my duplicity but as far as this crowd is concerned, I am straight or at least I don't mention that I am gay."

I wasn't horrified. Surprised but not horrified.

"Of course, my father knows the truth. He says he is okay with it, but I suspect he wouldn't want to let his friends in on what is, admittedly, a very badly kept secret."

That didn't sound okay to me.

"I know the world is supposed to be a different place but my father was fifty when I arrived. He's not that much younger than old man Parry. He reacted really well when I came out. At least, within the four walls of our house. He tried hard. So I don't lie. I avoid. I'm not proud of the deception but I understand how it would be hard for him to advertise to his cronies that he has a son of my ilk. He wouldn't lie either. I suspect that he simply hopes the question doesn't come up."

Not my place to judge, or to offer a better course of action.

"I hope you appreciate that I put on this suit for you. Most of my clothing is not this dull. I hope none of my friends see me in this tie."

I thought the tie was lovely, but what did I know. Did I mention that I am sixty?

"It brings out your eyes." I tried to console him but failed.

"These baby blues don't need any help. I'd bat my eyes at you to underline my point, but here I behave to match my surroundings. Remind me to take the tie off as soon as we step out the door, although I'm unlikely to forget."

"I can't believe you did this for me, Alex. I am grateful for your help."

"No problem. God knows I owe Tracy for all she's done for me."

"Including landing you in some tight spots."

"All's well that ends well. When I broke up with the one whose name we do not speak—actually it was Adam—she really saved me. She's probably glad her housesitting gig is temporary. Otherwise, she'd have to worry if she would ever get rid of me."

"Well, I appreciate your bringing me here."

"Not to worry. I should come here more often. I might be able to take advantage of these contacts someday. And, if I am going to eat the minimum every month, I might as well do it with someone who actually wants to be here. And, to tell you the truth, I find it a little exciting helping with one of Tracy's capers."

I felt a little put off. I thought of this as my caper, but every caper was really Tracy's. I didn't protest.

After we perused the menu, I recognized that something else about the club had not changed with the times. I ordered a shrimp cocktail and prime rib, my favorite meal from the early sixties. Only then did I ask Alex about my *person of interest*.

"I don't really know him. When my parents still dragged me along to their events, I often saw him there."

"What did you think of him?"

"I didn't. Kids lump all members of the older generations together as uninteresting, especially the oldest ones. By the time I remember, his wife had died, so he would come alone or bring one of his cronies along. Sometimes he brought his son. I don't know him either. That is all my information about the family. Remember, even when I was young, your *person of interest* was one of the old guys."

I surveyed the crowd. Actually, the crowd's hair. Twenty-five percent gray. Twenty-five percent white. Forty-eight percent missing. "I am surprised these guys lived to be this old eating so much red meat."

"And smoking cigars, and drinking hard liquor," Alex added. "Maybe they are as special as they think they are." He paused only briefly. "No, no one is as special as these folks think they are. And here comes one of the most special of the special, the most elite of the elite, the most prosperous of the prosperous."

"I assume we're talking Henry Parry."

"One o'clock." He glanced over my shoulder ever so discreetly.

It is possible that my reaction was not similarly discreet. My glance over my shoulder developed into more of a long stare rendered less subtle when I moved my chair ever so slightly for a better observation spot.

Henry Parry, who according to my calculations had to be heading for one hundred, appeared fragile but walked to his table without assistance. Admittedly not quickly, but independently. Stooped by age, he carried far too little weight on his long frame. He still had hair, although not much of it. What he had was pure white. I wasn't sure if he had a deep tan or his age spots had merged. He might not have moved with speed but he did move with confidence. And, the staff responded with deference. I noted that *his* table, a table for four set for two, was not near the kitchen.

"Who's the guy with him?" I used my ventriloquist skills which were, at best, awful.

"You can speak up. No one they know sits at this end of the room." Alex surveyed the crowd. "Plus, do you really think most of these guys can still hear?"

I ignored his ageist remark and moved my lips. This time he understood my question.

"Edward Baron. Lifelong friends. Princeton, nineteen-thirty something, I believe. Also a partner at Parry, Shippen, Weathersby and Baron. You now know everything I know about Edward Baron."

I studied the two elderly men. Parry the taller, the leaner, and Baron the shorter, the rounder, both cut from the same cloth. "I bet they still wear seersucker in the summer."

Alex faux scowled at me. "I don't know any more than I told you."

"They must," I said. "They look like classics." In autumn their classic attire consisted of conservative pin-striped suits and striped ties, all of which might have hung in their closets since Cassie Kelly took care of the house.

"You're staring," Alex said through gritted teeth.

"I doubt if he can see me."

"That is an ageist comment." He threw my earlier accusation back at me.

"I'm old. I can say things like that."

"Compared to Henry Parry, you are a kid. He's got to have, what? Thirty, forty years on you?"

I calculated that Alex's estimate was correct.

"He's going to have a cocktail," I announced as if the news that the waiter had placed a cocktail glass in front of Parry were monumental—a ridiculous response since those who had been in their prime in the 1950s knew how to handle their liquor, even at lunch. "I bet they drink every day. I didn't see him order it. It must be his regular." These men had several decades on me, but if I had alcohol at lunch, I would head home for a nap, not back to work. "We'd better talk to him before he finishes that drink. Let's go."

"We? I didn't sign up for that. You're on your own. Just don't involve me in any way. Or make a scene. I don't care, but . . . ."

"I know. You don't want to embarrass your father."

He raised his shoulders and dropped his head to the left. I read the motion as agreement.

"Don't worry. As far as the rest of the crowd is concerned, I'm going to the ladies room and just happen to see someone I know."

"Good one. No one ever tried that before."

Chapter 11

"Mr. Parry." I sounded surprised and delighted.

He smiled and I detected admiration in his dark blue eyes as if seeing a pretty young thing, which in his eyes and few others, I could possibly be. Then I realized his pleasant expression was just his well-inculcated social graces kicking in. "Excuse me if I don't get up."

"I'm sorry to disturb you and I promised Alex Digby that I would take less than one minute of your time."

"Alex!" He sounded excited and looked in the direction I pointed. He flashed a friendly smile and controlled wave towards our table.

Alex forced a weak smile and a small wave. He raised an eyebrow.

"Nice boy that Alex. Are you and he?"

"No, no. I'm . . ." I almost said *old enough to be his mother* when I realized that might raise this issue of why I was there. Instead, I finished with "sort of an honorary aunt."

"Really? You look so young."

I think Henry Parry meant what he said, but only because his vision was failing. Besides, he had reached a stage in life when almost anyone looked young, when almost anyone *was* young. He could lump Alex and me, along with both of our generations, into the pile of younger folk.

"Let me introduce myself. My name is Julia Tracy."

"Julia. How nice. My wife's name was Julia. I always found it a beautiful name."

"Thank you."

"For a beautiful woman, Julia Blair Parry—and of course for you as well."

Unsure of a response, I simply nodded until the awkward silence forced me to speak. "I felt happy when I saw you come in. I am a writer and historian." That was a lie—I mean tactic—I had adopted from Tracy. "I'd love to talk to you at some point about a history project I'm working on. Philadelphia-centered." Carefully chosen words made my statement true, at least in my eyes. "I wonder if I might call you for an appointment."

Protection came from his companion. "I'm Mr. Parry's partner. I handle his calendar."

I turned to see a scowling expression on a face that if the ridges were any indication had displayed a large number of scowls over a long period of time.

"Why make an appointment? I'm here. You're here. Let's talk now." Parry waved across the table at an empty chair.

"Henry, we have a schedule." The other gentleman was not pleased.

"Edward likes to think that people care if we get back to the office on time." He chuckled and then grew suddenly serious. "How incredibly rude of me. I must introduce you to my colleague, Edward Baron."

Baron appeared to hear a command in his name. He raised his rear from the seat with his body bent forward at the waist at forty-five degrees. If I discounted his age, I could have interpreted his position as a bow. In truth, I think the gesture was simply a manifestation of the most motion he could muster. "Edward Baron." He introduced himself. "Mr. Parry's partner at the firm and lifelong friend of the family."

When I offered my hand, I noticed that he wasn't expecting it, but he shook it lightly. He made a move as if he would pull out a chair for me, but a waiter materialized to seat me. I declined any refreshment saying I would be returning to my own table momentarily. Baron appeared relieved to hear that, but Henry Parry didn't seem to mind my visit at all. Even after I told him what I wanted to discuss.

"This is such a coincidence, seeing you here. I am researching crimes against women in the 1950s." I appropriated Antonia Sadoski's topic. "And I noticed that one of the crimes involved a woman who worked for you."

He frowned. "I remember the terrible situation you refer to. A true tragedy."

"We don't speak of it." Baron wanted to end the conversation. "It upsets." He nodded at Parry. "Anything violent does."

I expected the man to raise his finger to make circles conveying the universal meaning of cuckoo. But, Henry Parry didn't come across as crazy. I judged him to be remarkably alert when he spoke of the incident.

"I must say that I'm a bit surprised you want to talk to me about that horrific event all those years ago. It is quite sad but today a situation like that one would be considered rather ordinary. I believe we call those crimes carjackings."

"Do you recall talking to the police in 1956?"

"That type of violence doesn't touch many lives. Especially in my world. Especially in those years. I remember those events as clearly as I remember anything these days."

"Don't let Mr. Parry fool you. He is still as smart as a whip. The Parrys are from extraordinary stock." Baron beamed.

Sure. That was what he said when Parry was watching him.

Parry, apparently used to sycophancy, waved off the compliment.

I tried to steer the conversation back to 1956. "The victims met at your house. Did you see both of them the day they died?"

While claiming to hate to do so, Baron interrupted. "I'm curious about this line of questioning. This content sounds more suitable for a tabloid than a historical publication."

I didn't have to defend my imaginary project. Parry did. "The times have changed, Edward. History is much broader than the accounts of wars and treaties." He smiled at me. "One must keep up with the times. Now what was your question?"

I repeated it and he had a quick response.

"Of course, I saw her, the maid. I forget her name."

"Cassie Kelly." Edward Baron compensated for Mr. Parry's memory lapse.

"Of course. Cassie. Yes. It just happens sometimes at my age. A name will slip away, but I remember her. She served as our downstairs maid. I believe I told the police that I'd seen nothing unusual in Cassie's activities or in her demeanor that day. As usual, she served dinner, cleaned up and left to catch the trolley. "

"How did she get to the trolley?"

He labored over his answer. "To my knowledge, she walked to the loop—that's what they called the top of the hill where the trolley car turned around. Every night the same."

"And that night?"

"I assume that young man . . . ."

I figured he had a lot of years to sift through to get back to Jonathan Brien's name. I filled him in.

"Yes, that was it. Mr. Brien offered her a ride."

"Had he done that before?"

Across the table, Edward Baron cleared his throat as if to indicate that Parry had already been far too nice. After all, they did have that schedule to stick to. Parry ignored him.

"Mr. Brien was not a regular guest." He shook his head with great theatricality. "Whatever possessed a nice girl like Cassie to take such a chance, going to a lover's lane with that young man? I felt quite shocked at the time. Still do."

So much for keeping up with the times.

"You didn't approve of Jonathan Brien?" I asked.

"Turned out his real name was O'Brien. I remember that.

57

Can you imagine being so ashamed of what you are?"
Parry's mind seemed to wander off.

"Henry?" Baron called him back from wherever he had
gone.

"Sorry. This O'Brien boy had somehow or other
befriended Chip and Blair, my children. He joined us for
dinner that night. I wasn't particularly pleased."

"You knew Brien, I mean O'Brien, well?"

"No, but I knew the type." Henry appeared to draw
strength from the recollection. He had a disdainful
expression on his face as he recalled April 21, 1956.

*****Henry Parry*****
Parry Estate
Philadelphia, Pennsylvania
April 21, 1956

*Henry Parry, Sr. loved sitting at the head of an elegantly
set table. He'd sat at beautiful tables for his entire life, but
sitting at his own, with his wife across from him and his
grown children on either side, gave him the feeling that all
was right with the world. That night, however, things were
not normal. A young man named Jonathan Brien—Blair's
guest from what Julia told him—sat beside Chip, across the
table from Blair.*

*As if that weren't bad enough, Henry felt concerned at
the way Chip smiled at their maid as she cleared. He had no
doubt the desire to see Cassie explained Chip's ridiculous
excuses for an excessive number of trips home from college.
Henry understood the attraction. He understood how
tempting having a beautiful woman in the house could be.
Years before, he'd been infatuated with the family upstairs
maid. He'd been only a little older than Chip when the pretty
redhead with eyes as green as the Emerald Isle came to
work in his family home. She spoke with a lilting Irish
brogue. Her laughter was musical, hearty and real. He had*

58

never met a female with whom he'd had so much fun, with whom he had any fun, actually. He fantasized about how jealous his buddies would be seeing her on his arm until his parents pointed out the futility of pursuing such a relationship. Now he had to carry the same message to his son. Cassie Kelly might be a very nice girl, but hardly suitable wife material. Not for Chip. Not for a Parry.

Cassie left the room carrying a silver tray full of dishes and Chip's attention went with her, leaving his family to deal with their dinner guest.

Julia, always gracious, took the lead. "Henry, Blair tells me that our guest is a law student."

"A fine career choice." Henry reacted with surprise to the insincerity of his own smile. He did believe the law was a fine choice.

"Yes, sir. I'm at Penn."

"A good school. I went to Harvard, myself. After Princeton. That is what Chip will do when he finishes at Princeton. Right, Chipper?" His son seemed surprised to hear his name. Henry had to repeat his thought. "You'll do law at Harvard."

Chip smiled at the Brien boy. "Father decided I'd become a lawyer the moment Mother told him I was expected." Chip got to his feet and Henry knew why. He could tell by the smile on his face. "If you'll excuse me for a moment."

Did Chip think that everyone in the room was blind? His behavior made it clear he was following Cassie.

Ever polite, Julia continued to converse with their guest. "The Parrys have been attorneys for generations."

"The law is in our blood," Henry bragged.

"Jonathan wants to do corporate law," Blair explained.

Henry understood what Blair was saying. Jonathan wants a job. And that would turn out to be only the first step in the boy's plan. Henry felt sure. He knew Jonathan's type.

Jonathan smiled. Kind of an earnest expression. Horatio

Alger wanting to make good in the law firms of Philadelphia. "I'm hoping to join one of the better firms in the city. Of course, I realize there is no better firm than Parry, Shippen, Weathersby and Baron."

The kid made no effort at subtlety. He'd blatantly solicited a job. At the dinner table yet.

Henry remained polite. "There are many fine firms in our hometown. The term Philadelphia lawyer didn't come into existence because the city has a shortage of attorneys." Henry remained civil beyond the point required after an assault like that. He didn't stomp off; he made his excuses. He even forced a polite smile as he spoke. "If you'll excuse me, I am going to practice my putting while there is a vestige of light left in the evening sky."

Julia wasn't nearly so polite but her annoyance wasn't directed at the rudeness of their guest. Icicles hung from her words as she ignored Henry's kiss on the cheek. "Try to pull yourself away from your golf green early enough to spend a little time with your family tonight."

Henry ignored her, but something in her hostility made him feel bad about the way he spoke to Jonathan. He brightened his tone as he addressed their dinner guest. "Enjoy your dessert. I trust that Cassie has turned out a fine confection for you. I'll say good-night." He started towards the kitchen but stopped with his hand about to push the door. He'd have to take care of this eventually, why not now. "Blair, may I see you for a moment?"

Blair appeared apprehensive as she rose from the table. "Excuse me," she said to no one in particular.

Henry noted that their visitor was also worried. He watched Jonathan's face as Blair exited through the door he held open. At last, the kid figured out that something had gone amiss.

As if a daughter inviting people like Jonathan Brien to the dinner table wasn't upsetting enough, in the kitchen he found his son trailing their downstairs maid around like a puppy dog. Extraordinary-looking woman or not, Cassie Kelly was an uneducated domestic servant, and, like any good father, Henry would use his parental authority to block any fantasy Chip had about breaking with tradition when choosing a mate. One glance from Henry said it all. Chip got the message. He headed back to the dinner table exchanging nervous glances with his sister as he passed.

Henry turned, trapping Blair between himself and the door to the dining room. He kept his voice low but strong. "I don't want to find that fellow at my table again. I don't like him."

Blair glanced over her shoulder as if she could see sound traveling into the next room. "You didn't give him a chance," Blair whispered.

"Did you hear him? He practically asked me for a job at my own dinner table. Most inappropriate."

"But Father . . . ."

Henry raised his index finger to silence her. "I don't want you to see him. And, I don't want to hear that he's been at the Cricket Club with you."

Blair couldn't control the surprise on her face.

"You bring a young man that no one knows with a name that no one recognizes into our club and you think I won't hear about it?"

Afraid to point a finger, Blair waved an arm in his direction. "I thought you, of the great love story of 1935, would be more tolerant."

"Don't ever paint your mother with the same brush as that social-climbing, fortune hunter." He spoke through gritted teeth.

"But Father . . . ."

"You're too young to see what he's made of, but I'm not. I may not know him but I know his type."

"Father, I'm not serious about him. I get a kick out of him. He'll do anything for me."

"He'll do anything for your money, your name, your

position. I'm only trying to protect you. I don't want you to see him again. End of discussion."

*****

"Perhaps my behavior sounds harsh in light of today's standards." Parry let his eyes meet mine. I saw pride. He enjoyed painting himself as the effective father figure. "I had to protect them, you see, although I do fear that my insistence that Blair reject the Brien boy may have altered the course of events that night."

"Mr. Parry was always a dutiful parent," Baron interjected.

"And Cassie was aware of all the romantic intrigue going on around her?"

Again, Baron interrupted, "I don't understand why . . . ."

Seeing him on the verge of making a good point, I scrambled to come up with an answer as I finished his question for him. "…why this matters to my history? People today like personal stories to demonstrate social history. They want to know what drove people, what their world was like. Although I disregard many of them, I like to know as many details to create a backdrop for those stories. I simply wondered if the maid found herself witness to household events. That is why I asked Mr. Parry if Cassie overheard. Maybe she felt sorry for Jonathan."

I smiled at Parry and he shrugged, the weak motion of an elderly man. "I assume so. She was there. I spoke freely in my own home."

"Was that the last time you saw her?"

"Yes. I didn't stay for dessert."

"Did you like Cassie?"

"Hardly a matter of liking or disliking her. She was our maid. As I recall, she proved herself to be extremely competent. I can't speak to her personality, although when I walked into the kitchen that night, she had coerced my son into helping her prepare the dessert plates." Over sixty years later, he retained a tone of disapproval.

Henry Parry had noticed that Cassie was beautiful, but I guess that since she wasn't his type, he didn't notice much else about her. Except that his son had become inappropriately involved. It must have pained him to see a son and a daughter making such ill-advised choices.

"I didn't see anything in the newspapers saying that Blair and Brien were romantically involved."

Baron spoke up but this time with a recollection, not a question. I thought perhaps he wanted to spare us from another of Henry's long ruminations. "I recall that period. Henry expressed concern that the two were moving in that direction."

"Do you know if she broke it off with him that night or not?" I addressed Parry.

"As I said, I do fear that my words drove that young fellow into Cassie's arms and put them both in harm's way."

"So you believe that's what happened?"

Baron made it clear he was tiring of the walk down memory lane. "The police concluded they stopped for a romantic tryst." The exasperation in his voice asked *so why don't you*?

I continued to address Mr. Parry. "You mentioned other staff. Cassie was not the only domestic you employed?"

"Oh, heavens no. We had several girls working in the house, some boys who took care of the grounds. Lawn. Hedges. Pool. Tennis courts. The usual. I am sure you know."

"Of course," I lied. "Did any of these *boys and girls* live on the estate?" Controlling a sarcastic tone wasn't easy.

"Not for a decade or more by the time of the unfortunate incident. After the war, World War II, when running a household became a bit less complicated, Julia, my wife, decided she wanted more privacy. I don't suppose you remember the war years, but they were quite tricky what with ration books and all that."

I would have loved to hear about running a household in World War II, but I could feel Baron getting edgy. Before my time with Henry Parry ran out, I needed to get the information I came for. "Would it be possible for me to get the names of people who worked for you in 1956? They might be able to provide information for this story. Or suggest others. Other stories, that is."

Baron's expression told me he found the request ridiculous and inappropriate, but Parry silenced his protests with a single hand gesture. "I am sure Edward would be happy to do that. After my wife died, he took charge of the household records. He has a list. I imagine any number of our workers would be happy to contribute to a history of Philadelphia."

I felt sure Parry was correct, but had he taken into account the number of disgruntled employees who would be more interested in participating in the history of the Parry family? From the little I'd heard, I bet there were more than a few.

Baron was polite to his boss. "Henry, I don't think we are entitled to make that decision for our former employees." He spoke to me with condescension. "Confidentiality issues." His tone provided an addendum for me, *you wouldn't understand.*

Henry Parry did not agree. "I think they would be proud to contribute to a history. Any Philadelphian would. What was the name of that other girl? She stayed for years, until she was far from a girl. Remember she came all the way from West Philadelphia."

Baron spoke reluctantly but he would not withhold information from his colleague. "Mancini. Maria Mancini."

"No. That's not it. She had a political name." He turned to me. "You know anything about Italian politics?"

"Only Berlusconi." I named a man known for his scandals not his policies.

"No. No. Historical."

"Mussolini?" Baron tried to divert the conversation with a joke, but Parry was not to be put off.

"Older. Older. Garibaldi," he all but shouted. "Maria Garibaldi. Mancini was her maiden name." He stared at the plate the waiter slipped in front of him. "What day is it?"

Baron's tone remained kind. "It's Wednesday, Henry."

"But on Wednesdays I have the flounder."

"No, on Wednesdays you have pot roast."

"Ah, yes. Good but not as good as the one served at my mother's house." I had the feeling he planned on reciting the entire recipe from his mother's era, but I excused myself so the serving in the present era did not get cold.

Chapter 12

After I left the Philadelphian Club, I returned to the twenty-first century and checked my phone for messages. I found four. I strained to make out the low and hesitant voice on the first. Background noise made hearing difficult but the content told me I was listening to Jonathan Brien's brother.

"I remembered something. Someone. A cop. A good cop. He listened. I remembered his name. I couldn't for a while. Remember his name. I didn't even remember he existed. When an experience is so traumatic, when I think about it, and I try not to, I don't mean . . . ."

The recording ended but the same voice returned in the next voice mail. "Sorry. I didn't mean to say that I don't think about Johnny. I do, but not the mess when he died. Anyway, you got me thinking and all of a sudden I remember this nice guy. Name of Bernardino. I mean he couldn't do anything to help us, not really, but he made a crack about old man Parry and how he liked to throw his weight around."

Once again he outlasted the allotted time for a message, but I heard his voice again on the next one. "This is Tim O'Brien but I guess you know that. I have to give you the cop's name. Bernardino. Valentino Bernardino. They called him Dino. Nice guy. Dino." Then he left a lot of dead time on the line before he hung up.

The fourth message came from Tracy, just checking in. I returned her call and recorded a brief update on my lunch with Alex. Then I set off in search of a Valentino Bernardino who would have been old enough to work as a policeman in 1956. Finding him, even from the deep cushions of my sofa, turned out to be less difficult than I imagined. Let me rephrase. Finding his obituary proved to be less difficult than I imagined.

Tim O'Brien's assessment turned out to be correct. The policeman was a good guy. Many honors while working. Many charitable efforts when retired. He followed his beloved wife, Carolina, in death but left behind a large family that included one son who bore his name, four daughters, seventeen grandchildren and three great-grandchildren. As I settled into a night of couch potato inactivity, I felt dejected. If Bernardino had anything bad to say about the investigation into the deaths of Jonathan Brien and Cassie Kelly, he had taken it to the grave with him.

Or had he? I asked myself as, still on the couch, I awoke to the sound of the local news broadcast repeating for those who returned home from work shortly before the rest of us got up.

Bernardino might have shared stories of his time on the job with his children. Maybe not names and dates but maybe tales of his investigations. What harm could it do to ask?

Finding Valentino Bernardino Jr. proved even easier than finding his father's obit. I didn't even have to open my computer. The local news ended and Val's voice boomed from my TV before he stepped on-screen in evening clothes. Turned out I had seen Val Jr. many times but never retained his name. Dino Bernardino's son sold cars and when I say he sold cars, I don't mean he worked on the sales floor and sold a half-dozen vehicles a week. No, according to the dealer's website, Val had a staff of twenty selling fine driving machines at a dealership that carried his name and could be identified by an oversized caricature of his face on top of the showroom. The business offered a wide selection of cars but specialized in vehicles unlikely to find a home in my garage, even with a winning lottery ticket. But Alex would love them.

I considered renting a luxury car for the trip to the dealership, just to guarantee a warm greeting, but decided deception wasn't necessary. Actually, I decided that getting moving wasn't necessary. I'd already accomplished my main task for the day—before 5 AM. I rolled over and drifted back to sleep plotting my visit to Valentino's Motor Cars.

It was afternoon before I rolled into the car dealer's parking lot. I had low expectations for any man with a thirty-foot caricature of his face on top of his business but, as the owner greeted me, I learned for the umpteenth time you can never judge a book by its cover.

Val Bernardino, stylishly dressed and gracious, eyed my car like the professional he was. The expression he tried to hide said that I, or anyone really, should not own such an automobile, but he did not make a pitch for a new one. Based on my current ride, he probably understood that, unless I was on the way home from the reading of a rich uncle's will, every car on his lot lay far outside my price range.

Despite my lack of value as a customer, at the mention of his father's name, he smiled and welcomed me into his office. He didn't offer me a seat, but rather a place at the picture window overlooking the showroom full of luxury cars that stretched into the distance. "If he were still alive, I would let my father come in and pick a new car to drive every morning. Rolls. Bentley. Ferrari. Of course, I wouldn't let him out on a public roadway. I would buy him a farm with a lot of roads where he could drive it. He'd be close to one hundred now. Where did you go to high school?"

That might have seemed like an abrupt segue but no Philadelphian is surprised by any effort to locate common ground. They expect questions like his. I was a few years older than the car salesman but had gone to school with his best friend's cousin. He had sold cars to classmates from my high school class, who had done much better than I had—at least financially. He played golf with the husband of a friend from grade school. That's the way it goes in Philadelphia.

When he believed we had exhausted all channels of possible connection, he asked. "So tell me what I can do for you?"

So I told him. I not only gave him the usual spiel but added that I had developed an emotional attachment to the victims. I wondered if his father had ever mentioned them or the case.

"I don't remember that case. He didn't talk much about specifics but my father would complain that back in the day those old-money Philadelphia society types could make a cop's life miserable. A lot of them were lawyers, knew every loophole but, more important, knew everyone, tried to pressure cops. I am pretty sure that type of stuff still goes on in the city—I'm just not sure if the same guys are doing it. Ever ridden in a Bentley?" The king of the delicious deal proved himself to be the king of the sudden segue as well.

I had been in a Bentley before, but I had the feeling my host would be disappointed by the truth. He wanted to give me a treat. I lied.

"Come on." He continued to chat about his father's life as a cop as he led me down the stairs to the display of luxury automobiles. He changed the subject only to lapse into salesman mode. "Can't beat it for comfort." He bypassed the current models and pointed to a classic. "Ever since you mentioned that case from 1956, I've been thinking about this car. Not '56 but close. 1958. Hop in."

I hopped and sank into soft leather the color of caramel.

"Nice, eh?" He asked with the tone of a salesman who knew how to get a buyer hooked.

A door I didn't realize existed in the glass wall slid open and Val and I rode out of the showroom.

I worried that he had forgotten why I had come, but he hadn't—even if he interspersed the relevant information about his father's career with details about the car. "Look at this dash. Gorgeous, isn't it? My dad was kind of a snob. A reverse snob, my mother called him. He didn't like bigwigs like the one you asked about. Watch this guy next to us. When you drive a flashy car, and I'll admit this is flashy, people react in odd ways. Some smile, wave, give you a thumbs up. Others don't know cars, don't care about cars, so they don't notice. My favorites? The ones who pretend not to notice but do. They try to peek out the corner of their eyes. See he's doing it. I love that."

I didn't have to prompt Val to return to the topic of his father.

"I was a baby during that case you talked about. Nineteen-fifty-six, right? A year after I was born. I don't remember that but all my life my father would talk about two cases that bugged him. The frustration he felt in both instances came from the same place. I don't know the names, but he felt he got sidelined by those types you talk about. You know, my customer base." He laughed. "Not in those days. I think they were afraid to be too flashy. Thank heavens, tastes have loosened up."

"Do you remember any specifics?"

"One death was of a young black woman. The other involved two victims. Young people. Guy and girl. May be your guy and girl. I don't know. He felt he got shut down on both cases. Could have done more. He didn't like that. What I really remember are the lessons I took from his stories. No one is better than anyone else. Everyone deserves equal justice, no matter what end of the social scale they occupy. I do know that he felt the victims of crime did not always get justice. Bad things happened to a lot of people, good people, trying to do their best, who found themselves in a situation that got completely out of their control."

I couldn't be sure that one of those cases was the Kelly/Brien case, except in my heart where I knew. If Dino Bernardino—the father who had raised this lovely son—thought something smelled fishy at the Parry house, I believed something smelled fishy.

"You know this car is reasonably priced."

"Not the way I reason." I didn't apologize.

He chuckled. "You can't blame a guy for trying. I hate to see you miss an opportunity. You look great in this vehicle."

But I looked, and felt, more at home in my compact. Alex, on the other hand, would have loved and looked good in the Bentley. I felt a little guilty that I hadn't invited him along on this outing, one he would have actually enjoyed. Maybe I could come up with an excuse to return.

Chapter 13

I wasn't surprised that I didn't receive a list of Henry Parry's staff. If I had been in his position, I wouldn't have given it to me. That he even considered doing so provided a clue to his mental capacity, which was, apparently, not what it used to be. I had, however, gotten away with one name: Maria Mancini Garibaldi.

According to Parry's memory, Maria had traveled to his family home from West Philadelphia. I checked online but, as expected, discovered no trace of Maria Mancini Garibaldi in the old neighborhood. The population of the area had changed during the white flight of the mid-twentieth century and I assumed, like most former residents, she had abandoned the city for the suburbs, probably for a western neighborhood. I did find several Garibaldis online. A search of the white pages and Facebook brought me to a Maria married to a Frank Garibaldi. I hoped this Maria was the Maria who worked for Parry all those years ago. Her age wasn't given. I took the age of the thirty-year-old woman in her profile photo, judged that her hairstyle represented the height of fashion forty years before and calculated her age at seventy-something. Several of her friends had the last name Mancini. If not the Maria I was searching for, she had to be a relative.

I didn't call ahead. I plugged the address into my GPS and pulled up in front of a brick cottage in a neighborhood of modest homes. The houses, none identical but all similar, sat on lots that boasted little grass but lots of lawn decorations. No mistaking the season at the Garibaldi house. Although there were few trees to drop their leaves directly on the property, many had blown from other locations creating an autumn spectacle. The last of the trick-or-treaters had departed weeks before, but the neatly maintained house still had carved pumpkins sitting on the cement porch in the arms of a giant skeleton.

I rang the bell but when I got no answer, I held the aluminum screen door open with my body and reached into the center of a gourd-adorned wreath, grabbed a brass knocker and dropped it on the wooden door. No answer. I banged the knocker two times. Three times. Four times. I deemed it unlikely that the Maria I sought still worked at a full-time job. If she wasn't at home, I hoped that she would return to her house from a quick errand before anyone on the block became suspicious of a loitering woman. I thought I looked respectable, but if I viewed myself through the eyes of a retiree home alone on an almost deserted block, I didn't necessarily fit the image of a welcome visitor. Nonetheless, I'd driven half an hour to get to the neighborhood. I decided to allow myself at least the same amount of time before I gave up. I hid from the chill air in my car and amused myself speculating about Maria Mancini, the person she had been and the person she might have become.

If this was the right Maria Mancini's house, she'd done okay in life. Not spectacular. Although I noted nothing wrong with the small brick bungalow she lived in, I wondered how a woman who witnessed the lifestyle of the Parry wealth felt about the reality of a life that matched the tiny house. I considered the topic for twenty-eight minutes. Two minutes before my deadline, a Toyota with dented sides and faded blue paint pulled into the short driveway beside the house.

The woman who climbed out was probably approaching eighty and definitely fit for her age. Well, maybe not fit, but skinny. Her build was wiry like her hair and her skin had spent too much time in the sun.

I climbed out of the car and caught up with her before she reached her front door. "Mrs. Garibaldi?"

She smelled like lilacs, even at ten feet. Her makeup, like her fragrance, was overdone. The woman's hair and nails were well cared for. A smile would have made a great accessory. None was forthcoming. She turned with a display of annoyance that quickly changed to anger when she saw a stranger standing in her driveway. "What do you want?"

"I'm looking for a Maria Mancini who used to work for the Parry family in Chestnut Hill."

She sneered. "They leave me money?"

"If they did, that's not why I'm here." I flashed her a smile that she did not return. I wiped the happy expression off my face before continuing. "I am checking into Cassie Kelly's murder."

"You're kidding me."

"It's not an investigation in the traditional sense. I'm not with the police. I am helping my niece. Her name is Tracy Shaw and she teaches at Wallmann College."

This woman had no interest in my niece or me. I plowed ahead.

"Anyway, she teaches a course that uses real cases to demonstrate what the era was like. She tries to make her students focus on how the times influence events and our perceptions of them."

"Oh yeah?" She asked a question but didn't care if she got an answer.

"There are occasions when Tracy's investigations lead to prosecutions." I immediately regretted letting that sentence out of my mouth. What if she was the killer? I backpedaled. "But that is not my main motivation. I am not an investigator. I am doing research for her class. I thought I would talk to people and see if that crime, Cassie's murder, was in some way reflective of her era."

"Nice aunt." She wasn't paying me a compliment. She found my support of my niece suspicious.

"My only niece," I offered by way of explanation.

"And you want to talk to me?" She sounded more

puzzled than annoyed, although I detected a trace of irritation in her tone.

"If you don't mind."

She mixed a shrug with a nod towards the house. "Come on in. Can't see what good it'll do, but then again can't see what harm it'll do, either."

As I followed her inside, it occurred to me that Maria Mancini might well have been a beautiful young woman, largely because of the contrast of her pale blue eyes against her dark black bouffant—assuming her current hair color resembled the color she'd gotten at birth.

But those pale eyes that grabbed my attention gave nothing away. The bungalow said a lot more. Sparsely furnished and so meticulously cared for, I would have eaten off the living room floor. Well, maybe not but I bet doing so would not have harmed me. The hardwood sparkled. Working as a maid had probably come naturally with the ability to clean like this. But working for the wealthy had no apparent effect on her style, or lack thereof. The house was bare, not stark as in a conscious decorating style, but unadorned. I had plenty of time to look around while Maria rested her gloves in a basket, put her keys in a brass dish, hung her coat in the closet and placed her handbag on a shelf and then went back to check that she had completed every step of the ritual.

She pointed to a sofa covered in chartreuse that fought with the greens in the cheap copy of an oriental carpet. "Have a seat." Although her voice suggested she might have been a heavy smoker, I smelled no evidence of her habit on her or in her house. Facing me, she settled on a chair built for comfort, certainly not style—at least not twenty-first-century style. I couldn't think of any century that it suited, but it served the purpose, making the same impression the house did. Functional. Cold. Utilitarian. Certainly not designed to impress, or to welcome.

My seat provided a view of the living room's only

adornment, a dated wedding photo placed prominently over the mantel of the faux fireplace. The bride wore the type of dress that, even as a kid perusing 1960s magazines, I found over the top. The wide skirt pushed at the edges of the photo. Lace was pulled into ruffles and ruffles were tied with bows and all were decorated with beads. Several kinds of beads. The dress may have been unattractive but the bride herself was not. She stared into the future with the intensity that many brides of the era expressed in their portraits. I detected no hint of joy but I did note that my guess had been right. Maria Mancini had been a pretty young girl. Standing next to anyone, besides Cassie Kelly, she stood a good chance of being thought beautiful.

"You like my wedding picture?"

I guess I'd been staring.

"I keep it there to remind my husband what a prize he got. He tells me I shouldn't remind him of what the girl he married looked like."

A weird noise escaped from my mouth. I hoped she took the sound for a chuckle.

"Yeah, he's a charmer. Speaking of charmers, did old man Parry tell you to talk to me?"

"He mentioned your name."

"I'm surprised. The old man couldn't remember my name when I traipsed in and out of his bedroom all day."

"You didn't like the Parrys?"

She raised both her shoulders as if to ask what could anyone expect. "I guess they were no worse than any other family to work for. Snooty. Oh so polite, but under the surface? Not nice. I'm not sure rich people are the same now, but back then they didn't even try to hide their disdain for the simple folk. But, you know, times changed." Maria paused. "But, never the Parrys. Not as long as I worked for them."

"Were the Parrys upset by Cassie's death?"

Maria shook her head with exaggerated motions. "They

were upset they had to get their own dinner until they found her replacement. I don't think I ever heard her name mentioned again after they told us what happened."

"Who told you?"

"Old Man Parry. He tracked me down right after I got to work. He had this snobby way of talking." She lapsed into a not very successful impression. "*Maria, I have some rather unfortunate news to report. Blair had a visitor last night and it appears that Cassie and that fellow hit it off and drove away from here together. They were both killed. The police are investigating, but apparently the two fell prey to a random act of malfeasance. Nothing for you to worry about. Nothing at all. The family will be fine.*" She chuckled. "I thought he meant Cassie's family but he meant his family. He said he did not expect any difficulty in replacing Cassie. He told me to see Mrs. Parry for information on how I could help."

"That was it?"

"Pretty much." She twisted her features in a show of concentration. "I remember being annoyed at the time because he never mentioned the kid's name. I forget it now, myself."

"Jonathan Brien."

"Brien. Right. The kid had two names. Rather confusing. I remember talk that he'd changed it. Not that I heard that from Old Man Parry. He never even said the name to me. When forced to mention the 'random act of malfeasance,' he talked about 'the boy.'" She took a few seconds to gather her next thought. "I guess the Parrys weren't all bad. They sent Cassie's mother a check to help with the funeral, but none of them bothered to attend."

"Did you?"

"Yeah, I could because they had the service on my day off, although I remember that Mrs. Parry wanted me to work because they were short-handed, what with Cassie's absence."

"Were you and Cassie close?"

"We worked together. I did the upstairs. Cassie did the downstairs until the cook ran off with a traveling salesman. I'm not joking. A guy came to the kitchen door selling pots and pans or something. Nobody really knows, because the cook dropped her spatula and left, never to be heard from again. Anyway, after that Cassie did the cooking and served the meals. Probably got a raise."

So many years later, I sensed that Maria resented Cassie's windfall.

"Did she like working for the Parrys?"

Maria affected a theatrically thoughtful expression. I was shocked. So far she'd given no indication that she could be, or would be, pensive—at least in front of a total stranger. The rasp in her voice softened. "She said the work wasn't bad but the knowing hurt."

"The knowing?"

"Knowing other people's secrets." Her tone was surprisingly soft.

Secrets! I hoped I didn't give away my excitement. "Did she tell you what those secrets were?"

The gentleness left her tone. "She didn't have to. When you're a maid, you're invisible. You see it all. Rich or poor, people have problems."

"Did you think any of the Parry's problems could have something to do with Cassie's death?"

"I don't see how. Wasn't like we were part of their world or anything." She smirked. "The parents were not especially happy together, but Old Man Parry never had an eye for the help. Not like some other houses I heard about. I can't testify that the old guy stayed faithful to Mrs. Parry, but if he had any outside activity, I am sure he restricted the action to someone of his own class. When it came to the household staff, he may not have been nice but he always behaved like a gentleman. A haughty gentleman, but a gentleman. I worked there for a lot of years and no one complained to me.

At least about the boss being a lech."

"And Mrs. Parry?"

"I never had a personal conversation with her. The family doesn't have relationships with the help, you know. I didn't talk with the family the way that maid on *Downton Abbey* does with Lady Mary. Sometimes the old lady would forget I was around and I'd hear her talk about how unhappy she felt in her marriage, but she never mentioned any suspicions about her husband and anyone in the house. About anyone really. She just found him distracted. Distant, she would say all the time. 'Too devoted to the firm.'" Again, she smirked. "Never his job or his work. The firm. You're thinking that Parry got involved with Cassie and offed her because of . . . because of what?" Her tone told me she found the idea laughable.

"I don't mean to imply." I protested although, in fact, I was trying to imply something untoward. I just didn't know what. "I am just trying to learn about Cassie. Did she talk to you about any problems?"

"Just money. She worked every minute she could. She was thrilled when the cook ran off and she could make those extra bucks."

"Was Cassie interested in the Brien kid?"

"Not that I know of. I saw him around the house a few times. He wasn't a regular visitor. I probably wouldn't have remembered him at all if he hadn't died that way. If he and Cassie spoke, I never knew it."

"So why do you think they were together that night?"

"Mr. Parry convinced the cops that the Brien boy offered Cassie a ride to the loop where the trolley turned around."

I nodded. I knew. Even if Henry Parry hadn't explained, I was old enough to remember trolleys. "You don't think that's what happened?"

"They didn't end up at the loop, did they? Besides, there was no way that kid, Brien, would be seen in the company of the hired help. Not *his* type."

"His type?"

"Hungry to move up, to become a socialite. He wouldn't have let a maid in his car—even a maid Chip Parry had an eye for."

"Chip Parry had a romantic interest in Cassie?" I feigned surprise.

"Followed her around like a puppy." Maria sounded annoyed. The detective in me speculated that the tone actually betrayed bitterness.

"Was Cassie interested in Chip?"

The way Maria shook her head seemed most emphatic. "She had other dreams, big dreams. She wanted to move to New York and become an actress. She could have. Cassie was beautiful."

"So she was leading Chip Parry on?"

She shrugged. "She liked him. They had a genuine friendship. She believed he could do a lot more than his family thought he could."

"She told you that."

"Not exactly."

I interpreted her smile as rueful.

*****Maria Mancini*****
Parry Estate
Philadelphia, Pennsylvania
April 1956

Maria was nearing the bottom of the backstairs when she heard the singing coming from the kitchen. "Oh, What a Beautiful Morning" in Cassie's soprano echoed in the large tiled room. Bad enough Cassie had to sing, but what was so good about her life that she selected such a cheerful tune?

Maria turned the corner and stopped. She pulled back so Chip wouldn't realize that she saw him sneak up behind Cassie at the kitchen sink. Suddenly, the strains of the show tune were interrupted by a squeal.

"Be careful. If I break your mother's French crystal, I'll be out on Germantown Avenue in the blink of an eye."

"If you marry me, you can live here forever and break all the crystal you wanted."

Marry him? Maria's hand flew to her mouth as if it could suppress her gasp. The move must have done the trick because the conversation in the kitchen continued.

"Is that what you're going to do? Stay in this house forever, socializing with the children of the people your parents socialize with? And no one else?"

"It's not such a bad life." Chip sounded amused, not defensive.

"I'm not saying it's bad. It's just . . . ."

"Restrictive." Chip offered.

"And restricted." Her voice softened almost as if she was afraid to address the issue head on.

"You know that my family is not that way. My mother wasn't born SR. Sorry, Social Register."

"I know SR, Henry. It's impossible to spend time in this house and not know that, or the story of your parents' great love."

"I like that you call me Henry. You're the only person I know who doesn't call me Chip."

"Chip is a name for a child, not a grown-up." The clattering of dishes stopped. The playfulness left Cassie's voice to be replaced by earnestness. "Don't you want to be your own man—to live in a place where who you are matters, not who your grandfather was?"

Chip didn't respond. Maria thought she understood what the silence meant. It went on and on. She didn't know what to do. They would hear her if she tried to slip back up the stairs. If she turned the corner, they would know she had been listening. She stood frozen in place until Cassie commanded Chip to make himself useful and help her carry the dishes to the dining room.

Chip not only said yes. He laughed. Maria grimaced. The

pretty blond got away with so much.

*****

"A few weeks later she was dead." Maria made the statement matter-of-factly without a hint of sentimentality.

"The silence," I prompted. "Were they kissing?"

"We'll never know, will we?" She shrugged. "Although I can't think of another explanation, can you?"

I couldn't. "Did Cassie ever mention that Chip came on to her?"

"She didn't have to mention it. His behavior wasn't what I'd call subtle. He came home from college every chance he got. Drove the old man crazy. I never saw the kid try anything with Cassie, but I'd be surprised if he didn't."

"You saw her the day she died?"

"Briefly. On my way out. She worked late in those last few months. Like I said, to take care of dinner."

"Did you have the impression that anything was bothering her?"

"No, she seemed happy. She told me she was close to quitting. I asked her if Chip knew yet."

"Did you think he'd be upset?"

"I did."

"You thought Chip would respond badly?"

"I told Cassie I didn't think one of us had ever told him no before."

"One of the maids?"

"Maids and the rest of us common folk. One of *us*. Not one of *them*."

Chapter 14

Maria Garibaldi gave me the names of her coworkers, the ones she could remember. A short list. The list grew shorter when I asked her to indicate anyone that knew Cassie well. According to Maria, Cassie was friendly to all, friend to none. She only ever chatted with a driver named Martin whose last name eluded Maria since they had worked together only a few years. I couldn't locate any of the people she mentioned.

I seemed to be at a dead-end by Thanksgiving when I arrived at Tracy's to find a table beautifully set not with the casual dishware that came with the house, but with my grandmother's china.

"Mother insisted I take it when she closed down her apartment. She said she wouldn't be cooking any more family meals."

"I can see where Limoges china doesn't fit with her new lifestyle. Did you tell her you were using it?" Bad question, I realized quickly.

"I haven't talked to her this week. Couldn't reach her."

To avoid unpleasant topics, I returned to a discussion of how elegant the table looked.

I felt relieved when Tracy's friends arrived during my discussion of the linen napkins. There's only so much to say about white squares even ones with fine embroidery and lace tips.

"Is Alex joining us?" the fashionista in the crowd asked.

"Not tonight. Family dinner," Tracy explained.

"And that fellow, Trevor? I thought we might get to meet him," the lawyer asked.

Tracy sneered. "After the big buildup?" There had been

flowers and candy and music. "We only had one date."

"Not interested in another?" The lawyer asked a follow-up question.

"He looked so handsome. He seemed so sweet. He was soooo boring."

"Didn't have much to say?" the librarian asked.

"True, but he never stopped saying it."

Good riddance, Trevor.

Without Trevor around to monopolize the conversation, the evening was full of light banter and laughs. No heavy topics until my project came up. I told them the basics and what I knew about the victims, which was essentially nothing—the newspaper talked largely about their place in the Parry household.

"I think I get the picture," the lawyer said. "I used to listen to my grandmother talk about people like Jonathan. Things were so snobby. What am I saying? People were. My grandmother was. I suspect there are still people like that around, but I try to avoid them—and that includes some relatives."

"When exactly did the murders happen?" the librarian asked. When I explained the crime coincided with the royal wedding in Monaco the conversation veered onto Grace Kelly's gown.

"Still a classic," claimed Tracy's friend from the fashion industry.

"Even I know that gown," said the lawyer. "It still shows up in magazines."

"She looked so beautiful," the fashionista added.

"She always did but that day she defined elegance," the lawyer said.

"So regal," I added.

"So virginal," offered the librarian.

"So duplicitous," said the attorney. "I think she had fun in her Hollywood days."

"I wonder if most people were as pure back then as we

thought they were," said the librarian. "Like your victim." She turned to me. "Was it common for a young girl to go parking with a man she just met in 1956?"

"I wondered the same thing." Then I realized something about her question required explanation. "I wasn't in school yet. The only thing I parked at that point was a tricycle."

"Maybe the male victim looked like a good catch to her. A law student." Of course, that opinion came from the lawyer. "For most women back then, finding the right husband represented a career."

"Yes, but in those days I think if she were truly interested in him, she would have played a little hard to get," the librarian offered.

"I agree, because back then wearing white on your wedding day meant something," the fashion professional told us.

"According to the bios I've read, Grace Kelly dissembled when she picked out that white gown," the lawyer followed up.

"But no one would have admitted her image was a charade, not in 1956," I explained.

"You know what I like about you?" The lawyer held up her wine glass to toast me.

"Not a clue." I smiled. "But whatever it is, I'll drink to it." I clinked my glass against hers and the Baccarat crystal sang.

"You don't talk about the old days as if everything was perfect then and everything is horrible now."

"I do wonder if I idealize some and demonize other parts of the past. I would love to go back, do a little time travel, just for five minutes to see if things were the way I remember them. Looking back, everything seemed so formal, so controlled, but I wonder if it actually was."

"The textbooks all say the fifties were a time of great conformity," the librarian added.

That was the way I remembered it. "Every year my older

sister, Tracy's mother, would hem her clothes as soon as Paris dictated the hemline for the year. My memory said it only might have been an inch or even half-an-inch change. But everyone would make the adjustment and then everyone's skirts were the same length. I don't know if every family was that way, but mine was."

"Was it really that restrictive for women?" the fashionista asked. "I mean that Cassie you talk about wanted to be an actress."

"That made her unusual. I was younger but I didn't know of a single contemporary of mine who considered a career. We were probably the last age group that didn't think about a future vis-à-vis working. We knew what our choices were. Secretary. Nurse. Teacher. Until we got married. Although a lot of women figured they wouldn't have to choose any of those jobs at all. They would just get married."

"And wives didn't work?" The lawyer asked.

"They stayed home with the kids. A few in our neighborhood stayed home without kids. When I was growing up, I thought those women had the cushiest life ever. I'd see my father get up early every morning, get dressed and head out to the office. But my mother? I remember her sighing one day. 'I have to get dressed. I have a card party at noon.' Apparently she felt overwhelmed. To me, her schedule looked good but as I got older, I realized how stifling her way of life was."

"Did she love being a homemaker?" the fashionista asked.

"Not only did she dislike housework, she didn't like witnessing it. I remember coming home from school and finding her watching soap operas with the cleaning woman."

"But that was your mother's generation. Surely things were different for Cassie."

I did some quick math. "She would have been about fifteen years younger than my mother. Things hadn't changed that much. Another fifteen years, however, and she would have been living in a much different world."

"After World War II life got more restrictive for women," the librarian offered.

"Jane Wyman movies." The lawyer provided proof.

"But they had great clothes," the fashionista added.

"Always for dinner at the country club," the lawyer said.

"Which is where Jonathan Brien wanted to be. I suspect the closest that Cassie Kelly wanted to get to that life was playing one of those women in a movie. She wouldn't have wanted Jonathan." I offered my opinion with the conviction that I spoke the truth.

"But did she want a fling?" the librarian asked.

"That's the $64,000 question." Then I had to explain how the name of a quiz show became a catchphrase in the 1950s.

Tracy laughed and smiled but rarely joined in. Something continued to bother her. I could tell. I hoped the problem wasn't having her aunt at dinner with her friends.

"Tracy, what's wrong?" I asked her over our clean-up activities. I worried she wouldn't talk, but I was dead wrong. The dam burst.

"My mother."

I found it hard to predict what my sister, currently going through a delayed mid-life crisis, might do, or have done.

"I didn't mind that my mother didn't want to fly up for Thanksgiving, but I hinted that I would be happy to fly down to see her in Florida."

"Maybe she didn't get the hint."

"I was not subtle. I think she did get the hint and felt terrified that I might show up and ruin things for her and her new beau."

Parental mid-life crises can't be easy on children, even children over thirty. I tried to rationalize my sister's actions but Tracy wasn't having any of it. While I, and just about everyone who knew them, saw her parents' split coming, Tracy had been caught completely off-guard. She wasn't the only child who chose to see her parents' marriage as she wanted it to be. After almost five years, she still couldn't see, or wouldn't see, how happy both her parents were in their new lives.

"You take more interest in my life than my mother does. Maybe you would have been a better mother."

"Tracy, never say that. Yes, your mother might be in an odd phase." At least, I hoped it was a phase. I knew it was odd. "Yes, it's a little unsettling that she is acting like a teenager five decades too late, but she has always been a wonderful mother to you."

"She never did anything but stay home and cook and clean. Even now, her idea of a good time is cooking and cleaning for a man. Just not my father and just not in their house." She slammed a dish into the drainer.

"Easy on the china." That serving dish had served four generations of our family and I hoped would serve many more although I'd done nothing to create those descendants.

"She's just living the same life in a different location. I am telling you, you would have been a better mother."

"I would have been a horrible mother," I exclaimed without hesitation. "Why do you think I never had kids? You know how when you were sick, your mother would sit up all night with you and cuddle you to make you feel better?"

Tracy nodded.

"I would have stayed in the other room so I wouldn't catch whatever you had. You would have been on your own."

"You would not."

"I would have. And, you would have been sent home from school because you smelled. Know why? I would have been too tired to give you a bath every night."

"That's crazy. Mom always said bath time was fun." She chuckled.

"Not to me. Kneeling on hard tile hanging over the side of a porcelain tub and getting splashed is not my idea of a

88

good time."

"But you would have taken me on all your adventures."

"Sure, as long as you wanted to eat in first-class restaurants and talk about cinema noir."

I got a smile out of her, a small one, but a smile.

"I am not kidding. Do you know how you and I bonded? Trust me, not over the Muppets—although that is a bad example because I do love the Muppets. When you were about three, I would make little movies of you and we would edit them together. I wasn't doing kid things. You were doing my adult thing." I stopped. I was selling my own inadequacies a little too well. "You know I don't want to undersell my role as an aunt. I am a great aunt. Just not much of a mother. But your mother?"

She stared at me as if daring me to go on.

So, I did. "Your mother was born to be a parent. She and your father waited a long time for you. She was so excited when she heard you were coming. During her pregnancy, she used to knit little outfits for you—unless she felt sick because she didn't want to stitch her cold into the sweater. There were more toys in your house on Christmas than at Toys"R"Us. She had a Ph.D. in Fisher-Price. And she loved being a mom. She doesn't remember a single bad thing you ever did. To her, you were perfect."

"She ran away."

Okay. That I could not deny. My sister did disappear. "But you were over thirty! She wanted to hold on until you settled down, but that didn't happen. I guess your parents always figured if nothing happened, you'd end up with Mitch."

I realized I had talked myself into a corner.

"But after he . . . ." I never liked to use the word died but now that he'd been missing for over seven years, even I found it hard to believe that he would return. I changed tacks. "Look, if your mother felt the need to run off and act a little crazy, accept it."

"But what about Christmas? She didn't even invite me for Christmas."

"Maybe she'll have a change of heart by then and if not, you can create a gorgeous Christmas here. This house was made for the holidays with the big windows and the high ceilings and that fireplace. Santa will have no problem getting down that chimney."

She could barely find the energy to shrug.

"The owners won't be back by then will they?"

She sniffed as she shook her head. The tears welling made her gray eyes gleam a silver-blue.

"I can't say that what your mother does, or rather doesn't do, isn't painful, but forgive her this one transgression in a life devoted to you."

Tracy glared at me with tear-coated eyes.

"Two. Okay, two transgressions. You could count Thanksgiving and Christmas separately, but they both make up one holiday season if you figure the Christmas season actually starts today."

Tracy stared at me.

"The defense rests."

I didn't say a word while she considered what I said.

I felt relieved when she finally spoke. "I wasn't perfect?" She forced amazement into her tone and a smile onto her face.

I ignored her question. "Why don't you give me advice on how to pursue this killer?"

Chapter 15

Although doubtful they would have much to contribute, or to be willing to contribute, Tracy found nothing ridiculous about my interest in the Parrys. I decided to interview the rest of the family before following any other leads. An easy decision since I didn't have any other leads.

I did a quick Internet search for the two children whose love life had caused Henry Parry concern. At that point, the family tree became scrambled. Both Parry offspring had multiple marriages, although Blair appeared to be carrying the ball on that play. I counted at least four weddings. Chip had apparently stopped at two. Counting the children's life events was complex enough. Identifying all the grandchildren proved impossible. That didn't worry me. In the time period that concerned me, I only had to worry about the first generation of Henry Parry's offspring.

Since I'd already met Chip's father, I saw no point in surprising Chip Parry. He probably knew someone was out and about, asking questions about the Kelly/Brien murders. He probably figured that someone would eventually want to talk to him. He probably had his speech prepared. I looked up the younger Parry's number in the membership guide I'd picked up in the coatroom at the Philadelphian Club, ignoring the "for member's use only" on the cover, and called. Chip Parry registered no surprise, or displeasure, at my call. If the younger Parry had appeared at all reticent to see me, I might have concluded the family was up to no good, but Chip appeared happy, almost anxious to see me.

His front door opened as I raised my hand to grab the knocker. I assumed the man standing in a wide hallway with a golden retriever beside him was Chip Parry. Still energetic and preppie in his late seventies, the son definitely represented a chip off the old block. At least when it came to his physical appearance. He had the same tall, slim build but he still appeared muscular. Chip Parry's features, although fine, lacked the patrician cut of his father's. More cute than handsome, I could see the twenty-year-old in the face that had aged gracefully. Heck, I could see the six-year-old. Still, despite the differences, the family resemblance could not be denied. Besides, the man said, "Hello, I am Chip Parry."

"Julia Tracy."

"Yes, you said that on the phone. My mother's name was Julia."

"Your father mentioned that."

"Did he mention that she was a lovely woman?"

"He did."

"Good, because she was."

I found our last exchange a bit odd. Checking to see if his father praised his mother sufficiently? Making sure I admired his mother? I couldn't know. Did the strangeness of our exchange mean that Chip was strange? I always trust that dogs are a good judge of character and this one seemed to like Chip. So I figured I'd probably like Chip. His eyes, somehow managing to twinkle despite the same dark blue tone as his father's, reinforced my positive impression.

"Did you have any trouble finding the place?"

"Not really." The two-story stone building was hidden down a long tree-lined lane in a northwest suburb. I didn't know how much of the woods Chip owned but there were no other buildings to be seen when I pulled into the circular driveway in front of the house. From all indications, he lived comfortably but not ostentatiously. I mean his home cost a lot more than I could ever afford, but, I suspected, a lot less than he could.

The twosome, man and dog, led me into a den, shabby in that way that did not cry reduced circumstances but rather screamed inherited wealth. The paintings on the wall were oils, and the books on the shelves were leather-bound. The photographs displayed—my guess would be of his children and grandchildren—were framed in silver, with monograms etched into the rims. Chip directed me to a well-worn armchair and sat in a similar, but not matching, piece on the opposite side of the fireplace, unlit but stacked with wood, awaiting the first frost. The dog curled up on the rug at Chip's feet as if I were Norman Rockwell just arrived to paint their portrait. As Chip and I chatted, the dog grew tired of posing and found his way to my feet. Chip stayed in his chair.

The retriever, that his owner introduced as Four, seemed the more enthusiastic party about my visit at least as long as I kept petting him. Chip gave me the impression that he too was happy until I dispensed with the small talk and broached the topic of Cassie Kelly. He still had a smile on his face, but he appeared to grow melancholy at the mention of the murder victim.

"Cassie." He took a deep breath. "Sad to think how long she has been gone. Cassie was beautiful, you know. Sweet. Kind. And smart. I know that if Cassie had lived she would have made something of herself. Cassie would not have worked as a maid forever."

His repetition of her name reminded me of a pre-teen girl with a crush. "Sounds like you were a little sweet on her."

"A little?" He chuckled. "I was in love with Cassie."

No need to get out the thumbscrews to coax the truth out of this guy. He seemed pleased to share the news.

"As I said, Cassie was lovely. I would have been a fool if I weren't."

Which might not have been such good news when tragedy struck in 1956. "So it must have hurt when she died." I wanted to sound sympathetic, not accusatory. "I mean you must have been pretty jealous that she was into Jonathan Brien."

"Cassie was not *into* Jonathan Brien."

I sensed no anger in his tone. He simply stated a fact.

"She would never have gone parking with him. Cassie knew what Jonathan was all about."

"And that was?"

He chuckled again, this time a bit ruefully. "Marrying my sister Blair."

"Jonathan was in love with your sister?" I feigned surprise. Day by day, I grew more and more alarmed by my ability to fake a variety of emotions.

"Jonathan loved that she was rich and in the Social Register. You know, *a rose by any other name would smell as sweet*? Not to Jonathan. He loved that Blair was a Parry."

"And Cassie was different?"

"I know. You're thinking how stupid is this fellow? He could see Jonathan Brien playing his sister but couldn't see the maid playing him. It wasn't like that."

"What was it like?"

"I had to pursue Cassie."

"Were you serious about her?"

He straightened his back as if preparing for battle. "I was willing to fight my parents so I could marry her."

"They didn't want to have a maid in the family?"

"A maid. A Catholic. A Hibernian. You would think my parents would have been more understanding. My father loves to talk about how he fought to marry the Catholic woman he loved. Of course, when he isn't presenting himself as a social rebel, he describes her as a French Catholic and implies she had aristocratic ancestors. Of course, by the time I grew old enough to understand, she was *formerly* Catholic." He shook his head as if still mystified.

"So your parents knew how you felt about Cassie?"

"My mother disapproved. I'm not certain my father knew until the night Cassie died."

*****Chip Parry*****

94

Parry Estate
Philadelphia, Pennsylvania
April 21, 1956

He loved to watch Cassie spoon ice cream onto the Peach Melba. He loved to watch her do anything. Chip Parry loved Cassie Kelly, full stop.

"If you're going to follow me everywhere, you should at least help. Here." She shoved a silver tray in his direction. "Hold this."

Chip obeyed while Cassie topped off the desserts and placed them on the tray.

"When you get off tonight, I'll drive you to the trolley stop."

"Henry, your parents don't want you to be seen with a girl like me."

"What's wrong with a girl like you?"

"Don't act naïve. Even Jonathan, who does everything in the world to fit in, is wrong in your parents' eyes."

"They'll come around."

"No, they won't. I heard your parents talking. And, I wasn't eavesdropping. They discuss whatever they please around me as if I'm a piece of furniture."

Chip didn't argue her last point. He could not deny that was true. He did the same in front of the household staff. At least he had until Cassie came. "Cassie, you can't think because my parents disapprove of Jonathan that they disapprove of you. Even you say that Jonathan's a phony."

Tray in hand, he spun around when he noticed the creaking of the door. His father's eyes focused on the tray. He made no attempt to hide his annoyance. No, he would have been annoyed to find Chip chatting with Cassie. He appeared furious seeing Chip helping her out with her duties. "Chip, dinner isn't over. Get back to the table. Cassie has work to do." He emphasized Cassie's name to make sure Chip understood that meal preparation was hers to

95

do—and only hers.

Cassie got the message. She took the tray from Chip's hands and set it on the counter.

His sister appeared in the doorway. Blair sized up the situation in an instant but her expression wasn't teasing. She shot Chip a nervous look. As he passed his sister and father, Chip glanced back at Cassie. Unconcerned and unintimidated she continued topping off desserts. He felt incredible admiration for her composure. She really knew how to annoy his father. Henry Parry wanted to see fear in those he dominated. He saw it in his own children but could not raise the slightest discernible discomfort in their downstairs maid. Her attitude made Chip love Cassie all the more.

*****

Six decades later, tears clustered in the corners of Chip's eyes. "After Cassie served dessert, I never saw her again." He forced a smile. "Sometimes I think how different my life would have been if I had insisted on driving her home that night. I might be a happily married man living with my loving wife, instead of a lonely old divorcé rattling around in this big house."

I didn't know how to comfort him. I didn't try. "Did you ever notice Jonathan coming on to Cassie?"

He made no attempt to hide a smirk. "Jonathan Brien would not have risked a future with my sister to pursue a roll in the hay with Cassie."

"Even if he thought things had ended with Blair?"

"He would not have given up so easily."

"Then why did Cassie end up in his car with him?"

"I assume he offered her a ride."

"But they ended up in a lover's lane."

"I am telling you. Neither of them would have wanted to go parking with the other. Maybe he had engine trouble or ran out of gas. It was a carjacking, plain and simple. It just didn't happen when they were parking as the police thought, but I am sure that someone wanted the convertible. Certain elements would be attracted to a fancy vehicle like that."

"But those certain elements didn't keep the car."

"Ms. Tracy, I don't know what happened, but something must have spooked the criminal. Maybe he noticed someone coming, saw a cop nearby. I can't know. What I do know, is they would not have gone there to canoodle, as my father claimed."

Canoodle—a word I hadn't heard in many years and maybe never without a sardonic overtone.

"I read articles about the funerals in the newspapers. You weren't in the picture at Cassie's."

Chip bent forward with his elbows on his thighs and cast his eyes to what I suspected was an authentic antique Persian carpet.

"I wasn't at the funeral. None of us went. My mother said we would draw too much attention to ourselves, but I knew the real reason. She didn't want the family associated with a scandal."

I noted the catch in his voice but couldn't see his eyes.

"Do you know anything about Cassie's family?"

"Hard-working, kind parents. I never met them. Immigrants I believe. One brother. Still in high school at the time. I heard he passed."

"High school?" Why wouldn't he?

"No." He looked at me and I saw that his smile was amused, but not mocking. "I heard he died."

"In high school?"

"No." The left corner of his mouth twisted bringing his expression perilously close to a smirk, but his eyes remained kind. "In his fifties."

How did Chip know that? How had Cassie's brother ended up in contact with Chip Parry's world? *If* he ended up in contact with Chip Parry's world? Maybe Chip kept track

97

of him. In the age of the Internet, tracking people wasn't hard.

Before I could ask, Chip who had just spilled his guts, asked, belatedly in my opinion, "Exactly why are you collecting this information?"

Again, I called myself an amateur historian and, eliminating the statistical element, appropriated Antonia Sadoski's thesis topic and went with the need for social context. I hinted at a possible book and threw in a reference to Tracy's class just to cover all my bases. I wished I could remember exactly what I had told his father. Then again, would his father?

Chip nodded at my explanation, such as it was. "Social history is rather interesting, especially when written from the viewpoint of the individual."

"Individuals," I lied. "I'll be looking for other stories, so if you know of any similar situations . . . ."

"No. No. I've lived a charmed life, untroubled by tragedy, except that one." He paused. "I still regret that I allowed my parents to stop me from going to Cassie's funeral, to her viewing, to see her one more time, to say good-bye. But they would not hear of it. They ordered me to stay at school. Ironic, isn't it? Cassie's claim that my parents wouldn't want me to be seen with her proved correct." He lifted his head and I saw that his face and his tone were overwhelmed by regret. Suddenly, I saw a smile that was both sweet and sad. "You remind me of her."

I found that hard to believe. In sixty years I had never been deemed beautiful, even on my best day which was, in fact, July 10, 1973. "Thank you, but she was a beautiful young girl."

"Beauty doesn't fade. It evolves. You have lovely bone structure."

Right. That and a good personality.

"Do you live nearby?" he asked.

"In Center City and I'd better get back there. I'm late." I

lied and fled from Chip Parry, not because I considered him a suspect because I didn't, and not because he was unattractive because he wasn't. I don't know why I practically ran out the door. But I did—without considering that an extremely wealthy man had just flirted with me.

Chapter 16

When my phone rang the next day, I didn't recognize the voice on the other end but found it easy to identify my caller. "Ms. Tracy. Calling to see if you changed your mind about that Bentley."

"If you hold on, I can check my lottery numbers."

"Good one," he said with the patience of a man who had heard the line hundreds of time. "It's Val Bernardino."

"I guessed. How are you?"

"Fine. Did you have a good Thanksgiving?"

I assured him I had.

"I had a great Thanksgiving. That's why I am calling."

I didn't get the connection until he explained he had told his sisters about my visit.

"My sister, Valerie—she's a few years older than me—she hosted our dinner. She lives in Haddonfield. Nice house. Big enough to hold all of us. At least, all of us who are left. Anyway, when I told her about you, she remembered that investigation you asked about. Not a lot, because it was a long time ago, but she had met one of those Parry people. They had a daughter?"

"Yes, Blair."

"Well, I am not sure about that, but Valerie remembered because she had met someone my father was talking about. I mean she met the girl years later and my father didn't talk about the crime at the time, but, at some point later on, he mentioned that case and she recalled meeting that kid."

"And your sister remembered something?" I was hoping for a piece of evidence.

"Only that my father said he worked his butt off on that case but could never get anywhere. She was too young to understand much, but she knew that my father didn't like the family."

"Did he think any of the Parry's were suspects?"

"If he did, he didn't say so. He pounded the pavement and knocked on doors, but couldn't find anyone who had seen a thing. No one noticed the victims or the car between the Parry house and the spot where they were found. I thought I should tell you."

After I thanked him and hung up, the phone rang almost immediately. This time I recognized the voice at the other end.

"Julia. Chip Parry here. I spoke to my sister on your behalf. She'll be home all day today."

"Well," I sputtered. I hated to be ungrateful but I had made other plans for the day. My schedule included a lot of couch time, but plans.

"Yes, she did express some reluctance, but I cannot see why any of us should hesitate to shed whatever light we can on Cassie or Jonathan. We should be eager to assist you in your efforts. I'm not foolish enough to believe that telling their stories makes up for what they lost in life, they were fine people and should be remembered." Chip continued in his self-congratulatory tone. "Blair is a rather private person but I asked her what possible harm talking to you could do? It isn't as if we have anything to hide. I thought you'd want to move fast before she changes her mind. My sister is not comfortable with anyone she hasn't known since high school." He released a theatrical sigh. "Actually, she isn't comfortable with anyone she hasn't known since grade school. She's married her way through her kindergarten class." He chuckled, paused and then chuckled some more. Chip Parry really liked his own joke. "Do let me know if you need anything else. Perhaps we can chat again. I'd be happy to review any information you found."

And in that moment, I decided that Chip Parry wasn't flirting with me. He was using me. Chip Parry played the charming gentleman, but under the surface lurked a bully, a manipulator and, perhaps, a killer. Maybe his sister would slip up and confirm that. So, despite a reluctance to do what Chip Parry scheduled for me, I took down the information and headed right over to Blair's.

In an illogical show of rebellion, I didn't rush as I'd been directed by Chip. I drove under the speed limit all the way to her house in Gladwyne. And, let me be clear, I arrived at a house, not a home. The architecture made it clear. The furniture made it clear. And, my hostess made it clear.

Blair, now close to eighty, sat with a ramrod-straight back on a settee in her formally furnished drawing-room. Her expression and tone were just as formal. When the uniformed maid led me to the lady of the house, Blair didn't get up. She offered her hand for what was almost a handshake. Her skin touched mine but she applied no pressure. "You might as well sit down," she offered. "I have no idea why my brother thinks we should speak to you." She all but huffed. "Except that he had that ridiculous crush on that ridiculous maid of ours. The whole episode was . . . ." She fought for a word and I had a feeling when she found one, she'd settle on *ridiculous*. She did. "Chip," she continued, "had no taste in women." She eyed me from head to toe.

Luckily, I hadn't been wearing one of my jeans uniforms. I had on a slightly more dressy uniform, all black and stretchy and easily accessorized to make me appear presentable. At least I thought so. Apparently, Blair didn't.

"I guess at a certain age men get desperate." She patted her wool slacks and straightened a seam that didn't meet her standards.

Was she telling me that I was the object of her brother's desperation? Her expression said she found me wanting. In what particular respect, I didn't know. I also didn't care. I wouldn't want to look like Blair Parry Middleton Foster Braddock Mills Parry. Not that she wasn't attractive. She

102

was, in her fashion, the fashion of 1962. The maroon velvet hairband that held back her gray hair matched the buttons on the plaid jacket she wore over black slacks. I would have loved to own that outfit. In 1962. As a matter of fact, I felt pretty sure I did own that outfit in 1962.

"Is that you?" I inquired about the oil painting over the mantel, the only depiction of a human in the room—no messy pictures of children or grandchildren for Blair. I noted the resemblance of the woman in the painting, and her angular bone structure, to the homeowner.

"Painted at the time of my debut."

So, Blair would have been younger when painted than Cassie was when she died, yet the figure in the picture appeared older. It might have been the fault of the artist, or it might have been because Blair's hair and dress were decidedly matronly. Proper, but a little dowdy and certainly without any trace of sensuality.

"It's lovely," I lied.

"Yes. It's a lovely remembrance of a wonderful tradition. My father looked so proud to present me. I don't think that I ever felt closer to him. Not even on my wedding day." She didn't specify which one, but I assumed she meant the first when she still might have gotten sentimental about marriage.

The conversation took a quick turn. "Chip said I should tell you about the night Jonathan and our downstairs maid died. As if I can remember what I did on a specific night in 1957."

"1956," I corrected her. There were few nights I recalled in detail, but call me crazy, if two people left my house one evening and ended up suffering gruesome deaths by morning, I believe that would have been one I remembered.

Blair's exasperation came through despite her tight-jawed speaking style. She might have called it an accent. I called it an affectation.

"I have no idea what right you have to pry into our

private lives, but since it is ancient history, I can see no harm in it. This is for an academic paper, correct?"

I moved my head in a manner that could be construed as a nod.

"On the social conventions of the time?"

This time I smiled and actually nodded.

"I guess ours was the story of a quintessential social mismatch."

"And that issue came into play that last night?"

"I do recall that when dinner finished, I told Jonathan it was over between us. As if there ever had been an *it* or an *us*. But Jonathan believed there was. Being young myself, I didn't realize how immature he was, how unrealistic. He thought we had a future. I know that he felt horribly disappointed. I feel terrible if losing me drove him into Cassie's arms." She flung a hand on her chest to make me believe what her tone couldn't. I didn't believe the hand either.

"You think that's what happened?" I asked.

"I could see how it might have. Jonathan wasn't appropriate for me, but he would have been quite a catch for a girl like Cassie."

I knew what she meant but wouldn't give her the satisfaction of thinking I did. "A girl like Cassie?"

She stared at me and sputtered searching for a response. *How can you not get my point?* Her expression asked.

"I didn't know her." I offered an explanation.

"Cassie was a maid," she said, stupefied.

"I understand that she aspired to a career."

"I would not have known. She was our maid." She repeated as if speaking to a child.

"Did you ever see Jonathan show any interest in Cassie?"

"When he could date me?" She let me know that she found my questions becoming more and more bizarre. "No. I did not. Jonathan was completely enamored of me. At least of my money, my position and my name. I'd label him a social climber."

"Didn't that bother you?"

Blair smiled. Perhaps, at last, she concluded that she was not dealing with an idiot. She leaned back, crossed her long thin legs and relaxed. I recognized her shoes from the days when I wore business attire. They were Italian, expensive and from the 1980s. "That's how things were in those days. Philadelphia was a tight little club back then. People wanted in."

"And Jonathan wasn't *in*?"

"Hardly. Although he wanted in—badly. He had no interest in sticking with his own kind. He aspired to a better life."

I nodded. Blair interpreted my gesture as knowing what she meant. And, I did. But that wasn't why I nodded. I made the gesture because she so perfectly fit the stereotype I'd expected. I forced my puzzled expression. "If Jonathan wasn't your kind, how did you meet him?"

"Chronic shortage of men to dance with all the debutantes. Most of the boys came from families you'd know, by that I mean you'd recognize the names." She rattled off a list of surnames straight from Who's Who in Philadelphia that she assumed would impress me.

I shrugged as if to say they meant nothing to me. And, that was true. I did recognize a few names but they meant nothing to me. Apparently, they meant a lot to Blair.

"Unfortunately those families couldn't provide enough males to fill our dance cards, so to speak. We had to call in outsiders. As I recall, a friend of Jonathan's from law school put him on the list."

"Did Jonathan lie about his background?"

"He omitted. But that didn't mean he fooled anyone. We all understood what he was, but he never caused our group any embarrassment. He could be very personable, quite witty. The Irish often are, you know. Jonathan had studied the WASP culture well. Knew his grammar. Knew his etiquette. Knew where to shop so he always showed up in the right uniform." She closed her eyes as if viewing memories on the inside of her lids. "Maybe not always." When she opened her eyes they showed amusement. "I should not say that. He was a good student and a quick learner. Perfectly presentable."

"But?"

"But he wasn't one of us. It's easy to spot someone who isn't your kind."

The way you spotted me. I didn't say that out loud. I bet she thought I grinned but, in fact, I grimaced.

"But you went out with him."

"On a casual basis."

I caught just the slightest trace of a smile on her lips.

"I was a foolish young girl and found him very cute. To give him his due, he *was* handsome. I suspect he would have aged well."

I imagined her internal dialog telling her to buck up and not get sentimental about someone like Jonathan.

"Where was Jonathan the last time you saw him that night?"

Blair looked sad. When she spoke, I detected true emotion. "On our terrace. That was the last time I saw him. On our terrace."

*****Blair Parry*****
Parry Estate
Philadelphia, Pennsylvania
April 21, 1956

Blair knew she had to get Jonathan alone. She had to tell him. Her father could hide extreme hostility under a cloak of civility. That was what he was doing that evening, but the civility would soon wear thin and she would bear the brunt of his anger. She did not want that to happen. Not over someone like Jonathan. Sure, she liked having someone fawning over her, especially someone as cute as Jonathan, but not enough to suffer her father's wrath for that pleasure. She guided Jonathan out a set of French doors that led directly from the dining room to the patio.

She knew he loved this terrace with the flagstone floor and the low stone wall surrounding it. She'd watched him react to the scene the first time she'd pushed open the wide doors revealing the expanse of greenery beyond. He tried to act blasé but his eyes took in the tips of the putting green flags to the right, the rows of formal gardens to the left, and, straight ahead, the meticulously tended lawns that rolled down to the small pond reflecting the last rays of the setting sun. The border of tall trees beyond emphasized that this was a private domain. The Parry's domain. He couldn't see the tennis courts or the guest house. She wished he could. She enjoyed impressing him—not simply because her family had money. He appreciated the kind of money they had. Old money. This patio shouted old money. And old money impressed Jonathan.

That night, Jonathan was flirtatious. Perhaps the setting inspired him. "What is so important that I couldn't finish my Peach Melba?" He reached for her but she pulled away.

"Jonathan, this is so hard." She turned to gaze over the grounds, but Jonathan moved into position beside her. She felt his closeness and the attraction that clouded her judgment in the first place. He seemed concerned, solicitous. For someone with his background, he could be quite the gentleman.

"What is so hard?" he asked.

"Jonathan, I am so sorry but I can't see you anymore."

"I don't understand." Despite his obvious confusion, his tone remained soft, comforting.

Why was he being so nice? How dumb was he? Couldn't he see the way her father treated him, the way her father looked at him, the way her father looked at her that night? "I feel terrible. Truly." She glanced at him but didn't want his warm, brown, puppy dog eyes to sway her. She knew what she had to do. "I have a good time with you. I do. Really. But, my father is concerned."

"Concerned? About what?"

"He's afraid we are getting serious."

"I thought that was what a father wanted for his daughter. To find a man with serious intentions. To find a good husband."

It angered her that Jonathan had the audacity to think he would make a good mate for her. *"Jonathan, you know my family. My father has certain expectations about the kind of boy I'll marry."*

"And I'm not that kind of boy?"

"Don't make me say this, Jonathan. You understand. I know you do."

She waited for him to agree, but he just stared at her, forcing her eyes to meet his. She looked away. He knew what she meant. He had to, but he was going to make her say it. Maybe he was more of a cad than she thought. *"You have to know that my father wants his children to settle down with people like us."*

At last, Jonathan couldn't hide his feelings. She watched as first pain, then humiliation and, finally, anger, took control of his face. She saw no sign of the puppy dog adoration in his eyes, only steely determination. He accentuated his feelings with a sarcastic tone. *"Your mother wasn't* people like us *when he married her."*

Blair hated having her mother's pedigree thrown in her face—especially by someone who had none. *"I know, I know. But I can't go against my father. He doesn't approve. He won't approve."*

"He has to get to know me. I'm going to talk to him."

The desperation in his voice surprised Blair.

"Where is he? What does he do after dinner? He's golfing, right?"

She didn't mean to agree, but her gaze shot towards the

putting green. Quickly, she turned her eyes towards the shrubs that hid the tennis courts but realized her ploy hadn't deceived him. "Jonathan, don't. It won't help. I know him."

But Jonathan remained determined. She laid a hand on his arm, but it didn't stop him. Jonathan shook off her touch and set off in search of her father.

She shivered watching him walk towards the putting green but not because of the evening chill. His strong stride and a confident attitude would never impress Henry Parry. She feared Jonathan was not ready for the brutal reality of her father's response. She turned towards the house, and, just for an instant, her eyes met Cassie's. The window to the kitchen was open and that maid had been listening. The little upstart was judging her. She'd not only formed an opinion but had the audacity to let it show on her face. Cassie pulled the window closed as if blocking an unpleasant sight.

What did Blair care? She didn't need the downstairs maid's approval. She did what she had to do.

*****

Blair let the hint of a smile show on her lips. "I have to give Jonathan credit. No one ever stood up to Henry Parry."

Did I detect a glint of admiration in her eyes for her former suitor?

"And that was the last time you saw Jonathan Brien?"

"Rushing off to find my father."

"And you didn't follow him?"

She shook her head so violently a hair on the right side of her scalp actually moved. "I did not want to be anywhere in the vicinity. I hid in my room."

"Do you know if Jonathan ever spoke to your father?"

"He never found him. I know because the police asked my father that question. I heard him tell them he never saw Jonathan after dinner. I assume when Jonathan couldn't find my father, he simply left."

She had more to say, so I waited, hoping for a theory of the murder.

"Jonathan never said he loved me, only that my father could not tell him he wasn't good enough."

I detected resentment in her voice. "That must have made you angry."

"I was angry that my father had been right about Jonathan all along."

It seemed to me she still was. Understanding that part of Jonathan's attraction to her was her money and position was one thing, but what if that was the only attraction? That must have rankled. I wanted to probe, but her expression told me to change the subject. "How well did you know Cassie?"

"Cassie? Not at all. I told you. She was our maid." She glared at me as if I were at best deaf and at worst crazy. "Don't frown at me as if I'm some sort of snob. Jonathan's family wasn't any happier about me than my family was about him."

She knew his family?

"That little brother of his made it perfectly clear."

"You met Timothy O'Brien?"

"Met is a polite word. I never told Jonathan because the kid backed off when I confronted him, but Jonathan's little brother was stalking me."

Chapter 17

The news that Tim O'Brien had met Blair Parry was shocking but wasn't what created the need to talk to Tracy. Neither of us liked a case without a driving force, and Antonia Sadoski hadn't provided one. Neither of us had heard a peep from the busy graduate student, but now I felt motivated. I could work for two people who had never been given the chance to speak for themselves.

Feeling the need to share my reaction with Tracy, I asked her to meet me in the Wallmann cafeteria where she had a sandwich and I had a side order of Brussels sprouts soaked in a substance that appeared to be addictive.

"I think it's grease," Tracy explained.

"I didn't come for the Brussels sprouts, although they are a great side-benefit. You know Cassie's story has been driving me. Yes, I'd love to help Tim O'Brien, but it is always Cassie that I am thinking about. But today at Blair's, there was a moment in her description of her last encounter with Jonathan when my heart broke for him. When Blair said he wasn't *people like us*."

Tracy didn't feel so sympathetic. "I notice you aren't claiming she broke his heart. A broken heart I could sympathize with. He didn't love her. Her father was right about his motives. Tim O'Brien confirmed them."

I had to agree with Tracy that Jonathan didn't love Blair in a conventional sense.

"In what sense then?"

"I believe he idolized her. She represented everything he wanted. It wasn't as if he hated her and was using her. He loved the package."

"And losing the package broke his heart?"

"No. What broke his heart was knowing he'd nurtured his dream for so long and with one sentence, when she said he was not *people like us*, she brought reality crashing around his head."

Tracy thought I gave Jonathan too much credit. "You like Cassie because you see her as a dreamer and a worker. I don't get the sudden affection for Jonathan. You describe him as a schemer and a manipulator."

"No. He was a dreamer. Just like Cassie. Sure his dream was superficial and foolish, but he worked for it. He didn't want to marry a rich woman and live off her. He wanted to be worthy of her."

Tracy's face made it clear she did not agree, but she didn't argue. She took a bite of her sandwich with a ferocity that spoke for her.

"But even if I acknowledge his plan was less than honorable, those words must have been like a punch in the stomach. All his illusions were shattered. All his effort—for nothing. He'd lost it all. I feel for him." The emotion in my voice shocked me.

"I am happy that caring about him motivates you, but I still view him as a social-climbing user."

"You girls talking about Gatsby?" Ed Hayley appeared beside the table, tray in hand.

"No."

I marveled at Tracy's ability to be gracious when I knew her annoyance level had jumped from zero to sixty.

"Just working on another case." Her tone remained pleasant but did not invite him to linger.

"Ah, the '56 Thunderbird. The joyrider? Cruising around with two bodies in the trunk. I looked it up." He added with pride. "There was plenty of space back there."

I hated to admit it, but Ed Hayley resurrected an interesting point. I'd speculated about the blood in the trunk but never focused on why and how the blood ended up there.

I pictured the handsome young couple driving away from

the Parry estate and into some sort of trouble, but if not to a lovers' lane, then where?

If the perp did move the bodies, why did he move them? And why to a place where they were likely to be found?

I waited until Ed finished a litany of self-aggrandizing memories from the 1950s and moved on, before I followed up. "If he's right and the bodies were in the trunk . . . ."

Tracy interrupted. "I will caution you. He is seldom right. Always certain, but seldom correct. The cops didn't find a murder weapon at the scene. Maybe the perp stuck it in the trunk and that's how the blood got there."

"And took it after the joy ride?"

"According to Tim O'Brien, the cops suspected it was Jonathan's own golf club and Jonathan always got himself the best. Why leave something so valuable behind?" Tracy's thought process was logical, but I didn't quite buy her conclusion.

"No. I am willing to bet Ed Hayley is right about one thing. I mean, admit it, it had to happen once in his life."

She looked doubtful.

"Eventually, Ed had to make a good point. I agree that the perp felt the need to move the bodies."

The question wasn't to where; the issue became from where.

Chapter 18

I didn't mind waiting for Timothy O'Brien on the bench at the end of the Boardwalk since the early December day felt like October. Even though he seemed to be in his natural environment, lounging on the bench with the bright sun bouncing off his shades and the gentle wind ruffling his curls, Alex was not so complacent. "Are you sure he's jogging up here?"

"No."

"So why are we here?'

"I'm hoping he is predictable."

"I am definitely predictable. It is almost one o'clock. I'm getting hungry."

"Well . . . ."

Alex interrupted me. "And, I don't want another package of peanut butter crackers. You promised me seafood to entice me into this drive."

"And you'll get some. In the meantime, enjoy the beautiful day. Enjoy the warmth of the sun, the rumble of the surf . . . ."

"The growl of my stomach," he finished. "We should have eaten first and then gone to his house when he got back."

Given the type of conversation I had planned, I thought it wiser to be outside of the house, in plain view. I hadn't shared my thought with Alex, but he was no fool. He figured out which way the conversation would be headed. "You think this guy killed his brother?"

"No," I answered quickly.

"So I am not along to protect you?"

"No," I aimed for a tone that dismissed the idea as

ridiculous. "Although the conversation could be unpleasant. I think he may know more than he told me before. Besides, you volunteered to ride along. I could have come alone."

"It did sound like fun. You play good cop. I'll play bad cop." Alex grew excited. "Tracy and I do this all the time."

"We're not cops. We are nice people helping this nice man solve the murder of his nice brother who died giving a nice girl a ride home in his nice car."

"No bad cop?" Alex was disappointed.

"No bad cop. I do, however, have good news. You'll get to eat soon. Here he comes." I pointed to the lone figure, dressed all in red, moving slowly down the Boardwalk. I recognized Timothy O'Brien's form.

He saw us but my identity didn't register until I called out. "Mr. O'Brien, I am sorry to disturb you again." I flashed a broad smile which, given the circumstances, probably seemed a bit inappropriate. "Remember me?"

"Of course." O'Brien smiled too, although not as broadly. "I am always a little distracted when I run. I apologize. I waited a long time for someone to investigate Johnny's case. I'm not likely to forget. You could have called."

I pointed toward Alex. "Well, my friend and I were going to be down here . . . ." If I stopped there, I hadn't told a complete lie. So, I stopped.

He glanced at Alex. If he wondered why I was traveling with a thirtyish Ralph Lauren model, he didn't ask. "You have a new helper."

He introduced himself and Alex rose to shake his hand mumbling something about being no help and just coming along for lunch. I detected bitterness in his pronunciation of the last word.

Nonetheless, I felt relief when Alex dropped the fake reason for his presence into the conversation. I didn't want to explain that Alex tagged along at Tracy's insistence that I never go alone when planning to broach a controversial

115

topic that might elicit a negative response. She also recommended subtlety so I avoided my first urge to blurt out *how did your brother take the news you were screwing up his plans for the good life?* "Another question popped up. "I didn't realize you had met Blair Parry."

O'Brien appeared stricken.

"You talked to her?"

I nodded.

"And she told you about the time we ran into each other?"

Again, I nodded.

"I'm not proud of how I met her. I wish I could tell you bumping into her was a coincidence but our encounter was no accident."

I didn't say anything. I prayed Alex would follow my lead. I hoped he, too, noted that the emotion rising in Tim O'Brien might lead to an explosion of truth.

"I never told anyone about the time I followed Johnny. Not even my wife knows. I tried to forget what I did. I still regret doing it. I was too young to realize my actions might embarrass him or jeopardize his plans. I wouldn't do that on purpose. I loved Johnny. After my mother died, when my father wasn't working, he was drinking. Johnny was all I had."

"Were you worried Johnny would move up and out and leave you with an alcoholic father?" I asked.

"No. No. I was too young. I didn't think things through to that conclusion."

"So you weren't angry at the thought he might leave home, leave you?"

"What do you think?" His eyes narrowed and his tone turned hostile. "You believe I killed Johnny so he wouldn't move out? Even as a kid, I would have seen the fallacy in that logic. I was old enough to know that either way I would lose him. You're crazy if you think I would have ever hurt Johnny. I loved him." He looked to Alex for support. Alex nodded but took a step back towards the railing.

I drew O'Brien's attention back to me. "Of course, I don't think you would kill him." *At least not intentionally.* "But you followed him to Chestnut Hill." I played puzzled. "I just want to know everything you know. You never know what insignificant piece of information might lead us to the person who killed him."

He watched the ocean pound the sand for what felt like an eternity before he spoke. "A stupid kid-thing to do. I had a learner's permit and the keys to my father's car. I wanted to see where Johnny went."

"I can imagine that finding out you were—I don't know what to call it—stalking his girlfriend got him a little fired up. Did you and Johnny talk about that, argue over that?"

"If the Parry girl told him, he never mentioned it to me. We never fought. About anything. Not even who got the last cookie. He was my big brother. I always got it. He was always good to me. I loved Johnny. I didn't want to lose him. And I wasn't stalking her. I just followed him when he went to meet her. Two times," he confessed. "And the one time I kept watching her after Johnny left, she spotted me."

"What did you expect?" I kept my tone soft as if I were just curious and concerned about the feelings of a young boy.

"To see his new world. So I could fit in. Johnny wouldn't take me along unless I changed, but when I saw that girl, I knew I couldn't be someone she would like." His eyes filled with tears at the recollection.

*****Timothy O'Brien*****
Chestnut Hill Cricket Club
Philadelphia, Pennsylvania
April 1956

Timothy hid on the other side of a fence behind a column watching Johnny play tennis with three people. His partner had blonde hair pulled back into a ponytail that curled under at the end. Even though summer remained months away, she had on a short white dress and her legs were already tan. She must have gone to Florida during the winter. One of the girls in their neighborhood went to Florida on spring break from junior college and came back all sunburnt.

Timmy could understand why Johnny would want to play tennis but not why he'd want to get all dressed up in white shorts and a white sweater with stupid stripes just so he could look exactly like every other guy on the court. Tennis was supposed to be fun, wasn't it? Who wanted to watch out for white clothes? If Johnny fell he would have gotten grass stains on his pants, and he knew how his friend's mother would go on and on about grass stains.

Timmy peeked around one of the brick columns that lined the fence. He didn't know much about tennis but he knew Johnny wasn't very good at it. Not horrible, but not as good as the other players. He was the one who hit the ball towards the fence, a shot that ended the game.

"I'll get it." The girl with the blond hair called. "Good effort, Jonathan."

Timothy hated that she called his brother by his new name. He hated his new name. His name wasn't Jonathan. He was John. Just plain John. Johnny.

The other players walked towards the clubhouse, but the girl with the tan ran towards him. Timmy ducked behind the post even though he felt certain she was the one he'd come to get a good look at, the girl his brother loved. She had nice hair and long legs like his father always mentioned when he talked about pretty girls. He waited a moment before he peeked around the pillar and there she was, picking up the ball that had rolled almost to his feet.

"Oh. Hello. You startled me." She popped up but didn't move away. She stood still, staring at him, bouncing the ball in her hand.

118

Timothy mumbled, "Sorry." He walked away, like a passer-by who had stopped to tie his shoe behind the post. He managed to take only a few steps before she called out to him.

"No. Please. Stop. I want to talk to you."

Timothy stopped but felt afraid to turn around. When he checked over his shoulder, she stood right at the fence, almost pushing her face through the rungs. She wore a big smile. A big smile tinged with confusion.

"Come here. I just want to ask you a question." Timothy didn't think hers was a natural smile, a nice smile. Her teeth were showing, but so did a shark's before it bit you.

Timothy walked back reluctantly and glanced around nervously. If Johnny saw him, how could he explain his presence? He hid as well as he could behind the column.

"Do I know you?"

Timothy shook his head.

"But you were watching us and then me. Should I know you?"

Timothy shrugged.

"Do you know who I am?"

"Kind of."

"How do you know me?"

"You know my brother." As soon as the words left his mouth, he knew he shouldn't have said them, he shouldn't have said anything, he shouldn't have come.

"Your brother?" She sounded amazed, and, he thought, a little horrified. "I know your brother?"

"Johnny O is my brother."

"Johnny O?"

"Johnny O'Brien."

"I'm sorry," she said although she clearly wasn't. Puzzled yes, but sorry no. "I don't know any Johnny O'Brien."

"Yes. You do. I just saw you playing tennis with him."

Blair was thinking over what he had said when the other

woman in her group called her. "Blair. Hurry. We're waiting."

The woman had more to say to him. He felt sure. He sneaked a peek toward the clubhouse and saw Jonathan in his all-white clothes waving from the patio. Timothy leaned into the brick pillar to make sure he stayed out of sight.

Blair waved at Johnny, looked to Timothy, and back towards Johnny. Her expression changed. She didn't appear puzzled anymore. She seemed what Johnny would call bemused. She had another smile, a not-nice one, on her lips as she turned to run towards the clubhouse.

Timothy experienced so many emotions as he peeked around the column to watch her go. Sadness. Jealousy. Embarrassment. But mostly fear, fear that she would tell Johnny what he'd done. He felt scared that he would lose Johnny to her world, but, at the same time, scared that he had done something to keep Johnny out of that world.

*****

"Did that happen the day he died?" I asked.

"Not long before. Only a couple of days."

"What did Johnny say?"

"Nothing. He never said a word. I waited. I was scared."

"So you don't know if she told him about talking to you?"

"If she did, he didn't tell me."

"I am curious why you didn't tell us you met Blair when we talked to you before."

He couldn't control the tears. They overflowed his eyes and left tiny circles on his Phillies jacket. "All these years I thought I was to blame. What if I blew his cover and that was the reason the Parry girl dumped him and he really did go with Cassie Kelly and that's why some creep found them in a place where they never would have been if I didn't mess things up?"

His sobbing grew so strong that he offered no protest when Alex wrapped an arm around him. He buried his face in his hands and let Alex comfort him. So much for the bad cop.

Chapter 19

I persuaded Liz to lunch with me in Chestnut Hill. She thought I felt nostalgic for our days at McNally's. That was kind of true, just not my main motivation. For one thing, I simply could not believe the little parking area on Cresheim Valley Road had vanished. I'd spent hours on the Internet hoping for a glimpse of the spot I recalled—that I thought I recalled—but found no videos, no photos, and no reminiscences. I visited the library and located books that indicated my memories might not be wrong but offered no proof they were accurate.

"Wasn't there a little parking area right off the road here." I pointed at the corner as we passed Cresheim Valley Road where it crossed Germantown Avenue.

"I remember something like that around here when we were kids. I kind of recall a picnic table, maybe two. I think the spot occupied that corner, but how could that be? There's no room. If my memory is right, it's been gone for years." Liz wasn't sure.

"But I swear I saw it a few years ago," I protested. "I remember one night I wasn't living here but I was in town for a conference . . . ." My voice trailed off. "I guess that must have been twenty years ago. Probably longer."

"I know." Liz sighed. "You turn your back on a neighborhood for twenty, thirty years and they change everything. It appears this corner has been spiffed up. Why do you care all of sudden?"

The light turned green and I made the left. Hoping the picnic area had reappeared since my last visit? "This is where it happened."

Liz knew what I meant by *it*.

"Well, where the bodies were found. Revisiting the scene of the crime is a technique I picked up from Tracy. The cops assumed it happened here."

"There is no here."

I kept looking around in the hopes I'd just been negligent on my recent drive-by. "Around here, anyway. Tracy always goes and sits at the scene to see if she gets any inspiration."

"And visiting the location helps her." Liz sounded comforted by the thought.

"No. It never helps, but she never gives up on the theory that one day it will. I follow her lead."

"You visit graves too?" Liz asked.

"I do. Tracy thinks going to the cemetery is a waste of time and, I have to say, for the most part, it is."

"For the most part?"

"Cemeteries yield family information, but do I get any mystical insight? Never. But, graves are quiet and I feel as if I bond with the victim."

"Who was probably never there."

"You sound like Tracy. Although I do like to point out that in the case of family plots, the victim often came for an earlier funeral."

"I wonder what the killers do. Do you believe they return to the scene of the crime and visit the graves of their victims?"

"Good question, Liz. I wonder if Chip Parry ever visited this location when it was still the *spot*, if it ever was the spot. I should have asked him. Not that I think he is the killer." I told her about Chip Parry's feelings for Cassie. Liz thought Chip's love for the family maid made a juicy Romeo and Juliet tale. "Jonathan and Blair? Not so much, but still a problematic match."

"If you are thinking Henry Parry killed Jonathan O'Brien and Cassie Kelly simply to break up their relationships with his children, you are forgetting what a powerful man he was. He had other ways of breaking up those relationships."

"Money?" she asked.

"Lots. Why would any socially prominent multi-millionaire kill two people that he could bribe with the money in his checking account?"

She thought over the idea. "I assume Jonathan Brien needed tuition money. And you said Cassie Kelly wanted to move to New York. Either of them should have leapt at the money. But if they didn't, if Parry couldn't buy them off, he had no choice but to kill Brien and Cassie to keep them out of his children's life. Unless . . . ." She paused for dramatic effect.

"Unless?" I prompted her.

"Unless Cassie changed her mind and we have two cases of true love. Chip and Cassie. Jonathan and Blair. Then, neither of them would have taken the money and they would have had to be dealt with differently."

"Possible, if Blair and Chip Parry are both lying about the status of their relationships. I could believe Blair would lie but I can't see why Chip would."

"To cover up the crime their father committed."

"I don't believe a man like Parry would resort to murder, let alone a double murder." I was skeptical.

"He wouldn't do it himself." Her tone added, *silly*.

"Whether he does it himself or has someone else do it, it is still murder. I cannot believe he would risk so much." I continued down Cresheim Valley Road but the picnic area did not appear. "He might have been a snob but is anyone that much of a snob that they would resort to murder for such a superficial reason?"

"My guess, yes. Preserving the purity of the family line might not have been a superficial motive in Parry's eyes. Maybe he thought he was above the law, that no one would ever suspect him, let alone prosecute him."

A possibility.

"You don't believe Chip would lie, let alone kill, but," she stretched the word out for dramatic effect, "he would protect someone who did."

"Aside from Henry Parry, any idea who?" I didn't mean to sound exasperated. Didn't mean to.

"I'm thinking."

"While you are, consider that the *upstairs maid* said Cassie thought she'd be making the move to New York soon. Where did she get the money? Maybe old man Parry did bribe her to get her away from his son, and she took the money."

"Perhaps, and that wouldn't have made Chip feel any too chipper." Liz nodded with theatrical flair.

"So you think he killed the woman he loved?" I asked, unconvinced.

Liz feigned anger. "I'm not as convinced of his innocence as you are." She spoke through clenched teeth. "*If I can't have her, no one will.*"

"That was very good." I complimented her impersonation of a desperate young aristocrat.

"I always wanted to be an actress. I can even play nefarious male characters."

"Nefarious." I considered the term. "Chip Parry didn't strike me as nefarious."

"Not at, what, eighty?"

"Close enough."

"So maybe he's harmless now, but at twenty with testosterone surging through his veins? Or the father, Henry Sr., circling forty?"

I agreed that the two Parry men would have been different people six decades ago. Either of them would have had the physical strength to overpower Jonathan O'Brien. Henry Sr. had the arrogance. I wasn't so sure Chip did.

"How tall is the young chip off the old block?" Liz asked.

I'm not good at height. "I would guess around six foot."

"What is his build like today?"

"Solid. He's slim but not skinny." I hadn't studied his form.

"Sounds to me like it's a safe assumption that he had the strength as a young man. And is he built like his father?"

I had to envision the father and son. "A little more bulk, but yes."

"So that means we have ourselves two good suspects. Not to mention what they could accomplish together. What about the sister?"

"She would have the internal strength to move a mountain, but physical strength? In 1956, it would be an unusual woman with the required physical strength, and Blair Parry doesn't strike me as the athletic kind."

"She played tennis. Maybe golf?"

"She's only about 5'3."

"So maybe the Parrys excel at teamwork."

I could see that the family would close ranks and why. "Maybe the Brien kid felt so upset at being dissed by Henry Parry that he threw himself at Cassie. That would have gotten young Chip's anger up. Of course, Blair wouldn't like that either. A snob like Blair wouldn't like being replaced by a maid."

"Or finding out she dated a man who wasn't what he claimed to be," Liz added.

"Or discovering that his love for her wasn't what he professed it to be," I offered.

Liz was growing excited. "We've got a list of motives. Brother and sister may have coordinated their efforts and then covered for each other."

"It's a shame we can't have them brought up on charges of malicious snobbery." I put on my blinker and pulled the car to the curb.

"Where are we?" Liz asked.

"This is the home of Henry Parry. Has been since before World War II. His father's before him."

Liz gazed up the long driveway to the tall stone Victorian barely visible at the top of the hill. "It looks haunted."

"Maybe it is, but I doubt we'll ever get inside to find out

what the ghosts have to tell us."

"How far does the property go?"

I didn't know exactly. "From what I could see online, it's deep. I can see tennis courts and outbuildings, maybe stables and a garage or two."

"It's pretty big but not flashy, fairly typical for the neighborhood." Liz didn't mention what a nice neighborhood we were sitting in. "Cassie had a pretty long walk to the trolley. If I were she, and Jonathan offered me a ride, I would have taken it. Of course, I would have taken a ride down the driveway."

"You know this is the first place I've been where I know Cassie and Jonathan actually were." I tried to envision the two victims driving off the property together, but found it easier to picture them separately. Jonathan driving his new wheels up the driveway. Cassie walking down the same pavement on her way to the trolley."

"Do you feel anything?"

"Just a little sad."

"No messages from beyond the grave?"

"Nada."

"Can we eat now?" Liz was ready.

Chapter 20

I hadn't given up on finding the site where the bodies were found, but I had other things to do, including, as did thousands of others, Christmas shopping.

I am sure Blair Parry would not view our meeting as accidental. If I were in her position, it never would have occurred to me the encounter could be anything but a carefully arranged coincidence. But the truth was, I hadn't planned it. It wasn't as if King of Prussia wasn't the largest mall in the area. It wasn't as if Nordstrom's wasn't one of the most popular stores in the mall. It wasn't as if the shoe department wasn't one of the busiest areas in the store. And, it wasn't as if I tried to engage her in conversation. I smiled. She smiled. I cradled a Jimmy Choo sequined pump I would never have any reason to wear. She held up a Prada slingback. She asked if I had discovered anything unexpected in my research. I said I hadn't. She said that was too bad. I told the salesman I was just browsing. She asked him for a size seven. While she took her seat beside a pile of shopping bags, I left the shoe department and took the escalator up to the restaurant.

I already had my food when Blair walked into the seating area clutching the folder with her order in it. I didn't wave to invite her over. I didn't even let on I'd seen her. She appeared beside my booth and asked, with what I took for a forced smile, "May I join you?"

"Of course."

She pushed her bags onto the bench across from me and slid in beside them. "Christmas shopping. Unfortunately, so far everything I've bought is for me." She chuckled. "Dressing for the holiday season is such a burden, isn't it?"

128

"Isn't it?" I agreed.

I let her lead the conversation. What had I bought? Nothing. What brands of shoes did I normally wear? Anything that fits my temperamental feet. What other stores did I like to visit in the mall? I gave her a short list. I'm not much on shopping. My closet is lined with identical items in neutral colors. I'd recently switched to my winter uniform of black pants, loose sweater and boots—with a scarf representing the only show of color.

Blair sent the conversation in a new direction. "Ever since we spoke, I've been thinking about those days quite a lot."

No need to ask which days.

She gazed into space. Thinking about them? I assumed yes. I didn't expect Blair Parry to bring up Cassie Kelly, but then again, I didn't expect her to sit with me. I didn't interrupt her reverie.

"I used to watch Cassie sometimes."

"Watch?"

"Observe."

"Why?"

"She seemed so happy. I couldn't imagine why someone with her background would be happy. No money. No connections. High school education. She was a maid for God's sake. But one afternoon I came home early and found her singing and dancing around our kitchen." Her expression asked, how ridiculous was that?

"She must not have minded her work."

"Being a maid wasn't my idea of a life. Maybe she sang and danced to make her existence more bearable."

I could have argued with Blair that Cassie wasn't *being a maid*. She was *working as a maid*. And working as a maid was not her life, but only a small episode in the one she had planned. A means to an end. I didn't argue. I preferred to sit silently, hoping Blair would continue. She did.

"She had a fairly nice voice. For a maid. I wouldn't call

it special. Accurate describes it better and she could hit some high notes."

Damning with faint praise. I kept that thought to myself. "Do you remember what she was singing?"

She scowled. "How could I possibly recall? After all those years." She chuckled. "Wait. I think I can remember."

I felt pretty sure she always had.

"Somehow or other, Cassie had gotten tickets to see *My Fair Lady* when there were previews in Philadelphia before it opened in New York. Seeing that show was a big deal to her. She gushed to my brother about it. I imagine she had rushed out and bought the album. I'd overheard her say that she used her extra money to buy LPs of Broadway musicals." She fell silent.

"So, what was she singing?" I prompted.

"Oh, you know that song. A huge hit." She made a great show of recollecting. "I Could Have Danced All Night." "I didn't care much for musical theater, but everyone knew the plot of *My Fair Lady*. I guess it made an appropriate choice for an urchin like Cassie."

An urchin? Number one, who uses the word urchin? Number two, who, aside from Professor Henry Higgins, would have the gall to call anyone over the age of five, let alone a beautiful woman like Cassie Kelly, an urchin?

Across the table, the person with a surfeit of gall remained oblivious to my annoyance. "Cassie didn't know I was watching, so she would check herself out in the glass doors of our kitchen cabinets. I found her a little bit vain. Apparently, she thought she was quite pretty."

Possibly because she was quite pretty. I'd go so far as to say she was quite beautiful. How did Blair, the one supposed to be the golden girl in the Parry house, feel about that? I recalled the portrait on her living room wall. The youthful Blair certainly suffered in comparison to Cassie. Besides being young and blond, Blair and Cassie had in common that their images projected a cool reserve. According to what

I'd learned about Cassie, if you scratched her cool surface you found a warm person underneath. I couldn't imagine that if you scratched Blair Parry's cool exterior you would find anything but a cold interior.

"Anyway, your visit got me thinking about her. We all do a bit of song and dance in school, don't we? But Cassie took it all so seriously. What a silly girl with her pipe dreams and all!"

Pipe dreams. Of course, Blair would dismiss them as such. The thought that Cassie could move up must have struck at the heart of Blair's belief system. She was the one meant to have it all.

"I think maybe she did wise up and see that Jonathan might be the right man for her."

"*Really?*" I made no attempt to hide my sarcasm.

"He would be a catch for someone like her."

Someone like her. Someone beautiful, talented and, from what I heard, someone above making snide remarks— unlike you. I kept the thought to myself since I didn't want to stop Blair's recitation of her facts, but she finished talking about Cassie a lot sooner than she finished her Salmon Salad Nicoise. I smiled and listened to the history of her life as well as the mundane details of her current lifestyle. By the time our meal together ended, I knew every school she had ever attended, every boy she ever dated, every man she had ever married, as well as every country she had ever visited. I knew everything that she could squeeze into a thirty-minute discussion. She knew my name. But then again, she'd known that when she sat down.

Chapter 21

I will admit I did a little singing and dancing to "I Could Have Danced All Night" as I emptied the dishwasher. My performance didn't honor Cassie Kelly as much as the family I had grown up in. My mother had also seen *My Fair Lady* in previews, something we were unlikely to forget since family lore recorded her deeming it a failure and admitting that she had slept through a large part of the first act. Nonetheless, as devotees of Broadway, my parents bought, as had Cassie, the original cast album, leading to a large number of shows in our family theater, better known as the basement, with my best friend and me fighting over the numbers from *My Fair Lady*. I occasionally got to sing the major hit.

I had moved onto Lerner and Loew's next show, *Camelot,* one Cassie did not live to see, when Tracy knocked at the door.

"They let me up." She was known at the front desk. "Did I hear music?"

"Some might call it that. I've been reminiscing about shows my friend and I put on in the basement. Sometimes your mother appeared as a guest star. Admission was a nickel for adults. I think we conned a couple of kids out of two cents each."

"Was that in the nineteenth century or were you a twentieth-century bargain?"

"We were priced to bring culture to the masses."

"And your life in the theater popped into your mind because?"

I told her to sit down, filled mugs with hot cider and related the story of my lunch with Blair Parry.

"Did it ever occur to you that she arranged to run into you?" Tracy had a lot more experience investigating than I had.

"Why?"

"Why would anyone in the Parry family speak to you? To get you thinking in a certain direction."

"But she said nothing meaningful. What she disclosed I would not have wanted to reveal about myself. She came off as conceited, self-satisfied and pretentious. And those were her good points."

"Yes, but what did she think she communicated?"

I took a moment to think. "That Cassie was a silly girl with pipe dreams."

"And, therefore, might have been impressed with Jonathan Brien or whatever his real name was. She's defending the family line." Tracy sipped her cider. "The question is why she would feel she had to. With apologies to Shakespeare, I think they protest too little. Blair and Chip are being far too cooperative. They don't have a full understanding of what you are doing, yet they spill family secrets? He claims he loves Cassie even now, so he must be innocent. Father says Cassie overheard his talk to Blair about breaking up, so he sets up Blair's story that she rejected Jonathan and he fell into Cassie's sympathetic arms." Tracy's tone grew harsh. "She didn't even pump you for an update on your research. She came to deliver information."

"The Parrys always wanted to control the story." I considered Tracy's proposition.

"The question is why."

"Something happened on that estate. Liz made a good call. That place is creepy looking."

"You've seen it?'"

I heard an element of concern mixed with surprise in Tracy's question and made my answer sound casual. "Just happened to be driving by."

"I'm sure." She wasn't.

"I didn't expect to see anything. I needed a physical environment where I could picture Cassie and Jonathan since I can't find the place where the bodies were dumped. If only there were some, any, physical evidence."

"In all my investigations, I don't think I've ever laid my hands on a single piece of physical evidence. I might suspect that such an item exists—or rather existed—and use that as a discussion point. Generally to crack any case, I rely on someone recalling a detail that fell through the cracks, one that opens a different line of inquiry. But to tell you the truth, I usually succeed by uncovering someone's need to unburden himself or herself, on finding a guilty conscience that has been waiting for someone to ask the right question, maybe for fifty years. It might belong to the killer or to someone close to the killer."

"The Parrys *are* talkative," I said.

"Just not genuine—based on what you tell me. Have you found people to gossip about them?"

"We don't travel in the same circles. Them or their exes."

"I suspect there would be a wall of silence around the former spouses—depending on their social rank and finances," Tracy offered. "And anything they knew would be hearsay. None of them would have been in the picture back then."

"I hope to find old employees who might dish. I probably have a better chance of finding a physical clue than I do of identifying anyone to talk about Blair and Chip Parry."

"But I saw some mention of fingerprints in one of the articles you gave me."

"One of the articles said that a few prints left on O'Brien's car were not matched. I doubt that most of our suspects ever had their prints taken."

When Tracy spoke, her tone matched her expression. Mischievous. "You might want to bluff. Tell the suspects their prints were found on the car and see how they react."

"You are way ahead of me. I wasn't thinking that way at all, but it isn't a bad idea. I'll get the spiced wafers while we think."

We ate cookies and gazed at my view of the PECO offices in downtown Philadelphia. I loved having sixteen-foot windows but I loved even more that they looked out at the time and temperature circling the building along with miscellaneous announcements pursued by neon energy-eating monsters.

"Does it bother you to have neon monsters peering in your window?"

"Not as long as all the monsters are electronic. And on that building."

In a conversation totally unrelated to monsters, I told Tracy about Chip Parry and his efforts to ingratiate himself with me.

"Maybe we are judging his motives for cooperating too harshly." Tracy gave me one of those conspiratorial grins that friends and relatives have been giving me for over thirty years. By now, I would think they would give up on seeing me settled romantically, but, apparently, hope does spring eternal. Not in my mind, but apparently in Tracy's. "Because he has a crush on you?"

"No, because he *acts* as if he has a crush on me."

Tracy called for a ruling. "Any proof of that?"

"Rich men do not go for older women, with the possible exception of women of any age who are even wealthier, and, of course, Jane Fonda and Sophia Loren. If Chip Parry is searching for Mrs. Parry the third, he would not be seeking a woman with an AARP membership card."

"You underestimate yourself."

"You overestimate Chip Parry. Our original assumption is correct. Chip Parry is working hard to get me on his side. Not so hard that he actually pursues me, but he wants to make sure he can control me. To me that says guilty."

"Of what?"

"That is what I intend to find out."

Chapter 22

When I spotted Chip Parry walking down his long driveway, he looked every inch the country gentleman. Not my country. Wearing wellies and a matching quilted jacket, he would have appeared at home in the English countryside even without his walking stick. I pulled up beside him and lowered the window.

Four jumped up and put his front paws on the door. Chip's greeting seemed almost as enthusiastic. "Ah, Ms. Tracy. What a lovely surprise. Four and I were just out enjoying this beautiful day. Weren't we, boy?" He patted the dog's head. Unwilling to be distracted by Four's charms, I didn't. The golden retriever lost interest in me and whatever might be inside my car and moved away. Chip Parry moved closer. He rested his arms on the bottom of the window. "Why don't you hop out and join us?"

Of course, I did. I had motive, as well as a desire to enjoy one of the last days of autumn, and technically the first weeks of December were autumn despite all the Christmas decorations on display. Four explored the woods and then returned to accompany Chip and me as we strolled down the gravel driveway.

"Gorgeous day, isn't it?" Chip asked.

"Autumn is my favorite time of year. Even after all the leaves are gone, the season still has a different feel. I looked forward to it all summer."

"Mustn't wish your life away. Not at our age."

Okay. That stung, but I had to admit that although fifteen years, or more, separated us, Chip and I were the same age in that we both accepted that our best years were behind us. He softened his comment with a slew of compliments. "You

137

look lovely today." "The autumn palate flatters you." "I can't get over how much you remind me of Cassie." The ultimate compliment—and not just in Chip's world. Cassie had been indisputably beautiful. And, looked nothing like me. That's how I recognized that Chip found false praise a good ploy.

"Have you discovered anything new?" he asked.

"A source told me they found fingerprints on Brien's car." I didn't mention my source was a sixty-year-old newspaper.

"And you've come to ask me why my prints were on his car?"

I felt guilty at the deceit but plowed ahead with my plan. "I need to cross off every name."

"Ah, so your role has evolved from historian to detective."

I laughed and said nothing.

"Well, I must say I have no idea how the police would have gotten my prints back then—subterfuge I assume. Over the years, my prints have gone on file with the state for so many licenses, but I am surprised the authorities went back and checked. Hmm." His facial expression said he was pleased with law enforcement's interest. "At any rate, it would be surprising if my fingerprints weren't on the Thunderbird. Jonathan let me take it for a spin." He stopped and stared into the woods, remembering. "That car *was* incredible."

"When did you drive it?"

"The day Jonathan died." He stopped and dug into a pile of leaves with his cane searching for . . . what? An explanation? "He made me kind of sad. Jonathan was so proud of that car."

"But I thought you said you liked it."

"I loved it." Chip continued to dig through the leaves. "Jonathan wanted to know why I wouldn't get one."

"Why wouldn't you?" Clearly, he had the money.

138

"My father would never have approved. That's what I told Jonathan when he asked the same question." He dug deeper and flipped a small stack of leaves into the air. "I avoided the word *vulgar*. I said my father would find it too flashy."

"How did Jonathan take that information?"

"He seemed embarrassed. He tried so hard to do *the right thing*. You know there were conventions in those days. No, not conventions. Rules. Strict rules. Oh, those of us who believed in them might try to appear cavalier, but we always knew what they were and recognized who else understood them. Jonathan studied and tried hard to live by them." He stopped his excavation efforts and turned to face me. "I had no reason to kill Jonathan and I know that's what you're getting at. I knew that if I lost Cassie, it would be to her dreams, not to Jonathan or someone like him."

I kept my tone soft and my approach sympathetic. "If you don't mind my asking, did it make you mad that Cassie didn't respond to you the way you hoped she would?"

"You mean that she didn't buy my act?" He chuckled. "I was young and arrogant. I didn't give up. I thought I could win her over. I tried buying her little presents. She loved Broadway shows, so I would buy her cast albums, but she wouldn't accept them. So, I listened to them and tried to impress her with my knowledge. That didn't work either. I worked to remove any possible obstacles. I even asked my mother to fire our upstairs maid."

Maria Mancini Garibaldi? Chip had asked his mother to fire Maria Mancini Garibaldi? "Was that Maria?"

"Wow." He paused for effect. "You certainly do your homework. Yes. Maria Garibaldi. She had a different name back then. Mancini. Maria Mancini. I asked my mother to fire her. Not that my mother did. I didn't tell her the true story about why I wanted Maria out. I made up some cockamamie tale about her dropping something under the bed and my returning to Princeton without it. There was more but I have long since forgotten. It would be too embarrassing to recall. My complaint was ridiculous and my mother saw that and told me so. I never told her the real reason."

"Which was?"

"I harbored a nagging fear Maria would turn Cassie against me."

"Why would Maria do that?"

"It seems silly now. Maria ended up staying with us for over forty years. We never referred to the incident again."

"The incident?"

Chip blushed. If he blushed at eighty, how shy had he been at twenty? "Maria wanted to—how shall I put this— initiate me into my manhood. I tried but I got scared and ran away. It happened before we hired Cassie. But I felt worried. What if my feelings for Cassie were obvious? What if Maria was jealous? What if Maria told her what happened between us? How would Maria tell the story?"

I wondered not if Maria would have told Cassie, but why Maria had not told me.

Chapter 23

My thoughts were on Maria as I approached Tracy's house, but I had something to run by Tracy first.

"Guess who sent me a list of their former employees." I paused briefly. "I guess the answer is pretty obvious. In my entire life, I've only requested a list of former employees from Henry Parry."

"You got a letter from Henry Parry?" Tracy was as shocked as I was by the development.

"Well, not exactly. It came from Edward Baron but I am sure Parry approved it." I slipped on my reading glasses. "Listen."

Mr. Parry and I discussed your request and concluded our employees would not want us to deprive them of the opportunity to assist you in your effort to learn more about the horrendous crime that stole the lives of those two lovely young people all those years ago. I regret that we do not have current addresses for our former staff members. The information included on the list is the most recent we have on record.

We hesitated to include the name of Joe Danton because he seemed rather a rough character as a youth. I would advise you to approach him with caution—although I would hope the years have worn down his rough edges. In the end, we decided that we must include his name because as the only employee who had run-ins with the authorities, he may be your best lead.

I finished reading aloud as I followed her into the kitchen so she could scoop ice cream. I took off my glasses and stared at her hard. "Written in the rather scratchy scrawl of Edward Baron."

"What's that disgruntled expression on your face?" Tracy asked.

"You mean the one that says I think there is something rotten in the Parry family?"

"Why is that your reaction?" Tracy appeared disapproving, not curious. "Maybe this is a heartfelt gesture, just as the note indicates. Maybe they appreciate the effort you are making and want to contribute to your success." She handed me a bowl. "Eat your ice cream. Chocolate improves your outlook."

It didn't. "The entire Parry family is just being too nice, too cooperative."

"Because they have nothing to hide?" She teased me with a smirk.

"Or because they have everything to hide and want to send me off in the wrong direction?" I took another bite in the interest of attitude adjustment, but ice cream could not dispel doubts about the Parrys.

"They are giving you the name of their former employees, people who know them well, people who were in and out of their house, people who may be aware of their deepest, darkest secrets. I don't see them doing that if they were worried."

"I think they are trying to manipulate me and I don't like to be used. Especially, by people who could simply bribe me." I savored the idea and my ice cream.

"Sadly, I hate to inform you that you have too much integrity to be bought off even if the Parrys wanted to—which I do not think is the case. I don't think you're wrong to proceed with caution, but accept the list with an open mind."

"Maybe they checked and all of these people are dead already. That way they can look like good guys and risk nothing."

"I guess you'll find out if that's true."

It was true for five of the six names. The sixth, and only surviving, individual was the notorious Joe Danton.

Chapter 24

I called Tracy from the car on my way to Danton's house. "So catch this. The only living person on Baron's list is Joe Danton, the man they cautioned me about. This is just a tad too pat. They direct me to the only criminal on the list. They weren't being helpful. They were trying to lengthen the list of suspects."

"Number one," Tracy sounded like the teacher she aspired to be, "you don't have a list of suspects. Nothing about the Parry family has given you any reason to add their name to any roster of possible killers."

"Number 2?"

"Number 2, they could have opted to do nothing."

"See that's what makes me suspicious. They are trying to ingratiate themselves with me."

"Or be helpful."

"We'll see."

"So what are you going to do about Danton?"

"I'm almost to his house. I'll let you know what I make of him. Bye."

I suspect I heard her start to say, "Don't you think you should wait until I, or maybe Alex, can go with you?" All I heard before I hung up was "don't ya . . . ."

I hadn't actually meant to hang up before Tracy finished speaking, but now that I had, I wasn't about to call back. She wasn't worried enough to call me back. Why should she be concerned? As far as we knew, Joe Danton's criminal life lay sixty years in the past.

If Joe Danton was a criminal, he wasn't a very successful one. His house stood in a row of homes, once respectable, never large, on a street lined with buildings that seemed to sag under the weight of their age. I had second thoughts about approaching Danton's front door and not just because I worried the roof on the small porch would crush me. Maybe I had been too glib, dismissing any concerns that Danton might still have criminal aspirations. He might have been in his golden years, but pulling a trigger did not require a youthful finger.

I knocked on the door with a strength, or lack thereof, that said, *it's okay if you're not home.* But someone was. I heard footsteps, but Joe Danton didn't open the door. A woman answered my knock. I couldn't tell if she had lived many easy years or fewer hard years. She seemed weighed down by her life.

"Hello. I'm looking for Joe Danton."

"My brother. Joey." She studied me and I fought the urge to babble. I waited for a question, but after what felt like a full minute, she screamed, "One of your bitches is here."

She disappeared into the house, leaving me standing on their stoop. She didn't ask me to follow, so I didn't. I held the storm door open, letting masses of cold air into the old house.

"She ain't one of mine." I heard Danton before I saw him. "Not that I'm against the idea." Danton leered as he came into sight.

I took an involuntary step away before I introduced myself. I think I would have done the same thing even if his name had not come with a warning. It wasn't his outer appearance that was frightening—although his bloodshot eyes, blotchy skin and ragged grin were off-putting. The scary thing about the man in front of me was the tough guy image he labored to project. From his position a step above me, physics dictated that he would loom over me but he leaned forward to turn the height advantage into a threat.

"So, young lady, what can I do for you?"

"I'm talking to people who used to work for the Parry family."

"Writing an expose I hope."

"Should I?" My heart soared.

"Not really. That family was a bunch of stiffs. Even the kids turned into jerks by the age of twelve. The boy was the best of the lot, but that ain't saying much. Who would care about them?"

"Actually, I'm interested in something that happened to one of their employees?"

"That maid who got killed?"

"You knew Cassie Kelly?"

"Knew is a strong word. We worked together for a couple of years. Not that long."

"I'd like to hear anything you can remember about her." I waited for an invitation to come inside while hoping I wouldn't receive one. I didn't relish the idea of stepping out of sight with this man. Yes, his sister was also inside but she didn't appear any more reputable than he did. Judging books by their covers? Yes, but what else could I do? Their rough and tough images were all I had to go on.

"Maisie," he screamed, "I'm stepping out for a smoke."

Danton reached an arm back. It reappeared with a Phillies jacket. I pulled the door wide open and stepped back so he could join me on the small landing. From his pocket, he pulled a pack of cigarettes—a brand I'd never heard of—and lit one. I maneuvered to move upwind.

"Have a seat," he gestured as if premium seating were available. Grasping the metal railing, he lowered himself onto the top step and patted the cement beside him. "Take a load off."

In the interest of open communication, I did as told although no more than ten seconds passed before the cold surface made me regret my decision. I wanted to slip my notebook between my rear end and the step but hoped I would need paper to record whatever Danton could tell me.

"So what do you want to know?" His exhale ended in a coughing fit.

I didn't bother with my spiel. He seemed willing to talk. "Do you remember how you heard Cassie Kelly had been murdered?"

"That I remember. Don't remember much, but that I remember." He let his legs fall open and I pulled mine tight together to avoid knee contact. "Another maid. Maria. She came out to the garage to tell me. I took care of the cars. Made sure they were gassed up and clean. Drove the old lady on occasion but mostly I just did odd jobs around the property. Kind of like a property manager, if you really want to know. Not that they paid me for that job. I did it out of the goodness of my heart. I see the gutters are getting stopped up, I'm gonna make sure they are all taken care of. They never appreciated me. Not mean to me or nothing. Just didn't realize what a good thing they had in me. If they had, if they had paid me more, I might not have made the stupid mistake I made." He turned to face me and I tried not to recoil from his sour breath. "Yep, my life might have taken a different path if I hadn't been such a stupid kid." His expression said he would love to tell me his story.

"You made a mistake?" I didn't even try to return to the subject of Cassie Kelly. I figured he'd get there. Possibly not before I froze my ass off, as he would have said, but eventually.

"Friend of mine talked me into helping him heist a bank. All I had to do was drive the getaway car. Seemed like a good deal. Thought we got away with it. At least I had time to spend the money before they came for us. Two years later. Who would have thunk it, eh? Those guys don't give up." He took a long drag on his cigarette. When he finished coughing, he continued. "Anyway, lucky I had some great times with the cash but, after doing ten years in the clink, robbing banks didn't seem like such a good idea. But I did my time. Never wanted to go back, so I kept my nose clean. Not so easy for a felon." He explained his life with the smooth delivery of a well-practiced, oft-repeated tale. I

147

imagined that most drinkers who sat on the next barstool or riders who took the bus seat next to his had heard it. "After I got out of jail, I could only get crummy jobs. Paid even worse than old man Parry did, but this time I didn't try to supplement my income with what my sister calls *ill-gotten gains*. So in the end, I guess it wasn't Parry's fault I robbed that bank."

No, it wasn't—and I stood ready to blame the Parrys for just about anything. I waited for him to go on, but he had gotten lost in his thoughts. I wanted to prompt him, but not jar him. "So Parry wasn't a bad guy."

"Bad? No. Not bad. Never yelled or screamed. But man, could he condescend. That's what Maria used to say. 'Condescending bastard' was her favorite name for him."

"Were you and Maria friends?"

He pulled out his best leer. "You could say that. Always interested in friending a really hot number. Beautiful girl. Beautiful. I wasn't so bad myself, which you can probably guess."

I wouldn't have guessed, but now that he mentioned it, I could surmise that his bloodshot eyes with the droopy rims could had once been seen as big brown beacons, drawing women into his orb. The way he flashed them convinced me he thought they still had that power. I imagined when he worked for the Parrys his rotund form had been sleek and strong, and the way he handled his cigarette could have been seen as seductive in a smoke-filled era.

"I still do pretty well with the ladies, but that Cassie you asked about? She wouldn't give me the time of day. Uppity, that girl was. Maria thought Cassie was beautiful. Maybe if you like those blonde ice princesses. Not my type. Had a hell of a time convincing Maria of that. She was jealous as hell of that girl. I don't know why. Maria had the goods." He drew her ample form in the air. "That Cassie didn't have much up top. Not that it mattered. She had this way of looking at you that you knew you weren't never gonna get close."

"Did you dislike her?"

He rotated his head slowly to let his eyes meet mine. "You asking me if I hated her enough to kill her?"

I felt frightened by his words, but couldn't stop myself from answering honestly. "Gee. Sorry. I guess I was. Occupational hazard, I guess."

"What is your occupation anyway?"

Forgetting my historian cover, I gave him a short explanation of how I helped Tracy.

"But this is about more than a course. You think you're going to find a killer, don't you?"

"I wouldn't mind if it happened. Do you have any idea who might have murdered her?"

He shook his head as he exhaled. "No one cared enough to kill her. Old man didn't have an eye for her. I think the son did, but he stayed away at college most of the time. At least when I worked, mostly during the week. There weren't a lot of us working there. Guy who did the gardening never came onto her. I had to fight him for Maria. You talk to him?"

"Would that be Gus Bailey?"

"Gus. Yeah. That's it. Gus. How's he doing?"

"He passed away. I don't know when."

"That so?" He lapsed into deep thought.

I tried to ease him out of his reverie. "So what did you think when Maria told you about the crime?"

"I already knew something was up. There were these guys at the house that morning. Not the usual type that came to the Parrys'. Regular guys. Not stiffs. Of course, that was before I hated cops. Then, I would have recognized them right away."

"Did you have any idea what happened to Cassie?"

"No clue. Like I said, I didn't pay her much attention. Maria, she was hysterical. She kept going on and on about how mean she'd been to Cassie."

149

"In what way?"

"Damned if I remember. Don't know if I even understood in the first place. Now Cassie's gone and the girl's sobbing all over the place. Got my shirt all snotty. Which made me mad because for months I listened to how she hated Cassie. Used to make fun of her all the time. A goody-two-shoes, she would call her. I think Maria just felt jealous, 'cause she thought everyone liked Cassie better. Not me, man. Just thinking of old Maria is getting me all hot and bothered."

I tried not to dwell on that thought.

"You seen her?"

"I met her."

"She mention me?"

I shook my head. He appeared so hurt that I felt compelled to comfort him. "Maybe she wanted to protect you. Maybe she thought I would try to pin the murder on you."

"On me? That's a good one. More likely you could pin it on her." He laughed, but the kind of chuckle that said he was speaking the truth.

Okay, Maria envied Cassie, but I couldn't see her as a killer. She wasn't big enough or strong enough, but she had been pretty enough to enlist helpers.

"Maria was jealous of Cassie, but why would she kill the Brien kid?" I asked.

"Maybe he acted like a snot. I don't know. Most of them kids that came to the Parry house did. I never bothered with them."

"But even if she wanted to kill them, she'd need help." I thought I was being subtle but, apparently, I wasn't.

"You accusing me?" He switched to a declarative sentence. "You *are* accusing me." He flicked his cigarette into the street. "I think we are done here."

Chapter 25

We both stared at it. One rose. One long-stemmed white rose, large and perfectly formed. Dead leaves had been pushed aside so the flower could rest against the foot of the headstone.

"Even I can't believe it." I shook my head to emphasize my sense of wonderment.

"It's been half a century," Liz said.

"More," I corrected her math.

"If we hadn't had dessert, we might have discovered the killer, excuse me, visitor, kneeling at the grave just the way you always fantasized." Liz sounded amazed. "Do you think it happens every year?"

"If it does, we can come back on Cassie's birthday every year and wait for the killer to show up. If we miss him or her, we could still visit until the flowers fail to arrive. Then, we figure out who died that year and we'll know who the killer was."

"You believe the killer left it?" Liz asked.

"Who else would bring flowers to a grave after all this time?"

"Not flowers. Flower. Maybe your friend, Chip Parry—although with all his money, he'd probably leave something a little more elaborate."

"Maybe not. One white rose is perfect. From the little I know of Cassie, a single stem would represent her perfectly."

Liz nodded. "Too bad they take the thorns off now. Blood would have come in handy."

"If we were cops, we might be able to get DNA off the rose," I suggested.

"And find out it belongs to a relative, and the single white rose is a tradition some family member carries on."

"Probably," I said, although I didn't believe that theory.

"Maybe you brought up memories when you talked to Maria Mancini and she felt guilty."

"Because she lied." I made a strong statement.

"She didn't actually lie." Liz understood completely why Maria would not tell the story. "I wouldn't tell some stranger humiliating stories from my past."

"What stories?" I asked a little too eagerly. I knew nothing untoward about Liz's past.

"Were you listening? I wouldn't tell you."

"But I'm not just some stranger."

"Now that I think about it, that's worse. You'll be around to remind me." She shivered.

Recalling the stories or reacting to a cold wind tearing across the cemetery? I didn't know.

Liz avoided my questions. "I will tell you one thing. If I were Maria Mancini, I would have hated Cassie Kelly."

"Because Cassie rejected what she wanted so badly?"

Liz pulled her coat tightly around her. "What was wrong with Cassie anyway? If you were washing dishes for a living and a cute guy, a nice guy, a guy you seemed to like, offered you marriage to more money than you'd ever need, would you find it so easy to turn your back on him? Especially in that era."

"Cassie had dreams. She may have been young but she understood the Parry money would come with plenty of strings attached." I reconsidered. "And I am sure she planned on making her own money by pursuing the career she wanted."

"I bet Chip Parry didn't want a wife who sang and danced in New York."

Probably true. Bad enough Cassie had a working-class, Irish-Catholic background, but becoming a performer, especially one who sang and danced on Broadway? Just how

152

broadminded could Chip have been? Loving her didn't mean he wouldn't try to change her. "I don't think Cassie would have given up her dreams for a rich husband. Cassie knew who she was and what she wanted."

"At least our idealized version of the girl. We don't really know what she was like at all."

Liz's discussion took a sudden turn. "That's a big headstone."

"Almost as big as the one at Jonathan Brien's grave. I wonder how these families paid for these monuments." The base came waist high and looked impressive amongst the plain, square stones even without the Celtic Cross atop it. "I pictured the Kellys and O'Briens as struggling, but impoverished people don't have the money for something like this."

"Jonathan's mother died first. You said he was into appearances. I can see him chipping in for a stone for his mother," Liz offered.

"Not until he finished school. Plus, I'm sure he did not pick the Celtic cross. On the other hand, I doubt Cassie had a problem with the cross, but the size . . . ."

Liz verbalized my suspicion. "The Parry money must have paid for this."

"A good possibility. Maria Mancini said they gave money for the funerals." I stared at the headstone. "James Michael Kelly. Mary Breen Kelly. Catherine Mary Kelly. All gone at early ages."

"Father. Mother. Daughter." She craned her neck with great theatricality to survey nearby gravesites. "No more Kellys. No more Breens. No siblings—at least here."

"I don't know why her brother isn't here. I couldn't find him."

"Did you check to see if she had cousins?"

"What am I supposed to do? Spend hours on Ancestry.com searching for a cousin who may or may not have kept in touch with Cassie?" I understood that Liz's response—*hmm*—said *if you cared as much as you say you do, I don't think a little time on the Internet would kill you.*

Chapter 26

"How did you find her?" Tracy asked the next day over lunch in the cafeteria after I informed her I'd found a cousin of Cassie Kelly.

"I spent hours on Ancestry.com to identify her." I sighed. "And then more time on other sources to find her."

"She must have been shocked when you called."

"Surprised and then pleased. Cassie was ten years older, and her cousin Gloria always looked up to her. They were first cousins. I'm seeing her this afternoon."

Given that Gloria Kelly Gibbs was Cassie's younger cousin, I hoped our similar ages might make it easy to bond.

I discovered relating would not be hard as soon as she opened the door. Warmth spilled out of the woman's home. "Come on in. Happy to meet you."

Before I knew it, I was sitting at the table in a bright kitchen that showed little sign of use aside from the coffee maker that produced the cup of coffee in my hand.

"Guess you're searching for the family resemblance. Don't. Cassie came from the gorgeous side of the family." Gloria laughed. "I got the athletic ability and physique to go with it."

From what I could tell, she still had the physique in her late sixties. Her sportswear suggested she might still have the athletic ability.

"Our family was so small. Cassie was my only cousin. Well, my only girl cousin. She had a brother, but he didn't want to hang out with me. Our families—our fathers were brothers—didn't see each other all that often, but I adored her. I thought she was perfect." She paused. "Actually, looking back, I think she was perfect. Beautiful but she also got straight As in school. Always. Her parents wanted her to try for a scholarship and go to college but she sang like a lark. Played the lead in the high school musical three out of four years. Gorgeous voice. Matched her face. Matched her body." Mrs. Gibbs laughed. "I wonder why I didn't hate her. Of course, when she died I was still young enough to think I could grow up to be a beauty like Cassie." She released a hearty laugh, a good-natured one, without a touch of bitterness. "I didn't know I wasn't going to grow up at all."

I smiled.

"Because I'm only five foot one."

I knew what she meant. She wanted me to laugh at her comment. I did.

"What do you want to learn about Cassie? I don't know much. Like I said, I was a kid."

I gave my usual spiel about Tracy's class and ended with a specific inquiry. "The bottom line is that I am trying to determine if there were any other theories considered when she died? The police called it a carjacking."

"I never heard anything different, and the grown-ups would sit around and discuss what possibly could have happened. No one could name a single person that would want to harm her. She worked for a very respectable and relatively nice family, so everyone knew they could not have been involved. No one ever said a bad word about the Brien boy's behavior. He and Cassie had nothing in common, no mutual friends or acquaintances, so it had to be a stranger. At least to Cassie. They wondered if she was an innocent bystander and the Brien boy was the target. No one could think of any other theories—although Cassie's parents could not, would not, believe she was playing fast and loose with that boy."

"She was a nice girl?"

"She was a determined girl. I would see Cassie at Christmas, Thanksgiving, birthdays and for two weeks every summer when we would go to Ocean City. She would be so nice to me. I am sure a cousin, ten years older, would have loved to ditch me but she never did. She tried to teach me things and she talked about her plans. Not just dreams. Plans."

*****Gloria Kelly Gibbs*****
Ocean City, New Jersey
July 1954

"Why do you put all that suntan lotion on?" Before they left on their walk, Cassie had rubbed white gook all over herself.

"So my skin stays nice and white."

Gloria did not understand. She liked when her skin got pink. It never got tan.

"When you look at Grace Kelly—do you know she grew up near us in East Falls—when you see her on the screen, do you see any freckles?"

"I never get to the movies. My mother doesn't let me. Only if it's a cartoon."

"Well, when you do, you'll see. No freckles. On any movie star except Doris Day. She's allowed to have freckles."

"Are you going to be a movie star?"

Cassie smiled. "Maybe someday. First I have to be an actress. Then who knows? Maybe Hollywood will need another Kelly from Philadelphia."

"Is that how they decide who'll be a movie star?"

"It's a joke, silly. You have to decide that you are going to be a movie star and then work really hard. I read about Grace Kelly to learn how to do it."

"Does the sun give you freckles?" Gloria went back to her original question.

"I think it does."

"My mother said I was born with these freckles on my nose. Does that mean I can't be a movie star?"

"Maybe when Doris Day gets old, they'll need someone with freckles to replace her." Cassie wrapped an arm around Gloria's shoulder. "You can be a different kind of movie star. There are lots of different types of movie stars."

She guessed when her mother let her see movies with real people in them, not cartoons, she would understand. When a wave came in, she stopped and jumped. She wanted to see how big a splash she could make. Cassie just let the water stream over her.

"What did you learn?" Gloria asked.

She saw Cassie's brow crinkle above her sunglasses.

"When you read about Grace Kelly. What did you learn?"

"I learned that I have to move to New York."

"New York?" Gloria yelped.

"Don't sound so horrified. It's not far. Not even one hundred miles away."

Gloria had never been to New York but she knew the city was very big and she found that scary. "Are you afraid?"

This time when Cassie answered, her expression looked different. She had a smile on her face but Gloria didn't see any of her teeth. "You know what, Glory, I'm not."

She liked it when Cassie called her Glory. No one else ever did. When Cassie became a movie star and called her Glory, maybe then everyone would. She couldn't believe how brave Cassie was, moving away from home. "Why aren't you scared?"

Cassie smiled that funny smile again, "I don't know why, but I'm not. I just have this feeling that everything is going to turn out okay."

"Why are we stopping?"

Cassie stood in the shallow water letting the low waves wash over her feet.

"This is the beach where Grace Kelly played as a kid. Her house is right over that dune. Come on, I'll show you."

*****

"Every time I ride by that house, I think of Cassie."

And now I did too. In a town that has seen many generations of tear-downs and rebuilds in the past six decades, the Spanish-style house on Wesley Avenue remained unchanged since the Kelly family vacationed in it.

"What happened to Cassie's brother?"

"He had his own business. Worked as a contractor. Did pretty well thanks to the family that Cassie worked for."

"Really?" I didn't do a good job of keeping the amazement out of my voice.

"The son was the one. I don't know the whole story, but I guess Cassie used to talk to him about Martin, her brother, about how she worried he wouldn't make anything of himself. I think the kid made sure Martin went to college. Pulled some strings, maybe gave him some money. I don't know for sure."

She considered the topic for a moment before she continued. "After Cassie's parents died, we didn't see much of Martin. I know he married and had three kids. Boys. He died a few years ago. We didn't keep in touch. I met his wife and children a few times, saw them at his funeral. I think he had a happy life, which is odd because he seemed kind of sullen as a kid. You'll see." She popped out of her chair. "Follow me. When you said you were coming I got out our old 8mm films. Not the films. I had them all moved onto DVDs. As I said, I didn't see my cousins that often. Only on special occasions. So every time I saw them, my father captured the occasion on film."

I settled onto a high-backed couch as she set up the DVD. As one of the few people who liked watching home movies of families I've never met, I would have been looking forward to what lay ahead no matter what, but knowing I would be meeting Cassie made me excited.

I had to wait through several weddings and more first

159

communions before I saw her, but I recognized her the moment she came on the screen, radiating beauty. She was so much more than beautiful. She appeared luminous, even in black and white. I had felt the sadness of her death and had worked on her behalf to solve the mystery of her death, but seeing her in live-action, smiling, laughing, interacting with the family who loved her, made her seem real.

"We got the camera a few years before she died."

In the movies, everyone moved with jerky motions and, in the early shots, Cassie acted as goofy as anyone. Standing still. Waving at the camera. Making funny faces. Well, faces funny to a teenager in the 1950s. Birthday cakes marked the passage of time, and, in the later years, Cassie acquired a calm in front of the camera. I saw a young woman having fun with her family, showing affection to her parents and being kind to the young cousin that clearly adored her.

"Don't you just love Cassie's dress," Gloria said. "She saved up and bought it at Wanamaker's. Perfect for her birthday. The roses were pink and with green leaves."

I admired the organza dress embroidered with flowers. The full skirt gathered into a belt at Cassie's waist. We used to have a name for dresses like that. Clearly for summer. Clearly for a party. A garden party dress. That was what we called them. Well, my parents did. Not that I went to any garden parties, but my mother bought a few dresses for me to wear for miscellaneous festivities. When I reached Cassie's age in the films—sometime during the Age of Aquarius—I wouldn't have been caught dead in a dress like that, although I always secretly wanted one.

On the widescreen television, Cassie and Gloria were again waving to the camera. Both looked so carefree. Cassie glanced away and the camera followed her gaze to a big white birthday cake covered with roses. I couldn't count the candles.

"The roses and the candles were pink and green to match her dress. Twenty roses. Twenty candles. She couldn't wait to be twenty-one. Of course . . . ."

Of course, we both knew she never saw that birthday.

"She looked beautiful. I do love that dress."

"She always wore that dress to summer festivities, so we got her a cake to match it. She didn't mind at all. Found it funny." Gloria froze the frame with Cassie, demurely gorgeous in a full-skirted shirtwaist, smiling into the camera and feigning exhaustion at the effort required to blow our twenty candles. "Her last birthday." She leaned forward, as if meeting Cassie's gaze in the camera.

"What color were her eyes?"

"Oh, they were phenomenal, blue but with a touch of green that combined to produce this turquoise shade I never saw in any other eyes. With her golden hair. Wow. Wait until you see her at her prom."

Cassie's dress fit the style for 1950s proms, yet had a quiet elegance about it to match the quiet elegance she possessed.

"Who was the fellow she went to the prom with?" Cassie, smiling but standing apart from her date, did not appear impressed or even interested.

"Bobby Fanelli. Adorable, at least to a girl my age."

"To Cassie?"

"She thought he was nice and she needed a date for the prom."

"Did she have a boyfriend when she died?"

"I think she wanted to wait, to meet someone in New York. One time I went on and on about falling in love, I think maybe with Robert Wagner, although he was married to Natalie Wood at the time. Anyway, she told me I had plenty of time to fall in love. She said love looked great at first, but the next thing you knew you were stuck at home with a bossy husband and a bunch of bratty kids. There have been days when all six of mine were little when I wondered if she was right." Gloria laughed to persuade me that she was kidding. I wasn't convinced. "Cassie wanted more. She wanted to get out of Philadelphia, although I don't know why. I like it just fine here."

So, Jonathan wanted what Chip offered Cassie. But Cassie, who could have gotten everything Jonathan wanted, aspired to something completely different, somewhere completely different, something more. To Jonathan, there was nothing more.

"Did she ever mention Jonathan Brien."

"No one in the family had ever heard his name."

"What about Chip Parry? Did she talk about him?"

"That's the kid from the family she worked for, right? Not a lot. I remember once she did. She thought he had a crush on her and she wasn't interested. She wasn't mean about him. She just thought she could never marry someone like him. He was nice. She said that. Me? I would have leapt at that life. Can you imagine never having a money worry?"

She didn't expect an answer to her question and I didn't furnish one. I had my own question. "Do you think she had the opportunity to marry him?"

"She thought he would probably marry her. At least that was my take. But what did I know? I was only a kid."

"Did she love him?"

"Now that I'm older, I understand that she viewed him as a good, decent, sweet boy but she knew he'd never give up his high society lifestyle. I thought he'd be a fool to give up a big house and fancy parties. Like I said, I was a kid."

Chapter 27

The code of conduct at Wawa convenience stores, unwritten yet freakishly adhered to by customers of all ages, races, creeds and possible combinations of those variants, i.e. everyone, states that each customer holds the door for the next. Going in. Coming out. The two teams coordinate. Just like players in a well-played soccer match, a customer on the inbound team sees the play taking shape while crossing the parking lot. The maneuvers, however, don't usually commence until each party has moved to within fifteen yards of the door. Generally, no words beyond *thank you* are exchanged.

That is why I reacted with surprise when a few steps out of my car, but a good thirty yards from the store entrance, I felt an arm wrap around my shoulder. An arm? It might have well have been a metal vice. With one expert move, the arm controlled me and the attached hand managed to immobilize my head.

"What a surprise! So good to see you," the man said while ruffling my hair with a gesture that a casual observer would perceive as affectionate.

"I can't *see you*." How could I with my head nailed to his shoulder?

"Julia Tracy, as I live and breathe." My name rang out in a ridiculously loud voice and an equally ridiculous Texas accent. I realized two things. This was not a random encounter and this was not anyone from Texas. "Great to see you." The roar then dropped to a whisper. "No one wants to hurt you. I will be gone by the time we get to the door."

The hand pulled my hair rather gently in what a passerby would consider an affectionate, teasing gesture. If there were any passers-by, which there were not. Our side of the parking lot was empty.

"Do not try to look at me. If you succeed, you'll regret it." The tone was not at all in the register of the friendly Wawa spirit. "You don't want to scream. Trust me."

In that matter, I tended to trust him. I didn't feel a gun in my side, but I had no idea who else might be nearby. We kept walking, the man holding me close, remaining unseen while hissing in my ear. "Do not turn around. I am going to walk you to the door. We are going to keep moving at this pace. You are not going to look at me. You are going to keep your eyes down. Do not try to catch a glimpse of my reflection in the door. You are not going to say a word. You are going to listen. If I were you, I would do exactly as told."

If this guy had too many more rules to run through, there would be no time for him to say whatever he came to say.

When a woman emerged from a pick-up truck five spaces away, he shook my head as if tousling my hair in an affectionate tousle and raised his voice, "So great to see you." The woman didn't notice.

My attacker lowered his voice again. "I have come here to tell you that, for your own good, you are going to drop this ridiculous investigation of yours. There is nothing to be gained by digging up this ancient history. The police solved this case decades ago."

Technically, not true. They diagnosed it. That, I would give them, but solved? No. But there was no time to argue. My companion had more to say and only a dozen steps left to say it.

"Bad things can happen to people who do not know when to let sleeping dogs lie." He squeezed my arm tightly. I felt pain, enough to make me grunt but not enough to make me yell. "If I were you, I'd heed this warning. Now, go in the store, pick up your purchases, and do not look back."

A customer coming from the other direction grabbed the door, held it open and smiled at me and then at my escort, who must have been giving a convincing performance of a devoted friend because I saw no alarm on the other man's face.

"So great running into you." My companion gave me a little shove, meant to appear playful, and kept walking. He kept moving, and I did as I was told. To a point.

As soon as I got through the set of double doors into the store, I went to the front window and looked out. I saw the back of a man in nondescript jeans, a plain blue hoodie and a cap with no visible logo, as he climbed into a black SUV. I caught a glimpse of his side as he pulled the door shut. I didn't recognize him or the car—one of the bigger models I'd seen used for purposes of transporting government officials, little league teams and drug dealers. In other words, the car didn't offer much of a clue.

I searched the store for the man who had held the door for me.

"Excuse me."

His eyes registered annoyance. So, I blurted out as much of my story as fast as I could. Not the whole story. Or the true one.

"Do you remember holding the door for me? I was walking with a man. Did you happen to get a look at him? He claimed to know me, but I don't think he does. He said he went to high school with me but I went to an all-girls high school. He must think I am someone else. I don't expect that you would know him, but did you notice what he looked like? He's gone now, so I am not concerned but it is kind of odd and I didn't get a good look at him."

On some occasions, I worried that working on cases with Tracy made me too facile a liar. On this occasion, the skill proved useful. The guy seemed to relax.

"I'm sorry, lady. He was kind of nondescript. White. Dark hair. I didn't notice much about him but he looked way too young to have gone to high school with you. Are you sure he didn't say you went with his mother?"

"That must be it. That would explain it." I refrained from kicking him in the shins. After all, he'd done what I asked and answered my question honestly.

I bypassed the fruits and vegetables, grabbed a candy bar and, after smiling at the cheerful clerk who took my money, charged angrily to the door, but there I instinctively lapsed into the Wawa code of conduct. I held doors and smiled at other store patrons which calmed me to the point where I found myself composed enough to do a thorough surveillance of the parking lot. I didn't see any sign of the stranger, but that didn't mean he couldn't see me. What is the point of issuing a threat if you don't check to see if the conditions are met? Somewhere he was waiting.

Even though I was less than a mile away, I decided to scratch my trip to Maria Garibaldi's house. For the day only. No way this episode would make me scrap my investigation. If anything, I felt renewed and revitalized. And thirsty. As soon as I finished my Babe Ruth, I stopped at another Wawa for water. Without incident.

Assuming, although unable to spot, someone on my tail, I traveled backroads through Delaware and Chester counties. Thirty minutes of aimless roving and I spotted no car consistently behind me. Just to be sure, I hopped onto the Pennsylvania turnpike at the EZ Pass entrance on Route 29. If anyone was following me, they did not have an EZ Pass.

I asked the Bluetooth to call Tracy but cut the call off after one ring. Did I really want to worry my niece? No. But just in case my attacker posed a serious danger, I really wanted to have an adequate investigation into my death. I told the car to call her back.

The message I left was jumbled, close to incoherent, and ended with "I'm finding this hard to explain on the phone."

Chapter 28

"I'll only stay a few minutes."

"Long enough for wine." Alex didn't ask. He shoved a glass of red into my hand.

Tracy patted the couch beside her. "What was so serious that you couldn't tell me on the phone?"

I told her.

"Why didn't you scream?" She asked.

"At first, I couldn't be sure he wasn't someone I knew, an old friend. Overly enthusiastic, but a friend. Then, I wanted to hear what he was saying. He said he wasn't going to hurt me."

"And you believed him?" Alex was judging me and I wasn't earning high scores.

"Kind of." I wanted to say that my reaction was well-thought-out, the result of a logical consideration of the facts, but it wasn't. "To tell you the truth, I just froze."

"Did he hurt you?"

"He manhandled me, but not to any real ill effect. I think the Parrys sent him."

"The Parrys?" Tracy seemed amused. "You were in Maria Mancini Garibaldi's neighborhood. You'd recently been sent away by a man of dubious reputation. Nonetheless, you finger the Parrys as the culprits."

"Number one, who told me that Joe Danton was a bit of a lowlife?" I asked.

"Your eyes and ears?" Alex's question dripped with sarcasm.

"Well, yes, I'll admit that, but the Parrys tipped me off to his tarnished past."

"Maybe because they wanted you to be careful." Tracy

defended the family.

"Or maybe because they knew he would send someone after me. That means the attack, encounter, whatever we call it, is still the Parrys' responsibility—direct or indirect."

"All speculation." Tracy waved her hand to dismiss my theories.

Alex's view was more sympathetic to my position. "Or maybe they figured you would perceive anyone they sent to be delivering a message from Joe Danton."

"Exactly." I pointed to Alex as if to say he was the most astute man on earth.

"You think the Parrys keep a team of thugs on retainer?" Tracy remained amused.

"They have investigators and this guy was a pro. He managed to look friendly enough that no one thought I was being abducted. And, I never got a good look at him. Actually, any look at him. Clearly an experienced professional."

"I understand your initial shock, but as the situation evolved you should have screamed," Alex offered advice.

"Why didn't you?" Tracy asked.

"I don't know." The realization hit me that I never considered making a scene. "He told me I didn't want to. The entire episode was over so fast. Maybe I was too curious."

"Next time something like this happens, scream," Alex ordered.

"It isn't going to happen again," Tracy said with authority. "There is no reason to continue if your inquiries put you in harm's way."

"She wasn't being followed," Alex spoke to Tracy as if I weren't in the room.

"Excuse me." I tried to get their attention. "What I was trying to say before we went on this tangent was that he was not your typical thug," I declared as if I had an encyclopedic knowledge of the world of thugs.

"I am sure competent thugs come in a wide variety of flavors," Tracy agreed.

"Well, this one was a premium flavor. He might have been wearing generic sportswear but he forgot to take off his $400 sneakers."

"Thugs like sneakers," Alex issued a proclamation.

"Maybe he is a well-paid freelance thug with expensive taste." Tracy shrugged, but the action looked weaker than her dismissive wave. She had to admit that those shoes were hard to explain.

"And good grammar. He used the subjunctive. Correctly."

"I know PhDs who can't do that." Alex supported my position with his words and an expression that suggested Tracy give up the fight.

Her expression changed. "Why do the Parrys want to hurt you?"

Chapter 29

The next morning, I drove to Maria Mancini Garibaldi's house with one eye on the road and one eye on the rearview mirror. I took the most indirect route possible, dodging in and out of neighborhoods, driving up and down random blocks. No one was following me, except for the last block. When I parked in front of the Garibaldi's house, a Toyota with dented sides and faded blue paint pulled around me and turned into the driveway.

"Hi, remember me?"

Her unhappy expression answered. Maria remembered. "You wanted something?"

"I wondered something." *Something* was why she didn't bring up the incident with Chip Parry.

My original wish—to confront her about why she held back information—had evaporated. Why would she tell a perfect stranger an embarrassing story? No, I needed to be nice and hope she would want to confide in me. I shadowed her and told her what I'd heard as she, refusing my help, moved from car to porch and back unloading groceries.

After all these years, she still displayed discomfort at the thought that anyone knew about her advances towards her boss's son, but she didn't say that. She said, "I didn't bring up the incident with Chip because it didn't seem relevant." She struggled with a particularly cumbersome package. "And, it was none of your business." She dropped the bag on the porch and took an inordinate amount of time to turn to face me, deciding how much she would say. At least that was my assumption. She let out a deep sigh. "I felt humiliated." Her tone asked *satisfied you made me confess my embarrassment?*

"But you stayed and worked in that house for years." I used a sympathetic voice.

"That was my job. I needed the job." She brushed by me. "I wasn't exactly a rocket scientist. I couldn't just quit and get a job with NASA. Actually, I'm not sure we had NASA back then."

I followed her to her car, speaking to her back. "If I were you, I wouldn't have given up on Chip so easily. You didn't, did you?" I tried to sound supportive as if I understood.

She stopped tugging at her parcels but didn't turn. "I am a realist. He had no interest in someone like me."

"But he did in Cassie." My tone added, *why not you?*

"You think I believed that Chip would change his mind about me if Cassie weren't around?" She spun around and although I heard anger in her voice, I saw tears in her eyes. "Are you thinking that I killed Cassie? Is that what you think? Trust me, Chip Parry wasn't that cute."

But he was that rich.

She tried to muster some bravado. "Look at me. How could I kill anyone?"

I didn't point out that even a tiny woman could swing a golf club. Or that she hadn't been close to eighty in 1956. Instead, I used my most compassionate tone. "I'm just trying to put together all the pieces and thought, given your interest, you might have noticed things." I didn't even try to relate my questions to my research for Tracy's class. I had moved into investigator mode. "I wasn't accusing you of murder."

Although I kind of was.

"It occurred to me that it must have galled you to see Cassie getting what you wanted. I can imagine how much that hurt. I thought you might have paid close attention. Chip dangled your dream in front of Cassie and she turned it down. You're right that I thought you might hate her for that. But I never thought you'd kill her." *Only because I couldn't figure out how or why you would kill Jonathan.*

171

"I don't have to talk to you." She slammed the trunk lid down leaving several bags inside the car and headed for her house. "I don't understand what you are up to, but it's not what you told me."

I explained that sometimes we delve into the details of a case. I repeated my story. "I'm not here to accuse you. I thought if you were interested in Chip, you would have paid attention—especially if Cassie decided not to take him up on his offer."

Maria stopped at the top of the steps, listening.

"I simply thought you might know something, something you didn't even realize you knew. Given what happened between you and Chip Parry, I understand why you might not want to think about that, why you felt uncomfortable." *It would have been worse, wouldn't it, working for her? Catherine Kelly Parry. Mrs. Henry Parry Jr.* Even though I withheld those thoughts, I expected, despite my sympathetic tone, that a can of soup would hit my skull at any moment. If it had, I probably would have deserved it. "I understand that if she had said yes, you would resent her, but never would I—would anyone—think you would kill two people because you resented her. What happened doesn't make you a suspect, it makes you a witness with a greater interest in the events."

This time when she turned, the tears were gone. "Sure, I was jealous. That is what you are really saying, right? That I would have been jealous. Who wouldn't want a cute guy with gobs of money?"

"And you wanted him?" I worked hard on a compassionate intonation.

"I never gave him a thought until he started following me around like a puppy. Then I figured why shouldn't I take advantage? I could hardly make a move that the kid wasn't beside me."

"But that stopped when Cassie came on the scene?" I infused my voice with kindness.

172

She released another deep sigh. "Before." All resistance drained from her and I felt pretty sure she was ready to talk. She took the few steps to the porch railing and grasped it with two hands. "I thought Chip was too shy to make a move. After all, he was younger and, I figured, less experienced. He certainly acted it. So I took the initiative." She shook her head. "Big mistake."

I waited barely daring to breathe lest I distract her.

"I scared him. I know that now. I came on too strong. I thought as the older woman—a high school graduate—I could initiate him. To quite a few things. I figured it wouldn't take much to get him all turned on." She grew suddenly pensive. "Although I don't think we used that term back then. I wonder what we called it."

She paused and I worried she would ever finish with semantics and get back to her point.

"I'd seen all those prim and proper Buffys and Muffys he took to the movies and maybe out for a little cuddle and if he got lucky, a little over-the-sweater action. He wasn't going to get from them what I could give him. I wanted to be different." She snickered. "I was different all right. I had his pants around his ankles and I could tell he was interested. Very interested. And then a door slammed in the distance, and he panicked. I think that's why he said the things he did. How I wasn't like him. How I didn't deserve someone like him. How people like him didn't do things like that with people like me." She paused to consider her words. "People like me. There I was with his . . . him . . . in my hand and he's telling me I'm not good enough."

The insult still rankled. If I were investigating the murder of Chip Parry, I would consider her a prime suspect even after all the years that had passed.

"Can you imagine how much I needed that job that I came back after that?"

She wanted my sympathy and got it.

When I finally spoke, I kept my voice soft. "It must have

173

hurt when he went after Cassie."

The tough Maria reemerged. "I thought Cassie should know the same thing happened to me. So I warned her."

I believed she warned Cassie, even if she didn't convince me about her motive. "If she rejected Chip, maybe Chip would look your way again," I suggested.

"I wasn't dumb enough to believe that. I wanted her to see that he was just playing her, that she was just like me in his eyes. But the truth? Chip loved Cassie."

And then I found out why Maria had not driven me off her property with canned vegetables.

"I've been over it a thousand times." She let go of the railing and stumbled to a porch chair. She slumped onto the hard seat. "Did what I told her cause her death in some way?"

"Did she tell Chip what you said?" Not if Chip told me the truth.

"I don't know. After she and Jonathan died, I tried every trick I knew to find out if she rejected him because of something I said. If she went with Jonathan because of something I said. I couldn't just ask Chip." She shook her head as if disgusted with herself. "I even pumped Lillibet. Pretty shameful since she was only nine at the time."

"Lillibet?"

She appeared more puzzled than I did, and I looked plenty puzzled. "The little sister. Elizabeth. Never called that. Always Lillibet."

"I didn't know there was a little sister."

"But you've been talking to the family."

"No one mentioned a little sister."

A knowing look. That is what I would call the expression on her face. A touch of amusement, a dash of bitterness and a whole lot of *I knew it*.

"The family said she was dead to them. I guess if no one mentioned her, they still feel the same way. In those days she was just a cute kid—cheerful, friendly, curious—not like the teenagers. When Jonathan came around, she'd take a break from shadowing Cassie and follow him all over. Always wanted to be near the big kids, especially Cassie. When her parents agreed, she'd eat dinner in the kitchen to be near Cassie. I think she liked Cassie a lot more than her own siblings. She would hang around and listen. I thought maybe she heard something."

"Did you find out if she did?"

"I don't think she did. I quizzed her. Not directly. I tried to be tricky. I felt kind of bad. That Lillibet did not have an ounce of guile in her. Can't figure out how that child ended up in that family."

"Where do I find Lillibet?"

"She went to Woodstock in 1969. By the time I retired in the late eighties, she hadn't gotten home yet. She does send a Christmas card now and then. The last card came from New York City."

"It shouldn't be too hard to find a Lillibet Parry."

"No longer Parry. Sadoski. She always signs her cards Lillibet Sadoski."

Sadoski? Coincidence? If Lillibet's name had been Smith, maybe. But Sadoski? I thought not.

Chapter 30

I made the call as soon as I got into the car. "Wait until you hear this one. Just wait." I spoke to Tracy's voice mail. "I'm on my way."

In transit, I left messages for Antonia Sadoski saying that I had a question for her but not what that question was.

"Nice to see you too." Tracy stepped aside to let me charge into the living room.

"Did you know the Parrys had a third child?" I took a position in the center of the room with my hands on my hips and my head tilted to the side. I stared hard at Tracy.

The news did not appear to upset my niece. "I did not," she said matter-of-factly.

"Do you want to know the child's name?"

"Why not?" She waved at a seat. "Sit and have a glass of wine." She checked her watch. "It's after noon."

"No wine until you guess the child's name."

"I don't know." Her head bobbled as if she thought she could shake a name loose. "Mary? Jane? Wait. I know. Cassie?"

I shook my head in disgust and plopped hard onto the sofa.

"I'm sorry." Tracy poured the wine as quickly as she could. In hopes of soothing the savage beast I'd become? A good possibility. "I don't have a guess." Her tone begged me to believe her.

I nodded as I ranted. "Her last name. You know it all right. It's obvious now."

Her face contorted as she sank on a chair across from me. "Not . . ."

I kept nodding with a ridiculously theatrical flair.

176

"Antonia Sadoski? She can't be; she's too young."

"But her mother isn't. Her mother, Lillibet Sadoski. Her mother Elizabeth Parry Sadoski aka Lillibet."

Tracy's face relaxed. "We should have figured that out, shouldn't we? Antonia's story didn't make much sense. Why go out of your way to instigate an investigation into a murder you have no connection to. We talked about that."

"I found the explanation sketchy when I used it as my own. I should have been more critical. I asked her and then accepted an obvious lie as truth."

"But why? Why would anyone initiate an investigation into their own family?"

"Lillibet loved the big kids. She was a lot younger than her brother and sister." I told her everything I had gotten out of Maria Mancini, which wasn't much, but enough to convince me that Antonia Sadoski knew more than she was telling. "Apparently, Cassie and Jonathan were nice to Lillibet."

"So nice that almost sixty years later, she launches an investigation into their death? Why? Why would she do that?"

"I guess there is only one way to find out. Fancy a road trip?"

Chapter 31

Locating Lillibet Sadoski was not hard. Listening to me go on about how Soho had changed since I lived in New York City was hard—at least for Tracy. "So many people," I kept repeating.

Tracy ignored me and led the way down the crowded sidewalks.

Finding Lillibet's building? Again, not hard. Sneaking into Lillibet's building? Not easy. We studied Lillibet's residence from a clothing store across the street.

Tracy reported, "Four floors. No doorman. It looks as if there is only one apartment per floor."

"Finding someone to trail inside will not be easy. Clearly, they all know each other," I mumbled as I pretended to look through a rack of clothes that I couldn't have worn at twenty, let alone sixty.

"We could just ring her bell," Tracy said.

"You are the one who taught me about the element of surprise." I eyed Lillibet's industrial-strength front door across the cobblestone street.

"We could approach one of the neighbors and say, 'Thanks for holding the door. We're going up to see Lillibet Sadoski."

"As long as we don't say it to Lillibet Sadoski." Tracy sounded skeptical. "The salespeople are getting annoyed with us. Let's go before I feel compelled to purchase this piece of cloth that appears to work as a skirt on people of a certain size, not mine."

Out on the sidewalk, I pulled out a printout of Lillibet's Facebook page. "Study the picture."

"If she looks like it." Tracy glanced at the paper and then

tucked it in her pocket. "We look suspicious enough without giving the impression we're checking a mug shot."

"It's New York. Pretend you're a tourist looking for famous people."

"I'm far too hip for that," Tracy protested. "I put her landline number in my phone. Let's just call it and tell her we're out here. After all, her suspicions are the root of this investigation." She handed me her phone. "I don't think she'll block it."

She didn't. Lillibet Sadoski cut me off as I tried to explain who I was—and where. "I know who you are. My daughter told me that you were Tracy Shaw's aunt. I've been expecting you."

I felt someone staring and looked up at the figure standing in the wide windows of the top floor loft.

"I would have gotten here sooner if I knew you existed." I met her eyes as I spoke.

I thought I saw her shrug. "You're here now. You might as well come up."

"This is my niece, Tracy Shaw." I nodded at Tracy standing beside me.

"She might as well come up too."

Lillibet disappeared and the sound of a buzzer carried all the way across the street.

"Well, here we go." I ran across the cobblestones and yanked the door open.

If I sounded annoyed when I greeted Lillibet Sadoski, it was not simply because she had wasted my time. She had wasted my time while living a life I fantasized about. I'd been an Upper West Side New Yorker but never a downtown type. Getting off the supercool freight elevator and entering Lillibet Parry Sadoski's apartment only confirmed what I suspected. Lillibet represented a quintessential downtown woman, attractive and dressed the way a sixtyish resident of New York's Soho should in a style that matched her residence, a casual and hip-looking loft with furnishings that were eclectic and expensive. Mementos on walls and shelves testified to a life of travel and adventure. Bookcases were full of photos, a fair number of them of her daughter Antonia. The only evidence the family had roots in old-school high society stood on a bookcase. A five-prong candelabra made an odd intrusion of her old world into her new.

Lillibet did not resemble her brother or sister, and her daughter did not resemble her. Her elfin looks made her an anomaly in the Parry family but not in her trendy neighborhood. Living the good life had left few wrinkles on Lillibet's smooth white skin, so she appeared younger than her years—even before she curled up on the leather sofa with all the flexibility of a twelve-year-old.

I sat on the couch opposite hers with my feet planted firmly on the floor. Beside me, Tracy matched my posture. After some formalities, I took the lead. "I think this process might have been easier if Antonia had made a full disclosure of her involvement with the Parry family."

Lillibet had no response. She stared at me without blinking. Did I detect a bit of the family hauteur?

"I have pursued this because I am motivated by the feeling that Cassie and Jonathan did not get the justice they deserved."

She continued to stare.

"So I have no issue with the time I spent, although I do feel somewhat betrayed by Antonia's lack of honesty."

She still stared.

"I don't understand why your family would want to resurrect this business after all these years?" I asked.

"My family?" Lillibet laughed a rueful laugh. "My blood relatives would never want this story to resurface. The Parrys don't like anything unpleasant, you know."

"I've discovered no proof of wrong-doing on their part. Why keep everything so hush-hush?"

"That's an interesting question." She reeled back as if hit

by a sudden realization but it had nothing to do with my question. "I'm sorry. I should have offered you something to drink."

I believed the thought simply popped into her mind and indicated no attempt to dodge the issue, but Tracy and I both declined. "Are you sure? I'm pouring something for myself."

I watched across the room as she poured scotch into a glass. "Breakfast scotch," she chucked before taking a long drink.

I got back on track. "Why did Antonia bring this up?"

"She did it for me. I'd carried this suspicion with me all my life."

She didn't specify what that suspicion was.

"As Antonia got older, I discussed the situation with her, how I had buried my suspicions about my father since I was a little girl."

Even though she fell into silence, I didn't interrupt. I was thinking about her father and waiting for her to say more about her suspicions.

"My daughter, such an old soul, so mature, understood what it meant to me. You don't know what it's like to grow up with the feeling that something is wrong. At least I hope you don't." She looked at me as if she expected some dark secret to come pouring out.

When I shook my head, Lillibet looked to Tracy who did the same. We had problems, but no secrets to confess.

"I grew up with a feeling of guilt, that I should have said more to the police but they never asked. What could I do as a nine-year-old? Call the cops and say I think my daddy murdered two people? Could you take a look/see? What could I do now? Write a letter to the newspaper that I had a story, a sixty-year-old story, possibly juicy but probably not? Want to interview me? Neither opportunity seemed promising. Then I read about you." She nodded at Tracy.

"You still haven't said how your daughter got involved,"

I said.

"Antonia picked her own thesis topic and her own school."

She sounded defensive, and I sounded more sarcastic than I intended when I answered, "That right?"

Lillibet ignored my tone. "She would be in Philadelphia, at Penn, conducting interviews about crime, I simply suggested that when asking about her thesis topic, she could ask around about the story. No one would find that odd—unlike asking a question like a bolt out of the blue. She discovered that I wasn't the only one with suspicions about my family's involvement." She sounded almost relieved. "I may have pointed out your niece's work, but approaching her was Antonia's idea."

"She didn't feel bad turning her family members into murder suspects?" I asked.

"For one thing, she's never met them."

"Another thing?"

"She never named our family. If your trail led to my father, my brother, my sister, it wouldn't be her fault. She had no intent to deceive. She sent you off without bias in search of the truth. And, since you are sitting here, I assume you did end up with my family. Did you speak to my brother?" Her voice softened just the tiniest bit at the mention of Chip.

"I did."

"Has he had a nice life?"

I didn't know. I could tell her what I saw of his current life which looked fine. Not fabulous, but okay. Comfortable.

"Chip was always kind to me. He was a nice boy. Weak, but nice. Probably still married to Clare, I suppose."

"Not married at all. Has been. Twice."

"Kids?"

"Yes, but we didn't talk about them. We discussed his earlier life. He told me how he felt about Cassie."

"I was just a kid but I could recognize infatuation. Of

course, I would have loved my brother to marry Cassie, but I knew my parents weren't crazy about the idea."

"How did you know?"

"Parents think kids aren't listening, let alone understanding, but they are."

"And that's why you questioned your father's involvement."

She nodded.

"But never Chip's?"

"Chip?" She all but yelled the word. "No way. And not only for positive reasons. Yes, he was too good and too kind to do such a thing, but also too much of a weenie. Looking back, I can see what a weak person my parents molded him into. My father spoke and he jumped."

"Blair is fine." I figured if I mentioned her sister's name she would run with the topic.

She laughed. "I am sure she is. Still married to poor George?"

"I doubt it." I didn't know George's last name. "She is Blair Parry Middleton Foster Braddock Mills." I counted the names off on my fingers.

"Blair knows how to take care of herself, and only herself. Now if you told me *she* was responsible . . . ." She paused for only a few seconds. "No, that's not fair. Blair could probably hire someone to kill for her, but she would never kill anyone herself. Too messy." Her eyes bore into mine. "Don't take that comment seriously. Blair had a lot of faults, but, at that point, she didn't have her own money. So hiring a hitman would have been out of the question." She took another slug of scotch.

"Did she have a reason she wanted to see either Jonathan or Cassie dead?"

"Are you serious?"

"Dead serious." I didn't intend the pun, but let it go.

"Blair was too arrogant to know she should have been jealous of Cassie."

183

"About Jonathan?"

"About everything. Cassie was prettier and probably smarter—Blair was no rocket scientist. She should have been away at college that year but she had to take make-up classes. Still, it never would have occurred to her that Jonathan could have been interested in Cassie."

"And Jonathan?"

"Are you asking me if she would want to kill Jonathan?"

"Yeah. I guess I am."

"Would you kill a puppy dog that followed you around so it could worship you?"

I knew *I* wouldn't.

She drifted off. Into recollections of her family? My guess was yes.

"Why now?" Tracy spoke for the first time. "Why are you raising this issue now?"

"My mother has been gone for decades. My father is headed for one hundred. He's not going to live forever." She paused to gain her composure. "God knows I am not that young. I could go first and I don't want to die still wondering about that night. It's unfinished business and I don't like unfinished business."

"You suspected your father of murdering Cassie and Jonathan?"

Her sheepish expression answered for her. "I don't know that I've always believed it—it took me a while to accept that the suspicion lived in the back of my mind, lurking there. It's a difficult thing to admit." She shuddered as if frightened by the admission. "If I'm wrong, I need to make things right with him."

"And if you're right?" I asked.

"He needs to face what he did."

"Why? I don't disagree, but he's not my father. Why do you feel that way?" Tracy asked.

I understood her point. It was one thing for us to feel Henry Parry needed to take responsibility. It was another for

184

his own daughter to take that position.

"Jonathan Brien and Cassie Kelly were nice young people with bright futures. The passage of time, the way things changed, only makes me feel more strongly they might have had great lives."

"But if you are wrong, the investigation could still damage your family name," I stated thinking that I sounded like a character from a Jane Wyman movie. And, apparently, like Edward Baron.

She huffed. "My family name? You sound like Uncle Edward. The Parry name. He would go on and on about it as if it were the most important thing in the world. And, he wasn't even a Parry. He's not a real uncle. No relation, just a good friend of our parents. An honorary uncle, you might say. And, he was the one who believed most fervently in the power of the Parry name. Having the right name should never put you above the law." She gazed out the window across Prince Street and into an apartment much like her own.

"I saw both of them that last day. Cassie and Jonathan. You know they were at our house."

*****Lillibet Sadoski*****
Parry Estate
Philadelphia, Pennsylvania
April 21, 1956

Cassie played the radio when she was alone in the house with Lillibet. She liked to hear Cassie sing along with the music. Cassie knew all the words and sang them in a beautiful voice. Blair said that Cassie's voice wasn't special, but Lillibet had never heard anyone sing so well in person. At least outside of church. Lillibet hoped she would be able to sing like Cassie when she grew up, but at nine she couldn't yet carry a tune.

But that day Cassie wasn't singing. Grace Kelly had

married a prince and the story was all over the newspaper and always on TV. While Cassie worked, she kept one eye on films of the wedding playing on the table-model television Lillibet's parents had provided—mainly to keep Lillibet in place for an entire meal when her behavior didn't earn her a place at the dining room table.

Mesmerized by the pageant on the screen, Lillibet slid onto one of the chairs to watch. She glanced from the royal bride to Cassie and back. People said that Grace Kelly was beautiful but Lillibet saw Cassie as more beautiful, even in the maid's uniform she had to wear in their house. She had no idea how pretty Cassie looked in real clothes. She never wore them to work. She arrived in the plain black dress and put on one of the aprons she kept freshly ironed in the pantry. At night she would take off the apron and walk to the trolley in the plain black dress, sometimes with a sweater or coat on top. Lillibet thought she still looked pretty.

Cassie was twenty, a half-year older than her sister Blair. Her parents always talked about how pretty Blair was, but she wasn't pretty like Cassie. They were both blonde and neither was fat, but that was all they had in common. Cassie was nice with a kind smile that made her look even prettier. Blair never looked kind.

"Can I help you?" Lillibet eyed the row of silver candlesticks Cassie had lined up.

"No need, but thank you." Cassie kept rubbing polish on a big candelabra from the dining room. Cassie took good care of all the silver and china and crystal. Lillibet's mother said she'd better. It was all expensive. Some of it was priceless, having been passed down for several generations already. She expected it to be passed down to many more.

"My mother says that might be mine someday."

"You are a lucky girl, Lillibet. You'll have many lovely things in your life. Just remember that beautiful things are wonderful, but life isn't all about what you own."

She believed Cassie was smart but maybe not about

fancy things. Lillibet didn't care much about plates and glasses but she did want pretty dresses and sparkly jewelry like she saw at the big events in Monte Carlo. "Can I stay to watch the wedding with you?"

"Of course, let me get you a snack." Cassie put down the silver and went to a bowl near the kitchen window where she plucked out an apple.

"Blair says that Grace Kelly's prince isn't much of a prince. Not like the little prince in England will be. Blair says that he's only a pretend prince in a pretend country."

"He's her prince, Lillibet. That's all that matters."

Lillibet heard the sound of the knife hitting the cutting board. "Can you cut the skin off, please?" She never took her eyes off the screen. "I don't like her dress."

"Oh Lillibet," Cassie sounded sentimental. "It's a classic gown for a classic beauty."

Lillibet had been watching the TV and didn't notice Blair come in from the back driveway. "Another day of the royal wedding? It slays me the way the press refers to Grace Kelly as a socialite from Philadelphia."

Lillibet turned to see her sister frowning at the television.

"Social Register or not, she is a beautiful bride. Cassie is right." Chip strode into the room and Lillibet noticed that although Cassie kept her eye on the apple when Blair came in, she glanced up to return Chip's smile.

"Is that your dream, Cassie? To marry a prince and move into his palace?" Blair stared hard at Cassie's back, but Cassie didn't respond.

That sounded like a good dream to Lillibet. Why did Blair sound so nasty when she talked about it? She made a mad face at her sister. She knew that Blair was being mean on purpose.

Lillibet heard the sound of a car crushing gravel in the driveway. She jumped up when she recognized the voice through the screen.

"Am I interrupting?"

187

"Hi, Jonathan." Excited, Lillibet opened the door for her sister's visitor. She'd met him before and felt happy he came back. She liked him. He was nicer than the other boys that Blair bought home and looked more handsome in his tennis whites.

Unlike most boys who came to visit, he talked to her and never called her kid. *He remembered her name and used it. "Thank you, Miss Lillibet."*

She ran back to her chair. Jonathan would stick around for a while. He always did, if he could. She didn't want to miss a moment of the royal wedding.

Jonathan always seemed so eager to make everyone happy, but she thought he looked kind of nervous standing in the kitchen doorway in his white shorts and sweater. She didn't understand why. He looked cute in his tennis clothes. "Am I interrupting?"

Cassie answered. "Blair was just explaining that Grace Kelly is not a socialite." She brushed by Blair to deliver Lillibet's apple and pick up a candelabra. She didn't even glance Blair's way when she carried it to the sink. Lillibet guessed that Cassie agreed that Blair was being mean. She probably was. She often was. Lillibet, wishing Cassie was her sister, returned her attention to watching the TV screen and eating apple slices

"I was simply making the observation that she is not, could never be, one of us. The press should not call an Irish Catholic girl from East Falls a Philadelphia socialite."

Two strong arms gathered Lillibet into a playful stranglehold. "From now on they'll be calling her Royal Highness."

Lillibet fought to extricate herself from Chip's grasp. "Her Serene Highness."

Jonathan paid no attention to their argument. He had come to see Blair. "I thought we were going to play tennis." Jonathan was a lot of fun. Most times. Other times he only paid attention to Blair. Lillibet didn't know why. Blair was

188

never any fun.

Blair patted Jonathan on the arm as she headed for the back stairs—the way her mother patted their dog when he was afraid of lightning. Well, the way she did before he got hit by lightning and died.

"Jonathan, explain the facts of life in Philadelphia to my brother while I get ready. It's only the two of us today. Let's just hit a few balls around here. I'll meet you at the court."

Jonathan looked confused but her brother told him not to worry about it. Jonathan didn't care about the bride and groom in a country that, as he put it, would fit inside his country's capital city, but he was excited about something outside. "Chipper, let me show you what I have parked in your driveway."

"Sure." Chip didn't look happy about leaving. Lillibet knew he wanted to stay and talk to Cassie. Chip and she both liked to talk to Cassie. But Chip was polite to Blair's visitor. "See you later." He smiled at Cassie. She nodded and smiled back.

Chip and Jonathan went out the door that Jonathan came in. At the sink, Cassie buffed the candlestick. Lillibet couldn't see her face to see if Blair hurt her feelings, but she wanted to make their maid feel good after Blair had been so mean. "You look like Princess Grace, Cassie." She wasn't lying. Cassie did look like Grace Kelly. "You have the same last name. Is she your cousin?"

Cassie chuckled. "No royalty in my family, Lillibet." She wet a rag and wiped the candlestick but she didn't look at it. She stared out the window. Lillibet ran over to the counter and pulled up a footstool to see what Cassie was watching. She saw Jonathan showing off a car to Chip. The two were looking at the inside of the convertible when her parents' Buick pulled up. Her father got out of the front passenger seat and opened the rear door so that her mother could climb out. Chip waved at their parents and his father nodded. He always did that when he wasn't happy. Even

Cassie knew. Lillibet saw a worried look on Cassie's face reflected in the window. "Your family is the royalty in this town, Lillibet." She looked kind of sad.

But Lillibet wasn't at all sad. "Mummy and Daddy are home." A head appeared over the top of the car. "And Uncle Edward." Edward Baron climbed out of the driver's seat.

Lillibet ran out of the backdoor and threw her arms around her father. He responded with a gentle pat on her back.

When she looked up, she found her mother frowning down at her. She straightened Lillibet's hair. "What have you been up to?"

"Watching the royal wedding. Her dress is so pretty." Lillibet had been swayed by Cassie's opinion.

"Whose dress? What royal wedding?" Her mother sounded confused. Although Lillibet didn't understand how anyone in Philadelphia could have missed hearing about the big story.

"Grace Kelly is marrying the Prince of Monaco," Uncle Edward explained, "and it seems our little princess has been watching."

Lillibet curtsied to Uncle Edward. He responded with an exaggerated bow.

Over by his car, Jonathan smiled, as if waiting for somebody to greet him. But her mother and father went into the house without looking his way or saying a word to him, let alone noticing his new car. Uncle Edward trailed behind and, following her parents' lead, ignored the visitor.

Lillibet didn't know a lot about adults but she felt kind of bad for Jonathan. She figured she could make him feel better.

"Jonathan, what a pretty car!" She thought that might make him smile, but it didn't. She shrugged and went back into the house without asking for a ride. She might be young, but she was old enough to recognize a bad mood.

*****

"Was that the last time you saw Cassie and Jonathan?" I asked.

"I saw Cassie all afternoon before I left for a friend's house." Lillibet had a way of speaking that was vaguely insulting. How was I supposed to know?

"And Jonathan?"

"Oh, no. I saw him later that night."

"Did you see him drive away?" I could only keep my fingers crossed.

"Of course not. I would have a better idea of what happened then, wouldn't I?"

She sounded a bit snippy for someone who owed me an apology.

I think she realized that because her next statement was an apology. "I'm sorry. This is just an extremely sensitive topic for me. The most problematic topic of my life."

"Mom." I heard the single word along with the clink of elevator doors laboring to open.

"In here," she called. "We have company."

Antonia Sadoski appeared happy to hear that but when she discovered Tracy and me in the living space, her smile faded. Her big leather bag landed with a thud on the hardwood floor.

Chapter 32

"Ms. Tracy."

I judged Antonia Sadoski to be surprised but not embarrassed. "I believe you've met my niece, Tracy Shaw."

"We met briefly on the Wallmann campus. And, of course, I know her by reputation."

"Of course," I said with a snippy tone I copied from Lillibet.

Tracy was more pleasant. She told Antonia it was nice to see her again. Very convincingly.

"Your mother was just telling us about the last time she saw the two victims of the crime you told us about."

I waited. No apology. No indication that she should have told us about her mother's involvement. Not even an explanation as to why she didn't. Stopping only briefly to shake Tracy's hand, she went to her mother's side. The student could not help looking elegant in her jeans and cashmere sweater. I could not help estimating the cost of her soft leather boots as she crossed her legs with casual grace. "I imagine you can see how difficult this is for my mother." She grasped Lillibet's hand although her mother's manner in no way indicated she was in need of support.

"Of course," I forced a concerned tone when I was really still feeling annoyance, "but we need to hear about the last time she saw Jonathan Brien." I turned to Lillibet.

She did not seem reluctant to talk. I think she had been waiting years for someone to ask.

*****Lillibet Parry Sadoski*****
Parry Estate
Philadelphia, Pennsylvania

April 21, 1956

Jonathan's mood seemed even more gloomy when Lillibet saw him after dinner. She'd gotten cranky too when she realized that by staying at her friend's house she had missed having dinner with Jonathan. But maybe it would be better to stay out of his way until his spirits improved. She didn't know what made him so angry, but he sure looked mad as he charged across the lawn. She peeked at the patio that he came from and saw Blair watching him go. Blair must have made him feel bad. Blair did not deserve a boyfriend like Jonathan.

Lillibet kept out of sight as she followed him towards the putting green where she had seen her father hitting golf balls, really, really hard. Too hard. The balls kept rolling by the hole. He had switched to driving balls down their long lawn.

Jonathan disappeared behind a hedge. Lillibet figured that he could see her father and her father could see him. She hid on the other side of the bushes to watch the action through a bare spot in the greenery. Jonathan tried to interrupt her father but he remained focused on the golf balls he had lined up.

"I thought you would be gone. Have you spoken to my daughter?"

"About how I am not good enough for her? She talked to me."

"Good."

Jonathan moved as close as possible, given that her father never stopped swinging. For a moment she worried Jonathan would pull the club out of her father's hands.

"Look at me. Look at what I've accomplished."

Her father didn't say a word. He just kept moving down the line of golf balls and driving them into the darkening sky.

"I don't understand how you can just dismiss me."

"Of course you do. You're a bright boy. Anyone can see

that. You're quite transparent."

"Then you should be able to see that I love your daughter."

"I see that you love her money, her status, her name, to be blunt, her relationship to me. My entire life I've seen people like you who don't know their place."

Without so much as a glance at Jonathan, her father rolled the small golf bag that he used at home towards the putting green. He dropped his driver in and pulled a putter out.

Jonathan followed. "My place?"

"Didn't you think that someone in my position could find out that you are not Jonathan Brien but John O'Brien, son of Leo and Mary O'Brien of West Philadelphia? That's nothing to be ashamed of, boy." Her father leaned over to set up a line of golf balls.

"Who said I'm ashamed?"

"You did by hiding the truth and pretending to be something you're not."

Lillibet heard the click of the putter striking the first ball.

"I am a promising young lawyer. I have prospects. The only thing I don't have is lineage."

"And that is something you can't acquire." Her father interrupted his putting practice and leaned on his club. "Take my advice. Finish law school. Get a good job in a firm interested in your kind. Marry a nice girl from the neighborhood. Golf at a club that caters to your type. You can be top dog. That will never happen where you aspire to go."

"Your own wife came from my type."

"Not that it is any of your business, but Julia Blair was a well-bred, wealthy girl before she married me. Yes, a Catholic but of fine French lineage with a small percentage of Irish blood. And, our circle accepted her because my parents and I insisted that she be accepted. That will never happen in your case. Now if you'll excuse me."

He sounded calm but he walked away without his golf bag. He swiped at the grass with his putter as he charged down the hill. He moved quickly but Jonathan didn't stop calling after him, his voice growing louder with each word. "You should appreciate what I've accomplished, what I am made of."

Lillibet thought that yelling at her father would only make him more angry.

Henry Sr. stopped and twisted his body halfway around. "I think that is where this conversation began, Mr. O'Brien. And this is where it ends. Good night."

Her father turned his back on Jonathan, made a great show of straightening his shoulders and walked away.

*****

"Even as a child, I understood that my father had been rude and mean and made Jonathan distraught. Realizing now how young he was, I find the way he stood up to my father amazing. He was confrontational, but he had tried to behave in a controlled manner. Even as a child, I admired him. As an adult, who understands just how difficult it is to control displays of frustration, I admire him even more."

"What did Jonathan do after your father left him on the putting green?"

"He paced around mumbling to himself for a few minutes. He kicked the bag my father had left behind. I thought that looked kind of funny. I wanted to figure out something to say to Jonathan to cheer him up, but he walked away. He followed my father towards the guest cottage."

"And you didn't follow?" I asked.

"I went to my room. I thought I could watch out my window, but it was really getting dark by then. The cottage wasn't that far away, but a thick row of bushes hid it from the main house. I couldn't see a thing. So, being a kid, I went downstairs and watched television."

For the first time, I saw emotion surfacing in Lillibet Sadoski. She fought tears as she struggled to get her words out. "I never wanted to admit, even to myself, what I thought, but, deep in my heart, at the moment my mother gave me the news, I believed my father killed Jonathan. How could I not after what I witnessed? They were so angry—both of them. And, then, one of them is dead." Her voice cracked and a moment passed before she continued. "But I knew whoever killed Jonathan had also killed Cassie, and I couldn't imagine why my father would do that. I felt so upset that Cassie was dead, but my parents told me to stop being dramatic, that her death had nothing to do with me. They called me self-centered and selfish and accused me of stealing her family's grief. I wanted to go to her funeral. I wanted to see her again. She had been my friend, my best friend in that house, but my parents said no. Cassie's death was none of our business. We should not interfere in the Kellys' lives."

Antonia let go of her mother's hand and found a tissue box. Lillibet blew her nose hard. "They ordered Chip to stay at school. He wanted to attend Cassie's funeral and felt devastated when he couldn't. I didn't understand then that he loved her, only that he liked her a lot."

She stared across Prince Street into the large loft where family life went on, oblivious to eyes taking in the scene. I don't think it mattered. Lillibet didn't see what she watched. "What if I had been wrong all these years? I hated them, punished them, my family."

"You realize if you had told us your story at the beginning you might have saved us a lot of time." In a tone much calmer and kinder than I would have used, Tracy spoke to Antonia but her mother answered.

"I wasn't interested in having someone confirm what I suspected. I wanted an independent investigation, an impartial opinion. What if I had made a mistake back when I cut myself off from my parents?"

"Your mother too?" I didn't even try to hide the shock in my voice.

"Do you think she was involved?" Tracy asked.

"As they often say these days, it wasn't the crime, it was the cover-up." She snickered. "I viewed them as a team. If he did it, I figured she had to know. I did not give her the benefit of the doubt. I don't believe she even noted a change in me. My spirit left that house long before I left physically—which I did with money from my grandmother that came through when I graduated from college. My mother seemed surprised. She didn't see my departure coming. I never discussed my suspicions or any of my reasons for going. My parents never asked." She considered that thought for a few seconds before she continued. "I hope I am wrong about my father and, if I am, I have to make amends before it is too late. I never had the chance. No, I never made the opportunity to make amends with my mother." Tears flowed down her cheeks. "I want to be wrong. So much. I want to be wrong."

"Did your parents tell you what they thought happened?"

"The carjacking?" This time she blew her nose hard to express her opinion of that story.

"An easy resolution for the police to swallow and maybe I would have too if the bodies had been found by the side of a road, near a red light, but in a lovers' lane. No way."

"They didn't like each other?" Tracy asked.

"They barely knew each other."

"Why didn't you tag along to see what happened when your father and Jonathan walked away?" I thought of my own behavior as a kid and figured I would have wanted to know how the drama played out.

"We weren't allowed to go to Uncle Edward's cottage unless he specifically invited us, which he seldom did."

"Uncle Edward?" Tracy and I spoke in unison. Tracy sounded confused. I sounded surprised.

"Edward Baron, a partner at the firm. He definitely

wouldn't have liked Jonathan." As she chuckled, her face contorted into a wry expression. "Probably because Jonathan hit a little too close to home."

I didn't mention that I'd met Edward Baron. "Social climber?" Neither did I mention that although I hadn't pegged him as one, I wouldn't be surprised if he fit the profile.

"Uncle Edward started life with a bit of money and a decent name, but working his way into the Parry family's social circle represented a huge step up for him. He had been a childhood friend of my mother's and part of her dowry, so to speak. Uncle Edward came with the bride. My father had been so determined to marry my mother, he would have agreed to anything. My father loved to tell the tale of how he so loved my Catholic mother that he forced his family to accept her."

Even though she wasn't good enough. I kept the thought to myself. I asked. "But your father didn't see Edward the same way he saw Jonathan."

"Those two were friends for years. Uncle Edward played the sycophant for years. He treated my father like royalty. Sometimes his adulation seemed a little creepy. He always talked about the family name like a treasure. My father thrived on the adoration."

"And Edward Baron was staying in the guest house that night?"

"Every night. He lived there."

I glanced at Tracy, who studied Lillibet Sadoski with narrowed eyes.

"My mother knew Uncle Edward from the age of three. He introduced my parents. After his divorce, he lived on the estate."

That's pretty cozy. Your mother marries one of the richest men in the city and moves her good friend into the guest house. Her male friend. I kept that thought to myself. At least, I thought I did. I think maybe my face was not

198

equally discreet.

"Uncle Edward was also a friend of my father's. They went to Harvard Law together." Lillibet answered an unasked question.

"Oh." I lowered my eyes and tried hard not to glance at Tracy. When I glanced up, I saw Lillibet staring at me with amazement. Antonia was staring at me with horror. Apparently, uncovering a murder in the family proved more acceptable than uncovering an affair.

"Are you implying that Uncle Edward and my mother were having an illicit relationship?" Lillibet stared at me as if I would admit it.

I had already created an entire scenario in my head that I did not share. Jonathan follows Parry, gives up, tries to leave the estate, happens onto Baron's love nest. Baron strikes Jonathan to protect Julia and his own lifestyle. Somehow Cassie must have caught him trying to dispose of the body.

Antonia finally spoke up. "Suppose your story about an affair were true, what would that have to do with Jonathan's and Cassie's deaths?"

I ignored her question and addressed Lillibet. "Your parents were happily married." My tone lied, saying I expected confirmation even though I didn't.

"I thought so." She sighed. "Until that night. I felt it was my attitude that changed but looking back on it from adulthood, something happened. There were no arguments. The topic was never mentioned. My parents were never the same. Even their relationship with Uncle Edward cooled. Looking back, I don't think I ever saw Uncle Edward in the main house again."

Maybe her father also stumbled on the scene at the love nest. "Didn't you ever wonder what caused the change?"

"Of course, I did. But, like I said, I thought it was me, my feelings. My parents held their cards pretty close to the vest. They were never the warm and cuddly types. As long as I lived in that house, I never understood what went on between them. I certainly didn't have a clue at the age of nine. By my teen-age years, I convinced myself that the way my father dealt with Jonathan and Cassie's death, dismissing it as a nuisance, made my mother admit what a snob my father actually was. She wasn't from the same social stratum, not Social Register. Maybe she worried that he looked down on her too."

"After twenty-plus years of marriage?" Antonia spoke for only the second time, asking a question I shared.

"I was a child." Lillibet sounded exasperated.

"But why would she steer clear of Edward Baron?" I asked.

"I didn't know. Only looking back did I realize that he didn't come around as often. Maybe the coldness between my parents made him uncomfortable. He'd always been nice to me, but I didn't care about him. I cared about my parents. If they argued, I am sure he would have backed up my father even though he was my mother's friend first."

"How long did he live in the cottage?" I asked.

"I think he moved in about a year before I was born. As far as I know, he still lives there."

Chapter 33

The confirmation that we'd been played might have been distressing, but I felt energized by our new information—by the supposition that Julia Parry was involved with Edward Baron—and, by a trip to one of my favorite haunts from the 1980s. We headed downtown to the Tribeca Grill, where I found old stand-bys on the menu and ordered them. Tracy followed my lead.

"I guess our confrontation didn't turn out exactly the way we thought it would." My words assigned blame to Tracy and me, but my tone expressed no guilt. Given that I was eating my favorite arugula and mozzarella salad, I sounded happier that I intended.

"I suspected we were in uncharted territory when you failed to nail Antonia to the wall," Tracy agreed.

"I was probably too polite," I admitted.

"And I concluded I was right when Lillibet ended up sobbing on your shoulder while Antonia fed her tissues."

"I like to think I'm not a softie, but I found it hard to stay mad." I made an understatement. "Especially when Lillibet explained why she couldn't confront her father herself."

"That was almost sixty years of emotion spilling out in one wave."

"It's not going to be easy to walk away after that." The fight had gone out of me, at least when it came to Lillibet Sadoski.

"Especially after you promised her you wouldn't." Tracy reminded me.

"I said that?"

Tracy just nodded.

"What else did I promise?"

"That you would talk to, but not confront her father and, when you do, you wouldn't tell her father about her suspicions."

"Did she say we could admit we met her?" I'd better get my story straight.

"Didn't say we couldn't."

"Did I happen to say *why* I would do that? Because, now that we're out of her apartment, and I'm no longer swept up in her emotions, I can't see what's in it for us."

"What is ever in it for us?" Tracy offered a pragmatic view.

I answered her rhetorical question to convince myself. "Making someone feel better. In this case, making a distraught woman feel better,"

"A distraught woman who tricked us." Tracy, again the pragmatic one.

"A distraught woman whose *daughter* tricked us." I offered a defense of Lillibet.

Tracy would not be dissuaded. "A distraught woman who helped her daughter trick us."

She was right.

"I don't owe Lillibet a thing."

Over our entrees, she changed tacks. "I can't argue with the idea that you don't owe Lillibet anything at all. But, you can't abandon the issue of uncovering the truth for Cassie and Jonathan."

"I can't do that, can I?"

Tracy's expression told me that I couldn't.

"So I'll have to talk to Parry."

"That's not for me to say." But Tracy was not saying it very clearly.

"Well, Lillibet did give us a new angle to explore. If Cassie knew that Julia was getting it on with Uncle Edward, that would give both Julia and Uncle Edward a motive to kill her. Julia came from money, but nothing like the Parry fortune. She had a lot to lose. Including her kids."

"Edward Baron had everything to lose, his job, his home. I have to think about this." Tracy stared across the restaurant. "Why that night?"

We considered that question and started our main course in silence.

I spoke first. "That night the Parrys showed Cassie what they really thought of people who were not *like them*. She saw how the family treated Jonathan and understood they would treat her no better. They could no longer rely on her to be discreet."

"Maybe she threatened them."

"But they would have paid her off." I leaned back in my chair signaling my disagreement with my own proposal.

"Remember her cousin said she had extremely high principles," Tracy countered. "Maybe she could not be bought off."

"Besides, Henry Parry was the one who had the money to buy her off. " I leaned forward, feeling positive again. "We don't know if Edward Baron did."

"But if Cassie revealed somehow, intentionally or not, that she knew about the affair, he had to find some way of controlling her."

"A confrontation of some sort might have developed. Maybe the situation escalated into a physical altercation. Seems hard to imagine among such circumspect people."

"It might have been an accident. That's easier to imagine than a cold-blooded murder," Tracy offered.

"Any argument can get out of control." I agreed but threw a wrench into the works. "And Jonathan?"

"Maybe he witnessed something he shouldn't have." Tracy came up with a quick answer.

"But he wanted into the Parry's world. He could have blackmailed his way in. Gotten Baron to be his mentor, defender. Wouldn't that have given him the best entrée ever?"

"Perhaps." Tracy considered my thought. "But he would

have known he wasn't wanted."

"What do you think? Should I try talking to Edward Baron before we approach Parry?"

"You could just let it go. You owe the Sadoskis nothing."

Back where we started.

"Yeah, let's forget about it. We were used." I sounded bitter. "At least the day in New York wasn't wasted. The food is as good as I remembered."

"I love it here. Food is great." Tracy thanked me for bringing her along on my trip down memory lane.

"You're welcome." I loved discussing my memories, our day, our meal and the dessert menu. We were polishing off our banana tarts when the topic of the Parrys came up again. "I liked taking an excursion with you even if we did hit a dead end." I hesitated. "Of course, we traveled a long way to get information we aren't going to use."

"And Edward Baron won't live forever and, after he's gone, we'll regret never talking to him," Tracy offered.

"And we weren't really investigating for Antonia Sadoski," I countered. "At least I wasn't. All my efforts were for Cassie."

"And Jonathan deserves justice," Tracy reminded me.

"And his brother would want to know the truth." I did feel an obligation to Tim O'Brien.

"Shall we stop to see Baron on our way home? We have a fairly good idea of where to find him."

"Actually, I know exactly where to find him. Remember, I did a drive-by. So, I guess we could do a drop-by."

Tracy shrugged as if to ask why not. "You know, often people are anxious to unburden themselves, simply waiting for someone to ask the right question."

"And we can do that?" I posed a question. "Without making him so angry he throws us out?"

"If we conspire on the train ride home, we can figure out a discreet way to do that." She sounded so confident. It might have been the Merlot talking.

"Maybe we should take a few days to think it over." My level of confidence, or alcohol consumption, did not match hers.

"No point in putting it off. Let's not allow the possibility to hang over our heads for the holidays. Besides, I think this is the type of feeling that could pass, but one we might regret letting go. How would we feel when one day in the not-that-distant future we hear the old guy has died—and with him our only chance to learn the truth?"

She was right.

"And, you do the talking. It's your case."

"I won't be accusatory." I made my intentions sound like a promise when in fact I understood I would be too frightened to be aggressive.

"Flatter him," Tracy advised.

"I'll flatter the Parrys. From what I've seen and heard, Edward Baron likes people who defer to the Parrys. I can discuss how wonderful Julia was and see if he runs with the topic."

"And if he doesn't?"

"I know. Be direct. Respectful but direct."

Chapter 34

"This place is nauseatingly tasteful," Tracy commented as we turned into the long driveway and stopped. At the top of the hill stood the old Parry mansion with a single white candle in each window lighting a wreath hanging above it. "At last, maybe I'll catch a bit of Christmas spirit."

"Yes, nothing brings out the holiday cheer more than the traditional murder accusation," I observed. No longer fueled by the buzz of our Christmas celebration, I wasn't feeling confident about our mission.

Tracy tried to reassure me. "No matter what you suspect, you have no proof that Baron killed anyone. You just want to eliminate that possibility to alleviate Lillibet's concerns and reunite her family so they can enjoy a happy Christmas." Tracy smirked. "Just keep reminding yourself of that," she said as if that had ever been our intent.

"Right, but we'll be clearing Baron. That does not automatically clear Parry. That does not do Lillibet any good."

"Maybe we'll find out something that clears Parry." Tracy had yet another rejoinder.

"We're way ahead of ourselves. We want the truth. Let's just see what Baron has to say, although the one thing I can predict about Edward Baron is that he will not incriminate Henry Parry."

The guest cottage on the Parry estate wasn't far from the main house but, tucked behind a row of tall pines, hard to see. Any other time of year we might have had trouble locating it, but not at Christmas when white lights made it look like a fairytale cottage in the middle of a fairytale woods. As if it weren't picturesque enough, light snow began to fall.

"No investigation has ever led me into a Currier and Ives print before." Tracy eyed the falling snow with wonder.

I viewed the precipitation with apprehension. "We should come back another time. The roads might get bad."

"Not for hours according to the weather report. Now, take your foot off the brake."

I did but wasn't feeling confident. "I don't know how to open the conversation."

"You'll be fine. Just . . . ."

"I know. Be direct," I said as we veered off the main drive. "We could pretend we are surprised to find this is the Parry estate. We could claim to be carolers out spreading seasonal joy."

"He doesn't need music. I can hear Mozart from here."

Ninety-year-olds, at least that particular ninety-year-old, played his music at a level that I could hear fifty yards away. So loud that we saw no indication that Baron heard the car pull up.

"Turn the car around," Tracy directed.

"Afraid of the snow?" I asked.

"In case of a quick getaway."

"That's not reassuring," I spoke to Tracy's back as she climbed out of the car.

I felt as if I were transported into a Christmas card as I caught up with Tracy on the path that led to a heavy wood door. Without hesitation, she lifted a brass "P" knocker in the center of a pinecone wreath and dropped it onto the metal plate. She then stepped aside and let me take the lead position.

"How will he ever hear us? Maybe we should give up?"

"Don't be so anxious to quit." Tracy rejected my proposal.

Tracy never gave up. Normally I saw that as a positive trait, but that night I wanted to give up.

"Try again." Tracy issued the order.

This time I handled the brass "P" but wasn't surprised that I got no response. I banged the knocker hard, so hard the door shook. If they couldn't hear me, maybe they would notice the vibrations. Luckily the music faded as I knocked again, but by the time Edward Baron opened the door the music blared even louder.

"Oh. Hello." The man seemed surprised and not at all pleased to see me. "I thought I heard something." His expression said he thought he also smelled something, and *something* wasn't good. He held up a finger and hurried away, the way someone his age hurries. After the volume on the music dropped, Edward Baron reappeared.

"Miss Tracy. Am I correct?" He hesitated only a second. "You must come in." Not because he wanted me to, but because it was night, it was cold, it was Christmas, and, above all, he was a proper gentleman.

As I stepped inside I found myself doing a pantomime: cold person warming up in welcoming environment. I rubbed my hands together and stamped my feet, albeit in a genteel fashion. I let my eyes reflect my admiration for the Christmas wonderland I had stepped into—a reaction completely at odds with my mission, but I didn't seem able to stop myself. I continued to rub my hands together with great theatricality as I introduced Tracy. "This is my niece, Tracy Shaw. I believe I told you about the class she teaches. Tracy, this is Edward Baron. Mr. Parry's friend and law partner." Even at the lower decibel level, Baron appeared to strain to hear me over the music.

"Nice to meet you, Ms. Shaw," he lied. Not very convincingly. The weak handshake that he offered each of us provided proof of his deception.

He crossed the hallway in six small steps and we followed him to the archway into a large room with beams so old that, at some point, they probably had been functional. They, like all the antiques in the room, appeared authentic.

"Henry," he yelled. "Henry." While he walked to the sound system and turned down the volume further, my stomach did a backflip. We hadn't planned on calling on Baron with Parry around.

Henry responded to lowered sound. He frowned at Baron. "Now I can barely hear the music."

Baron planted himself in front of Parry and pointed our way. "You remember Miss Tracy. Tonight she brought her family to see us."

I stepped into a sitting room lit only by the white lights of a tall Christmas tree and a small reading lamp next to Parry. Dressed in a smoking jacket as if he had escaped from a 1930s comedy of manners, Parry leaned on the tall arm of the sofa and covered his extended legs with a Hudson Bay blanket. He closed his book on his lap and rested his half-glasses on top. That took a full minute. All the while he held tight to a crystal brandy snifter.

"Ah. How nice. Do come in. Please have a seat. Edward." In his tone, I perceived a command as he waved his arms towards a cluster of chairs in the corner.

While Baron shuffled off to add overhead light and fetch seating, Parry called us forward. He shook my hand and then Tracy's as she introduced herself.

"Welcome. Merry Christmas to each of you. Excuse me for not rising, but the legs, you know. Not what they used to be. Sorry for the delay in getting you seated but we tucked those chairs away so they did not block the view of the tree. We don't get a lot of visitors these days."

"It's lovely," I said and Tracy murmured words of admiration for the tree, tall and full with long needles. Pine. Spruce. I didn't know. I did know it came from the expensive section of the lot. Wait, who I was kidding? This tree didn't come from any makeshift Christmas tree shop. It came from a florist, probably with the red bows and white lights attached. But not the silver ornaments.

"Every year I add at least one ornament. Of course, with

every year I require a taller tree. The poor thing labors under the weight of all that sterling. Over seventy years' worth." Parry seemed to drift off to relive every one of them.

Tracy grabbed the straight-back chair that Baron was trying to push toward us. When he shuffled back to get another, she did the same. With a crook of his finger that I saw as an order, Baron pointed to a spot facing Henry Parry who sat sideways on the sofa with a view of the tree that we now blocked. Tracy moved the two chairs into position.

Parry waited until we were settled to speak. "So, I imagine you have come here with news about our maid and that young man. Good news I hope." He smiled.

"Cassie and Jonathan," Tracy said pointedly. I felt fairly certain that neither Henry nor Baron got her point.

We'd come to talk to Edward Baron, but it became clear that no one talked to Edward Baron when Henry Parry was in the room. He had made himself the center of attention. Baron mumbled something about turning off the music and wandered off into a corner.

"Mr. Parry, we don't think that Cassie and Jonathan were attacked while they were parking. We think the killer moved the car to make the crime look like a carjacking."

I observed no reaction to the news. Parry simply gazed into space. "I guess that is a reasonable conclusion. But why did you decide on that scenario?"

If I thought I would feel uncomfortable directing carefully couched accusations at Edward Baron, I had no idea of the level of discomfort I'd feel doing the same thing in Henry Parry's presence. I thought of saying, *just wanted you to know that, thanks for your time*. I might have if Tracy hadn't been sitting beside me. But Tracy would be a witness to my cowardice. Fueled by her advice *people want to unburden themselves, you are doing them a favor,* I moved on to the difficult topic.

"As you know, I've been wondering what happened to those two young people so long ago."

"Tragic," Parry said.

"Tragic." From behind me, I heard Baron mimic Parry.

I wanted to say *maybe we should come back another time, maybe after Christmas.* I willed Tracy to say it, but she remained silent. We'd come this far. I couldn't back off, but my enthusiasm for confrontation was waning. The zeal that propelled me out of New York no longer exerted any influence over me. Perhaps all the symbols of the Christmas season placated me.

"And looking into things sometimes we hear rumors, ugly rumors that we have to dispel." I could not have sounded more uncomfortable. "You realize that maids sometimes see things they don't want to. Know things they shouldn't. Maybe they keep quiet about those things because the people they work for are nice to them. They make them think they are part of the family. But if something happened to make them feel unappreciated. Maybe they see how their employers really felt about them and *people like them.*" The very use of the phrase drove the Christmas spirit from me. I remembered my mission. "Maybe they wouldn't be as likely to keep those secrets."

Parry looked to Baron. "I don't understand what she is jabbering on about." He maintained a cordial expression. Was it the point I was trying to make that he didn't comprehend? Or the actual words?

I faced Baron. "From what we've learned, we think *you* do, Mr. Baron. Perhaps we could speak in private."

"I have no secrets from Mr. Parry."

I glanced at Tracy and she nodded encouragement. I continued. "It occurred to me, I mean I wondered if . . . ." I fought letting my innate politeness get in the way of my job. *People like us. People like us.* Remember what these men are really like. "I wanted to ask if, before her death, Cassie became privy to family secrets." Privy. *Who talked like that?* Well, these two would. "I wondered if she threatened you."

Baron forced a chuckle. "What could the Parrys' girl

211

possibly know about me that would allow her to threaten me?"

The Parrys' girl. Baron's choice of words provided an incentive to keep going.

"I don't want to discuss this in front of Mr. Parry." I glanced at the man on the couch, watching us intently and straining to hear. Aside from his preference for loud music, I had no proof that his hearing would not pick up our conversation. I lowered my voice in the hope that only Baron would hear.

"I would just like to clear this up."

"Why? Who are you? What does it matter?"

What does it matter? Yet another incentive.

"It matters."

"What is she saying?" Parry sounded irritated.

Baron raised his voice at Parry. "She asking about that night again." He stared at me with eyes full of defiance. "Go ahead. I have nothing to hide." Baron didn't sound so much defensive as disgusted by the idea that the likes of us might have discovered something unpleasant about the likes of him. With effort, Baron moved closer and sat on the arm of a leather wing chair. An old man affecting a young man's pose.

"I have to ask this question." I spoke to myself. Otherwise, I would have found a million reasons to avoid asking it.

Baron shifted gears. "I don't see why you are uncomfortable. You are not conducting an official investigation. As we've said, both Mr. Parry and I approve of your efforts, so we are happy to answer any questions you have. Any appropriate questions."

I felt a little nauseated. Baron would definitely consider my question inappropriate. "You can imagine how I hate to ask this. I have been led to believe that Cassie might have been aware of an improper relationship between you and Mr. Parry's wife, Julia."

Baron's anger rose to the surface in a nano-second. He tried to rise as well but instead slid onto the seat cushion of the wing chair. "That is a disgusting insinuation and a most inappropriate question. We are trying to be cooperative but that is a ludicrous charge and an insult to the memory of a wonderful woman." He leaned back shaking his head. "And if it were true, what possible link would there be to the death of those two young people? Disgusting," he mumbled. "If you continue with this line of inquiry, we will have to ask you to leave. I have no idea what makes you think that you have the right . . . ."

Part of me agreed that I did not have the right, but luckily the guy's attitude riled me, giving me the nerve to continue. Besides, I'd already offended him. Why stop now? I felt Tracy's support so I shifted in my chair to face him. "You were living here and working at Parry, Shippen, Weathersby and Baron. You were totally dependent on the goodwill of Henry Parry. He could not find out. You had to protect your lifestyle so if Cassie threatened to . . ." I fought for the right words ". . . blow the whistle, she would have had to go. She was only a maid. And maybe she told Jonathan. After the way Mr. Parry treated him that night, he wasn't about to keep any family secrets."

I couldn't believe what I was implying. Who was I kidding? I couldn't believe what I was saying. I had come into a man's home, an influential man's home, an influential man's secluded home and accused him of murder. Even worse, I had put my niece in danger by including her in my hare-brained scheme. Sure, she backed this plan, but responsibility for our safety fell to the senior person, me. I had not thought this through.

Baron also had an issue with disbelief. "I can't believe your audacity in coming into my home on Mr. Parry's estate and making such ridiculous charges."

I actually agreed. Silently. I figured Baron wasn't strong enough to eject me physically, but I waited for a brutal verbal attack. That didn't happen.

"Because you are here and because your charges are ludicrous, let me clarify," Baron said.

Suddenly I heard Parry's voice. "None of this would have happened if we were born fifty years later. There would have been nothing to hide."

Chapter 35

In response to Parry's voice, I turned to face him.

"Henry, I don't think these ladies are interested in our personal lives." Baron leaned forward but could not get to his feet. "Henry, do you hear me. Do not bore these people with the mundane details of our private lives." Now the lackey gave the master orders. "Do you hear me?"

I didn't know if Parry did or not. He ignored Baron. "You can't imagine the pain of living your youth adhering to strict conventions and your old age watching young people live with such freedom and joy. Showing the world exactly what they are, who they are."

I didn't notice it happening, but Edward had managed to get to his feet. He stepped in front of Tracy and me with his back to Parry. For the first time, I saw concern on his face. Not anger. Not condescension. Fear. Real fear, hidden under the façade of a jovial grin. "Mr. Parry's grasp of the truth is a little tenuous on occasion." His voice quivered.

I stood up and stepped around Edward so I could see Henry. He stared into space as he continued. "If only the boy had not behaved in such an insubordinate manner."

"Henry, think of your reputation, your descendants, your family name." Edward's tone revealed his desperation.

"Family name! Do you think anyone cares about our family name in this day and age?"

"People care." Edward sounded convinced.

"No. They don't. Maybe they never did. We thought they cared. We tried to make them care, but did anyone?" He stared into space considering his last thought. "It is time to tell them, Edward. I insist."

I redirected my attention to Baron.

"Henry, I see no reason . . . ."

Parry interrupted. Apparently, *he* saw a reason. "Edward. If you don't tell the story, I will."

Defeated easily by Parry's command, Baron sank back into the same leather chair from which he'd so recently escaped. He stuttered and made false starts for a minute before he found the right words. "We had a family rule never to intrude on Uncle Edward. No one came down here. But that boy. That aggressive, ill-bred wanna-be." Edward's voice gained strength as anger surged through him. He moved his head back and forth with slow but strong and deliberate moves. Whatever had enraged him over sixty years before enraged him again.

*****Edward Baron*****
Guest Cottage, Parry Estate,
Philadelphia, Pennsylvania
April 21, 1956

Even through the dusk, he could see that Henry was in an agitated state. An extremely agitated state. He'd been about to pull the drapes when he spotted Henry charging towards the cottage. The strength of his stride and the scowl on his face said something had happened. Edward abandoned the curtains and rushed to greet him.

He took the putter from Henry's hand and leaned it against the door so his arms would be free to pull his friend into the hallway and into his embrace.

"What happened? Tell me."

"The children . . . ,"

Henry became too upset to continue and Edward could imagine why. The next generation of Parrys had been making some very inappropriate choices.

"Now, Henry. Chip is barely out of his teens and Blair is still a teenager. These silly follies will pass."

"But after all we've been through to uphold the family

216

name. All the secrecy, the hiding, and they seem willing to throw it all away. They behave so inappropriately, so differently."

Edward patted Henry's back as he would a baby's. "Don't worry. It will be okay. I will make sure it is. Don't I always take care of things?" He put a finger under Henry's chin and raised his head so he could plant a light kiss on his lips. As he pulled back, he saw it. Just an impression of motion out of the corner of his eye.

"Edward. What is wrong?"

"I'm not sure." He grabbed the putter and ran out the door. He spotted a figure scurrying along the tall wall of pines that hid the cottage from the main house. He was sure he knew who the individual was. "Stop. Young man. Please. It's not what it looks like."

The kid turned his head and Edward realized he'd been right. He recognized him from the brief meeting that afternoon: Blair's unsuitable suitor. The boy looked back but kept walking. When he spoke his tone was harsh. "I may not be a socialite but I am not an idiot. It's exactly what it looks like."

"Brien?" Henry called from the cottage door with a voice that betrayed his confusion.

Confirmation. The interloper was Blair's undesirable date. A nobody. He felt his entire body relax. He could manage this situation. "Henry, our visitor appears to have gotten the wrong impression. I think you should tell him how distraught you felt about what happened between you." He looked over his shoulder to meet his beloved's eyes and nodded.

Henry's confusion melted into understanding and compliance. "I've been so upset. I am sorry for what I said earlier."

"If you aren't now, you will be." The punk paused to spit the words.

"Mr. Brien. Jonathan. Please," Henry called after him.

217

It sickened Edward to hear Henry beseech the young man in that tone, but it had to be done. The situation had to be managed.

"What was it you said to me about hiding the truth?" Brien pointed at Henry. "I was wrong to hide who I really was. Maybe I am wrong to be ashamed of where I came from. At least I'm not a pervert."

"Son." After the one harsh word, Henry erased the severity from his tone. When he continued, his voice was even, unemotional. "There is no reason to use that kind of language. Apparently, you've gotten a wrong impression."

"I saw."

"I don't know what you think you saw, but come inside and we'll discuss this reasonably."

The snooping intruder had the temerity to wave a finger at Henry. "Now you want to talk. Well, maybe now I am the one who's not ready."

Edward recognized these types, understood how to handle them. He stepped in with an attempt to pacify him. "Jonathan, we must resolve this misunderstanding."

"There was no misunderstanding here."

"If you insist on holding onto your notion of what you believe you witnessed, we can still resolve the issue. We can give you everything you want. Come back. Let's talk." He held out his arm, an offer to guide the boy into the cottage.

"Talk? What's left to say? Your fairy friend made it perfectly clear what he thought of me." Jonathan stared at the two men with contempt before he turned to walk away.

Edward took a step forward as if his motion could hold Jonathan in place. "Think of the possibilities. A career. A place in the Parry family."

Jonathan stopped. Ah, we have him, Edward thought. So predictable. These types are all the same. The young man looked over his shoulder at Edward. This type was always willing to listen. Edward remained calm as he addressed Henry. "Blair loves him. Let her have him."

"No, Blair doesn't love me." Jonathan faced the two men. "She loves the man Daddy tells her to. Big mistake, Mr. Parry. Big mistake."

Edward was growing exasperated. They could make the young man an offer he would not be able to walk away from if they could compel him to stop and listen. The question was simply how far the kid could push them. "Mr. Brien. I think you are under an erroneous impression, but you understand the damage such a false allegation could do."

The kid ignored him and spoke to Henry. "Nothing would give me more pleasure than telling the world." He raised his voice and yelled, "Henry Parry is a big phony."

Edward's exasperation escalated to anger. "Don't you raise your voice to Mr. Parry, you impudent upstart."

"I will talk to him however I damn well please." He resumed yelling. "Queer. Liar. Pretender. Phony. Pervert."

"How dare you speak to Mr. Parry that way? He is a fine gentleman and you are nothing but an inconsequential piece of garbage."

Jonathan threw a dismissive wave in Edward's direction, turned and walked away still screaming. "Pervert. Phony."

"Shut up. Come back here and apologize to Mr. Parry."

Jonathan threw another dismissive wave, this one behind his back.

"I told you to stop."

"Pervert."

"You listen to me. You stop and apologize."

But the boy didn't stop. Within seconds, he would make the turn around the hedges onto the wide lawn. Once he did, Edward would never be able to keep the situation under control. "Stop. I command you. Stop."

Jonathan took another step and Edward felt he had no choice. He ran forward and halted the kid's forward motion with a single stroke of the golf club to his head. The boy let out a low grunt and collapsed to the ground. He lay on his stomach with his head turned to the side, eyes open, too

219

stunned to move. Edward could see the puzzlement in his eyes. What did he believe? That he would let him walk away? That he could let him walk away.

The boy didn't resist or attempt to avoid Edward's blows. He stared into space as Edward brought the club down on his head repeatedly. "Who do you think you are? Talking like that. To Henry Parry. You aren't fit to polish his shoes."

Edward didn't count the strokes. He suspected there might have been a dozen before, shocked by his own behavior, he tossed the club aside and backed away.

"Edward. What have you done?" Henry's voice expressed despair.

"He had no right to talk to you that way. Who was he to talk to you like that? He was going to leave, to tell people what he saw. I had to stop him before he left." He pointed to the end of the hedges and that was when he saw her. Cassie, frozen in position. She wore a tan raincoat over her black uniform dress and carried a cheap plastic handbag. She, heading home, must have heard the commotion on her way down the driveway.

"I heard . . . ." She sputtered a few senseless comments before she made a full sentence come out. "Mr. Baron, what did he do? Why did you hit him?"

Edward moved closer to Cassie as he explained. "He'd gotten out of control, attacking Mr. Parry. I didn't want to strike him but I had to. To stop him."

"We have to call an ambulance. I'll go." She started to turn but Edward stepped forward and extended his arm as if to block her.

"No. Wait. I'll call. It's faster to call from the cottage. You come here and stay with the boy. He needs someone." He stepped away, making a show of going to the phone, not to the golf club lying on the grass.

Cassie took tiny steps towards Jonathan as if afraid to find what she knew she would.

"Is he breathing?" Edward pasted a concerned look on his face, but Cassie wasn't looking. Her attention remained focused on the youth sprawled on the grass. Edward bent slowly and grabbed the club.

"I don't know. He isn't moving." She knelt beside Jonathan's motionless body. "Jonathan." She leaned over the young man trying to get a response. "His eyes are open but . . . ." She focused on his bleeding scalp. "I don't understand. There's so much blood. What happened?"

"As I told you." Edward waited until he stood behind her, looking over her shoulder at the bleeding boy before he raised his arms and acted quickly before she could notice. He heard Henry's cry as he brought the club down on Cassie's head. Without a sound, she fell across Jonathan. Just to be sure, Edward hit her one more time.

When he turned away from the bodies, he faced Henry's accusatory look. "We had no choice, Henry. We have been through too much to lose everything, to lose each other."

Edward, feeling nervous and defensive, waited for Henry to respond. His heart filled with fear that he had lost Henry forever. After a full minute, Henry, staring at the two bodies, stepped forward and pulled a linen handkerchief monogrammed with the letter P from his pocket. He did not say a word as he handed it to Edward. Henry wrapped an arm around his lover as Edward wiped the blood from the golf club. He kissed his hair and whispered in his ear. "Everything will be fine. We will make everything fine." He pulled him into a firm embrace.

They both heard the gasp. The noise resembled the cry of an animal, a plaintive, frightening sound that Edward had encountered only once on the African veldt. He reacted to the horror on Julia's face with the most complex set of emotions he'd ever experienced. Fear. Dismay. Relief. But then relief moved to the forefront. She knew. At last, Julia knew.

She opened her mouth to speak but found no words.

221

Edward understood that it wasn't the sight of the bodies, but the sight of her husband embracing Edward that silenced her. Henry's arm remained around him, offering more than support. She had to see the way their legs and hips touched and sensed the bond that held their bodies together. He saw no surprise. He could imagine her filtering the memories of so many years. She'd known him longer than anyone. Until he'd met Henry she'd known him better than anyone else. On some level, she had to have known. Always. Just as Henry's parents must have known although they never admitted it. Why would they have allowed their son to marry at such a young age to such an unsuitable match, a Catholic, after such a superficial protest?

Edward loved Julia like a sister, but he wasn't responsible for her naiveté. Time she came to terms with reality. As her expression changed from heartbroken to defeated, he felt no sadness. At last, they would no longer have to live a lie.

But, of course, Julia offered another problem to be dealt with. As she took in the entire scene, she staggered backward. When she turned towards the house, Edward pulled himself from Henry's embrace. "You'll have to handle her."

Henry went after his wife, passing the bodies without a glance. Edward didn't mind being left to take care of things. That was what he did. He took care of things. He knelt beside the body and reached into the kid's pocket. As he hoped, he found car keys. He'd seen the vulgar little sports car up at the main house. He knew what he had to do.

Before Henry returned, he had devised a plan, moved the car from the upper driveway, loaded the bodies into the trunk, and put the top up. Fate had been kind. The social climber had a set of golf clubs in his trunk. Good clubs, he thought as he pulled the putter out of the bag. Same make as Henry's. What a shame to send a perfectly good club to the bottom of the pond when it could just slip into Henry's bag

222

to replace the missing putter. But the actual murder weapon and the alleged murder weapon both had to disappear. He couldn't help smiling at the irony.

He slammed the trunk closed and, figuring it would not be for the last time that night, he returned to the cottage and changed into clean clothes.

Getting the bodies into the car had not been half as difficult as getting them out. He had less time in the small parking area. He didn't know who might be watching. He pulled Jonathan's body from the trunk and dumped Cassie's on top of it. He didn't have time to figure out how they should be arranged. A killer wouldn't, he reckoned.

He figured no longer than five minutes passed between the time he drove into a corner of the deserted picnic area and the time he drove out, leaving two bodies in a heap behind him. He made sure to obey the speed limit as he drove into Germantown, to the spot where Henry waited. The flashy style of the kid's car concerned him but didn't attract any unwarranted attention, even when he pulled the convertible alongside a curb on a street with a park on one side and a row of houses opposite. As he walked, slowly and casually, towards the dark and conservative sedan he could see the light of Henry's cigarette. The light in the car did not go on as he opened the door. Henry had followed his advice to turn it off before he left home. He read that as a sign Henry had overcome his nervousness and his qualms about going along with the plan.

"I wondered if the Brien boy offered Cassie a ride home?" Henry appeared more amused than worried, proud of his contribution.

"That sounds like a possibility but we wouldn't know that would we, Henry, since we had driven out to get cigars. We should have known the store would be closed, shouldn't we?" Baron embellished.

"We should have but we so seldom find ourselves in the position of needing them. I think when I get home I will leave

*a note for Cassie expressing my disappointment that she
allowed my humidor to remain empty and reminding her to
remedy the situation before I return from work."*

"Good idea, Henry. Good idea."

*****

"We never spoke of it again." Henry injected when
Edward paused.

"Never?" I asked amazed and appalled. I could see by
the look on Tracy's face that she felt just as shocked.

"It was over. We could not change what had happened.
We dealt with the staff and contributed to both funerals but
never discussed how or why those actions were necessary.
What good would rehashing the situation do?"

"In all these years, it never came up?" I asked one more
time.

"Mr. Parry doesn't like to deal with unpleasantness. He
has the most positive attitude. We put the event behind us
and carried on."

I stared at Edward Baron, who appeared content with his
explanation.

"Until last summer." Parry spoke.

I turned to face him.

"I was surprised to find the recollection resurfacing on
occasion. A function of aging, I suppose. I had not thought
of that night in years. The situation had been handled. The
police never spoke to Edward. Naturally, I cooperated when
they came to inquire. And, of course, I had that discussion
with Julia."

"And *she* never mentioned that night again?" I asked. I
knew people who could compartmentalize, but this crowd
was ridiculous.

Henry closed his eyes. "Poor girl."

For a second, I thought he meant Cassie but he was
referring to his wife.

224

"She'd had quite a shock about our marriage that night. Although I always believed that, on some level, she'd understood all along. She'd known Edward since childhood. She'd been his best friend, but surprisingly she did not fully comprehend such things. I guess that level of naiveté wasn't that odd in those days, but I was still amazed. It took me some time to calm her, but I made her listen to reason. She agreed to keep up the façade of our marriage. After all, we had children to protect."

From the truth about their father? What about the truth of what happened to two innocent people that night?

Henry was still gazing into the past. "What I was, the kind of man I was, was scandalous in those years. Illegal, you know. There were a few fellows suspected of being queer, as we would say. They were great fun at dinner parties, you know, but they could not live the way Henry Parry needed to."

"And the murder?" I asked.

"Murder? You make it sound so sinister." He stared into space. His head shook but I wasn't sure the motion was voluntary. "I never thought of what happened as murder. It was an accident, a horrible misunderstanding. Had you witnessed the event, you would have seen that emotions were running high."

Had Parry become delusional or did he intend to rewrite history?

"If you viewed what happened as an accident at the time, why didn't you call the police?"

I could not read any emotion on his face as he spoke. "We couldn't have such a scandalous occurrence on our property. It would have been in all the papers. There would have been an investigation. We couldn't plunge our family, the firm, into scandal. I explained to Julia that when the police came she could honestly tell them she did not know what had happened to the two young people we barely knew. I never told her the full story so that was, in a way, the truth."

A very peculiar way.

I detected nothing of the supplicant in Edward's voice as he asked, "What are you going to do?"

Edward spoke to me but Henry answered. "We are going to do the right thing. God knows we can get the best representation."

Edward opened his mouth to speak but gave up. He looked lovingly at Henry Sr. "Please. What transpired wasn't his fault. Henry is a good man, a gentle man. He always was. That's why I love him." He moved to his lover's side and wrapped his arms around his shoulders.

Tracy and I had gotten ourselves into a situation that had moved beyond uncomfortable. We now knew a secret that Baron and Parry had killed to hide. Actually, we knew secrets far worse than the one the two men had originally conspired to conceal. And, we were alone with them in an isolated cottage. My eyes met Tracy's and I could tell her thoughts were moving in the same direction.

We could easily flee—I gave thanks that we had not let Baron take our coats—but a sudden departure might alarm the couple. I looked around for golf clubs and didn't spot any, but I did notice what appeared to be a complete set of fireplace accessories. However, a hefty instrument would probably not be the nonagenarians' weapon of choice this time around. I kept waiting for Baron to make a move for a gun, but he stayed put, with his arms wrapped around Parry. But wasn't a similar pose the last thing Jonathan saw when he decided to walk away?

Tracy's slight nod said, *we gotta get out of here.* I pulled a piece of paper out of my handbag and copied Lillibet Sadoski's New York number from my phone.

"You might want to give your daughter a call. This is Lillibet's number."

Neither man reacted to the mention of the long-lost Parry child.

"That's it?" Baron looked up but never loosened his grip on his lover.

"The rest is up to you." I decided as I spoke. "Talk to Lillibet. I will wait three days before I contact her."

With that, Tracy and I rose in unison and backed to the entrance, out the door and almost all the way to our car. "I guess they are just too old to follow us," Tracy said.

We turned and ran the rest of the way.

"Or maybe they don't want to harbor any more secrets," I said as I pulled the car door shut. But just in case they had other plans in mind, or weapons, I gunned the engine. We tore down the long driveway and out the gate before the twosome could decide they could not let us get away.

I was so focused on our getaway that we were in front of Tracy's house before I realized that I had at last located the spot where Cassie and Jonathan had drawn their last breaths.

Chapter 36

"You really didn't think this through," said Alex, the same Alex who had encouraged Tracy and me to look at the murder of Cassie Kelly and Jonathan Brien. "What did you think you would do when you found the actual culprit?"

"As far as we knew, no personal contact brought this investigation to us. What would ever make me think I would uncover a killer in the family of the individual who set me off on this hunt?" I was arguing with myself as much as with Alex.

"But why would it matter? You identified a murderer. A hundred-year-old murderer but a murderer. It's age discrimination if you don't turn him in. Not to mention obstruction of justice and possibly accessory after the fact." Alex sounded confident.

The smell of pine needles and the soft Christmas tree lights in Tracy's living room created an ambiance completely at odds with the conversation.

"What do you think?" I asked Tracy.

"I think we give those two old guys time to do the right thing." She curled up on the couch with a butter cookie from the tray of assorted pastries Alex had baked while we were out investigating.

"Why would they?" I protested in what sounded a lot like a screech.

"They wouldn't. They won't." Alex offered. "They got away with murder for sixty years. What do you care if you know that? It's your word against theirs. And, no insult, but even now they have a lot more clout than you do."

"So it's futile to do anything?" I asked. "But it must be a crime to do nothing."

228

Tracy remained calm. "You gave them three days to act before you call Lillibet. It isn't as if the police are going to burst through our door and arrest you for obstruction. It's been sixty years. What's the worst that could happen in three days? I don't think they are going to kill again."

"Unless they decide they need to knock you two off." Alex, studying the plate of cookies on the ottoman, didn't feel our stares. "What?" He asked when he sat back with a chocolate chip in his hands. "It's a joke. They are old guys. They couldn't hurt you if they wanted to."

"No, but they could hire someone." I pointed out what seemed obvious to me.

"Like the world's most polite thug." Tracy reminded us of my encounter at the Wawa. "I am sure Baron got some poor investigator they have on retainer to toss some scary words at you. Intimidation is one thing, but I don't think he'd find anyone to kill for him." She paused and I could tell by the look on her face that she doubted her own assertion. "Of course, if he sent one of the firm's senior investigators . . . ." She left the thought unfinished but I knew what she meant. We had no idea of the qualifications required to do investigative work for a firm that seldom lost.

"Say you do go to the police," Alex waved his cookie at me, "the cops will feel obligated to follow up. Do you really believe they will be able to arrest those two guys? No way. They have no evidence. But they might talk to the old folks and that will really make those guys mad. Who knows what revenge they would take? You have no obligation to go to the police at the risk of your own safety." He spoke the words as if he had received a degree from the Harvard Law School.

Tracy's was the voice of reason. "Let's give it the three days and see what the Parry family does."

They did nothing that we knew about until the third day when the front desk attendant at my apartment building announced that I had a visitor. Could she send Ms. Sadoski up? I said yes although I did not know which one to expect.

Lillibet appeared at my apartment door. I invited her in without asking how she found me. Finding people wasn't hard enough in the age of the Internet to warrant a question. Plus there wasn't time. She didn't even wait until we sat down to tell me. She was following me into the living area when she broke the news. "Uncle Edward died last night."

I stopped in my tracks waiting to see if guilt or relief was going to win the fight for my reaction.

"No, you don't have to feel responsible. I've processed all that guilt for you." She stopped to admire my view: electronic Christmas greetings running around the PECO building. "I wondered if his death was my fault, sending you, dredging all this up, upsetting old men. The story is not that simple. It turns out that my father and Uncle Edward have been arguing about taking the story to the authorities since last summer. Uncle Edward wouldn't hear of it. My father was told he has cancer and that compelled him to come clean about his life—especially that night. He told you the story and all that those events revealed?"

My eyes closed in time with the small nod that confirmed my knowledge.

"The news about their relationship was quite a shock, although now I feel naïve that I never considered the possibility that they were more than friends and law partners. But that is not what I came to discuss. Uncle Edward." She reset the topic. "The police took him away this morning after a tragic accident. It seems that last night after my father drifted off, Uncle Edward went out in his pajamas and a robe to bring in some wood. He slipped in the snow and apparently he couldn't get up. He froze to death." She stared at me. "I can see by your face that your first thought is the same as mine. Very convenient and easily staged. Difficult to prove, however."

She was as brisk as the cold night air that killed her Uncle Edward.

"What do I think? I believe my uncle was loyal to my father until the end. He did not want to see his legacy soiled. Poor Uncle Edward, so worried about protecting a name that wasn't even his. Among those of us who have heard the story, no one disputes that Uncle Edward was the murderer. I am sure that in his mind his death eliminated the need for confession. The killer is dead. There is no need to expose my father's role. Who even knows what charges could be brought against him?"

Even I, who was not a partner at a leading Philadelphia law firm, had some good ideas but I did not bring them up.

Lillibet continued. "My father will be dead soon. His days were short before, but I can't imagine he'll survive the shock of Uncle Edward's death, knowing what I now understand about their relationship."

"But you said your father wanted to come clean, to fess up to what happened. Now that your Uncle Edward is dead, he won't be there to stop his confession."

"Right now, my father's focus has shifted from a need to bare his soul to an unwillingness to speak ill of the dead."

She paused but I felt no need to fill the silence. She had more to say.

"I thought I wanted to know what happened that night but now that my worst fears have been realized, I regret that I did not let sleeping dogs lie."

I wished she had done that too, but I didn't say so. I asked, "What are you going to do?"

"I'm staying at the house with my father. Before this morning he seemed determined to make a clean breast of it. To the police I mean. But there were a lot of police in and out of that cottage today and he didn't say a thing. I am not sure I see the point of making all this public." Her tone melted slightly. "I thought I wanted to see him punished, but now I don't know. He's old. He's contrite. I mean given the circumstances of his life . . . ." I heard her take a deep breath. "I had no idea. He must have suffered."

231

I had little sympathy for her father and less for Baron. I felt tempted to feel bad, because of societal restraints when they came of age. I could relate to their sadness and frustration, but so many men and women suffered through those times and never felt they had the need, or even worse the right, to kill.

"I have to admit that in a way 1950s society killed Cassie and Jonathan. If there had been no need to keep secrets, the situation never would have happened." But then I recalled their arrogance. "But it did. For my own protection, I am going to assume that your father is going to handle the legal aspects of this case. I do, however, feel obligated to tell the victims' families what I've learned."

I conducted this inquiry on her daughter's behest, but I didn't do it for Lillibet. We had no contract. I felt no loyalty, except to the victims.

"I won't try to stop you. That isn't to say we won't deny the story if it is made public." Her tone got even softer. "I had fantasies of my father doing a perp walk, my proud, arrogant father, humiliated, disgraced. But that is not the man I've seen these past few days. The one I should get back to."

Chapter 37

On Christmas Eve Alex made an elaborate brunch for Tracy and me before he left for his parents' house. Talk inevitably turned to our investigation. How could it not after Tracy and I emptied our stockings from Alex? Latex gloves. Fingerprint kit. Plastic evidence bags.

"I figure if you girls are not going to stop these forays into detective work, you should have the proper tools." He raised a cup of eggnog to toast us. "To another successful investigation."

"Hear, hear." Tracy clicked her cup against his and then mine. "You might want to take the lead more often. Good job."

"It's not over yet. I'll contact Jonathan's brother and Cassie's cousin after the holidays. If they want to go to the authorities, they can. Although I have no idea what action they could expect authorities to take on the confession to a sixty-year-old crime by a man who is now deceased. The Parrys will deny the story. They'll never let their father confess even if he still wants to. And, there is no evidence. But at least the families will have the truth." I looked for Tracy or Alex to disagree with me, but neither did.

"Poor Cassie. All she wanted to do was help." Tracy's face expressed the sadness she felt for the young girl with dreams.

"Jonathan doesn't come out of it quite as well." I wondered how Tim O'Brien would take the story.

"You would think that I, of all people, would condemn Jonathan for his homophobia, but I am not convinced he believed all those horrid things he shouted at those guys."

Tracy and I both turned to Alex.

"I know. I sound terrifically understanding, don't I? What a mensch! But I am serious. He was a straight guy of the 1950s. He might not have thought their sexual behavior was despicable, but he knew the world would. Having said that, I doubt he approved of their relationship. But, I also doubt that he was the kind of fellow who would taunt gay guys on the street. He was a reflection of his times. And, he was angry. From the sound of him, that might have been the most emotional night of his life. If he were born in the 1980s instead of 1930s, we might have been friends." Alex paused. "Okay, the social-climbing thing would have been a problem. So maybe not friends, but I am not sure he would have been my enemy."

"I agree that his outrage wasn't sparked by moral indignation over their sexual proclivities. He died because he couldn't control his frustration at being called a pretender by the biggest pretender of them all." I might have reacted the same way.

"We don't know him. We never will." Tracy threw her hands in the air in a display of exasperation. "If he'd been calmer that night, he might have been perfectly happy to use what he knew to blackmail his way into the life he wanted."

Alex the Pragmatic turned to me. "Do you regret not letting the Parrys buy *you* off?"

"They never tried to bribe me."

"Too bad." Alex sighed. "Although the family might still try to purchase your ongoing silence."

"Aunt Julia wouldn't do something like that, would you?" Tracy defended my honor.

"Of course not." I defended myself with less certitude.

"But you might consider a date with Chip Parry?" An ever-hopeful Alex asked. "New Year's Eve is just around the corner."

"You want me to get mixed up with a family of murderers?"

"One. One accessory. Not even an actual killer. Aside

234

from one bad apple, the Parrys are a fine old family."

"You mean a rich old family."

"Maybe." Alex eyed the presents piled under the tall tree in Tracy's living room. "Not to be mercenary, but you give some pretty nice gifts as it is. I'd love to see what I might score if you had a fortune behind you."

"Keep dreaming. I doubt Chip is very fond of the woman who forced the truth to light."

Tracy disagreed. "You didn't put Henry Parry in his predicament. He put himself in that situation. I watched him while Baron told his story. I think Parry was ready to let go, to set things right. I believe he didn't want to die with the guilt on his conscience. If his family and advisors don't hold him back—and let's face it, it's likely they will—I bet he still would."

"The harder part might have been confessing to his family. I was responsible for that."

"You didn't force him. You just made it easier for him to confess." Tracy comforted me.

"And, Lillibet and her daughter paved the way," I reminded her as well as myself.

"Don't forget you reunited the family. I bet the Parrys are spending this Christmas together, after fifty years apart. You two can take credit for that." Alex waved his eggnog at Tracy and me.

"Now there is a wall where I'd like to be a visiting fly." Tracy expressed my thought. "And, one other good thing came out of the case."

Alex and I turned to Tracy. We couldn't find much good in the sad series of events.

"I got to tell Ed Hayley that he was wrong." She turned to Alex. "My know-it-all student." She toasted Ed Hayley. "Always certain, seldom right."

We consumed Christmas goodies in the seasonal ambiance of a house made for Christmas and discussed happier topics until Tracy asked if I'd like to take a ride.

"Let me check my calendar. Oh wait, I don't need a calendar. I've got nothing."

"I just want to stop at the garden shop on the way. I need a couple of wreaths."

I glanced around her living room and doubted it, but, at Christmas, more is generally more.

When we pulled up to the gate at our destination, I understood the need for the wreaths.

We drove through Holy Sepulchre Cemetery past many festive remembrances, wreaths, sprays and even trees. Designed for what? To assure the dead they were part of family holidays or to let the living keep the deceased part of family holidays?

"You know she's not here."

"You stole my line," Tracy admitted. "But I felt the need to come here, to tell Cassie what you did for her."

After Tracy positioned the wreath at the foot of the tall headstone, we stood at Cassie Kelly's gravesite in silence.

"I'm telling her what you did telepathically," Tracy explained.

"Is she answering?"

Tracy shook her head. "No, but that's okay. It would make me sad to think she and her spirit friends had nowhere better to be on Christmas Eve."

"I wonder if she ever sees Jonathan."

"We can ask when we drop off his wreath."

Our words were light-hearted, but hearts were far from light. I laid my hand on Cassie's gravestone. "So many years she missed."

"So many years were stolen from her," Tracy countered. "And Baron never looked back, never felt one ounce of guilt or regret. The only thing he was good for was making Henry Parry look sensitive."

I couldn't disagree with my niece.

"I am sympathetic to how they had to hide their love, but that doesn't excuse what they did. To both of them, Cassie and Jonathan were both completely disposable."

"Do you think Parry realizes just how arrogant he's been?"

No," I answered immediately. "I am convinced Parry confessed because of his own needs, not because of an ethical principle to see the truth come out."

A cold wind swept across the cemetery. I pulled my coat tight around me. "I want people to remember her. Jonathan too. I think I might give Chip Parry a call."

"For a date? I thought we agreed you blew that opportunity when you unmasked his father as a criminal. Dinner conversation might get a bit awkward."

"I have another reason in mind."

"Do you think he'll speak to you?" Tracy asked.

"I think he will if I call on Cassie's behalf."

Although initially suspicious of my stated purpose, Chip claimed to be happy I called. His response to my proposal was positive. "I can't believe I never thought of that."

"And you'll do the same for Jonathan."

"The family owes him."

And that was how Wallmann College came to be endowed with two scholarships. *The Catherine Mary Kelly Scholarship for Performing Arts* and *The Jonathan O. Brien Scholarship for Legal Studies*. The name of Jonathan's scholarship represented a compromise. At his brother's request, Jonathan Brien, nee John O'Brien, retained the O in his name—if only as a middle initial

Wallmann put together a lovely ceremony to thank the donors, but Chip wanted to remain anonymous. Not even Tim O'Brien and Gloria Gibbs knew the name of the donor. Since they knew the truth of their relatives' deaths—even if the world didn't—I think each of them had the same suspicion. When they met for the first time at the ceremony, they confronted me—as a team. When presented with a list of possibilities, I am pretty sure my face gave away the name I tried to hide. "I think the important thing is that deserving kids are going to become living legacies to Cassie and Jonathan."

Since I got the credit for bringing the endowment to the school, I was asked to give a speech. I thought that honor should go to Tracy, who was, after all, looking for a long-term gig at the college, but she deferred to me. So I took a few minutes to tell the assembled guests, and the first recipients of the scholarships, how Jonathan and Cassie dreamed. Admittedly, I struggled to put an excessively altruistic spin on Jonathan's goals but found it easier to talk about Cassie's aspirations. The two were bound by a desire to do better, to fulfill a dream and, most important to those who were benefiting from their memory, to work hard to do it. "Jonathan O. Brien and Catherine Kelly never got to reap the benefits of their hard work, but you can, you will and by doing so, you not only honor their memories but you will give them a way to live on, to achieve what they were cheated of in life."

I might have been the one on the stage listening to the applause but I knew the audience wasn't honoring me, or the anonymous donor. They applauded two people gone so many years before, long before their time.

Pinterest

To learn more about 1956 and the worlds that Cassie Kelly and Jonathan Brien lived in, go to: www.Pinterest.com/JaneKelly80.

Book Club Discussion Questions

1.   Grace Kelly was offered the dream of a lot of girls in 1956. How was the dream representative of the era? What parts of that dream remain relevant today?

2.   Social climbing was a well-documented phenomenon in the 1950s. Each locale has its own rules for social climbers. What are the peculiarities of Philadelphia's rules? How do they differ from rules of other cities?

3.   The Parry family had a lot of influence in 1956 Philadelphia. Do you feel there are families that exert that type of influence today? Are they the same families?

4.   How would your life be different if you were living it in the era that Cassie and Jonathan did?

For information on all titles by Jane Kelly go to:

www.janekelly.net
www.facebook.com/janekellyauthor
www.amazon.com/author/janekellyauthor

About the Author

Jane Kelly is the author of the *Meg Daniels Mysteries* published by Plexus Publishing, Medford, New Jersey and the *Writing in Time Mysteries and Widow Lady Mysteries*. She holds an MS in Information Studies from Drexel University and an MPhil in Popular Literature from Trinity College, University of Dublin. She is a past-president of the Delaware Valley Sisters in Crime and has served on the board of the New York Chapter of Mystery Writers of America. She currently lives in the Philadelphia area.

Made in the USA
Middletown, DE
28 April 2023

29298427R00139